Praise for bestselling author
KAIRA ROUDA

All The Difference

"A murder mystery that kept me guessing until the end, with lovable characters who made me laugh and cry. Kaira Rouda has done it again."

— *MELISSA FOSTER*

Here, Home, Hope

"... told with honest insight and humor, Rouda's novel is the story of a woman who takes charge of her life while never forgetting the people who helped make that change."

—*BOOKLIST*

"Inspirational and engaging, Rouda will touch readers who can relate to the frustration of being sidelined on the field of life, never allowed to play ... until finally experiencing the joy of full participation."

—*FOREWORD*

"I loved Kaira Rouda's book. I love its irony and its courage and humor. ...It's the real thing."

—*JACQUELYN MITCHARD*

"Witty and uplifting, Here, Home, Hope is a charming debut that explores the courage it takes to reshape a life and how to do it with a dash of panache."

—*BETH HOFFMAN*

"Reading Kaira Rouda is like getting together with one of your best friends — fun, fast, and full of great advice!

—CLAIRE COOK

"A warm, witty, engaging debut that left me laughing out loud."

—AMY HATVANY

"Endearingly honest, consistently upbeat, Here, Home, Hope is an inspiring read that left me feeling genuinely hopeful."

—JENNA BLUM

"If you've ever felt your own life contained a list of Things to Change (and whose hasn't?), then you will fall in love with Kelly Johnson. This funny, moving novel is a model of inspiration and reinvention for anyone seeking to find what's next in life."

—KATRINA KITTLE

"Relatable and inspiring. A perfect read for anyone experiencing one of life's 'what's next' moments."

—ROBYN HARDING

"A must read for anyone who's had their own midlife crisis, Here, Home, Hope reminds us that it's never too late to reinvent ourselves."

—LIZ FENTON

"A wonderfully warm read about finding happiness in yourself, Kaira Rouda's debut novel skillfully portrays the triumph of self-belief over society's threatening elements."

—TALLI ROLAND

A Mother's Day: A Short Story

"*Five stars. Nicely written - very quick read - sad moment but wonderfully heartwarming!*"

—STACY EATON

Real You Incorporated: 8 Essentials for Women Entrepreneurs

"*What I admire about Kaira is her can-do attitude. She knows what it's like to be in a man's world, but still accomplish things her way. She's the real thing, and after reading this book, you'll feel more confident of being your real you too. Go for it.*"

—KEITH FERRAZZI

"*Kaira Rouda empowers the woman entrepreneur by simply telling her to be herself. Where other books urge women to fit in with the boys, Real You Incorporated shows you how to create your own unique and wonderful brand. The secret is building it around the real you!*"

—BARBARA CORCORAN

ALSO BY KAIRA ROUDA

Here, Home, Hope

A Mother's Day: A Short Story

Real You Incorporated:
8 Essentials for Women Entrepreneurs

Published by Real You Publishing Group
Real You LLC
Laguna Beach, California

www.realyouincorporated.com

ISBN: 0984915109
ISBN 13: 9780984915101

Library of Congress Control Number: 2012900497
Real You Publishing Group
Laguna Beach, CA

Rouda, Kaira Sturdivant.
All the difference : a novel / by Kaira Rouda. – 1ˢᵗ ed.
    p. ; cm.
Suburban women—Fiction 2. Life change events – Fiction 3. Murder-mystery—Fiction

Cover design by Erin Corrigan.

To my friends

~

you do make all the difference

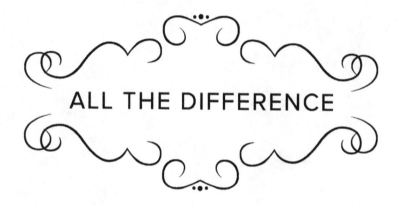

ALL THE DIFFERENCE

ALL THE DIFFERENCE

A NOVEL

KAIRA ROUDA

REAL YOU
PUBLISHING
GROUP

I shall be telling this with a sigh
Somewhere ages and ages hence:
Two roads diverged in a wood, and I—
I took the one less traveled by,
And that has made all the difference.

From "The Road Not Taken"

By Robert Frost

CHAPTER I

Friday, May 23

Tossing the script onto her desk, Dave told Laura, "Here, read this," as he sped past. "The teleprompter is set, Sunshine. We go live in two."

"Thanks, Dave," Laura said, not adding "you jerk," although she wanted to. She hated Dave Robinson, producer for WCOL-TV5, and didn't care that the feeling was mutual. Laura Mercer didn't care about much except ratings, beating the local competition to a story, and looking like big-city-market material. Laura knew she was the latter. She looked like the girl next door and sexy at the same time. That's what her adoring fans kept writing since she had leapt onto the screen in Columbus four years earlier. She was promoted from reporter to anchor of the noon and early evening news two years later. Already her name was a household word. Especially in households with male viewers.

Laura knew she was considered a draw at charity events. She agreed to lunches with local power brokers and marketing folks. Accessible, beautiful. And she was always perfecting her presence. Changing the tone of her voice, practicing inflections, tilting her head just a little farther left, or simply picking up a new adjective to drop into idle anchor babble. Laura was learning, absorbing, and mimicking everyone at the station. When the general manager asked her to do the news bulletin cut-in, she felt it was her big chance. Maybe this could lead to a network feed or even CNN Headline News pickup?

Eschewing a read-through for further primping time, Laura arrived in the studio with twenty-two seconds to spare, Dave's script in hand. Clipping on her microphone, she smiled at the cameraman, Rob. Soon, the cameras would be automated robots, but until then, she needed Rob to like her. Glancing up at the booth where Dave sat hunched over the control panel, Laura sneered—but it could have just been a squint because of the lights.

"Ready and three, two, one, music…"

"We interrupt our regular programming to bring you a special news bulletin from WCOL-TV5," the station announcer's voice boomed.

Suddenly, Laura's face popped into the middle of one of the station's highest-rated shows, prompting hundreds of calls from angry show addicts. Laura's hair was perfect—she was the brunette Breck girl. Her squeaky-clean image had boosted the number-three station in town to a tie with the perennial number-one. The soft orange and yellow backdrop complemented her skin tones. Set approval was part of her contract by now, and she exercised it.

"This is Laura Mercer, News Channel 5, with a special bulletin," she read from the teleprompter. "An hour ago, an explosion from unidentified causes ripped through a large home in Field City, five miles northwest of Grandville. Sources on the scene tell News

5 the two adult victims were airlifted to an area hospital in critical condition. We will have more about this story as information becomes available, and, of course, tonight on the eleven o'clock news. This is Laura Mercer. We now return to regular programming."

"And, we're out. Nice job, people." Dave's voice boomed from the control booth above the studio. Hoping to cover the story first, and thus smack an early, crippling home run useful for self-promotion for months to follow, he had obviously decided to break into programming with a news bulletin containing little news. It was May, sweeps week, a critical time to lure viewers to the station. It wouldn't matter to him how stupid Laura would look, interrupting a program to give no news.

"Goddamn it! Heads are going to roll for this one," Laura screamed after she'd removed her microphone. She held her breath then, waiting until Rob sauntered out of the studio. She needed him on her side until the studio was automated. The camera equaled power, since his choice of angles and camera position could make the difference between her nose seeming prominent or ugly. Someday she'd have the money to fix those faults, but not yet.

"Is it too much to ask to have a few facts before we jump on the air?" she yelled to Dave, her invisible producer above. "I know this is TV news, but facts, some facts, are important!" Feeling better after the tirade, she walked out of the studio, back to her desk.

Over the speaker, Dave said, "Have a nice day, Sunshine." Sunshine was the nickname he had given her two years ago when she arrived to save their sagging news ratings, fresh from a Dayton Fox affiliate. At first, he had seemed to like her. Six months later, he began complaining that "Sunshine" was raining on his parade.

The public loved her. Laura knew most of the staff at the station hated her as much as Dave did, but the station owners—the only people who mattered in the end—decided she was their "it" girl. Her ticket was written. She was biding her time until an anchor spot opened up in a bigger market at a sister station. Her departure could not come soon enough for Dave or the rest of the staff, Laura knew.

Once back at her desk in the center of the noisy newsroom, Laura thought, *Today was intriguing.* For once, the news registered. She'd actually felt something, deep inside, almost like a stomachache, as she read the story. *It had to be his house,* she thought. *But who was the woman?* Even now, Laura's heart was racing, and she realized her fingernails were drumming the fake wood veneer of her desk. Fortunately, no one else seemed to notice her agitation.

Turning in her chair, Laura yelled, "Tony, call all the hospitals in town. They airlifted the victims, so they're probably at Grant or University. I want the names of both people injured in that explosion, and I want their status. Now, Tony, move!" Laura knew the stone-faced assignment editor couldn't tell the orders were a personal request; she always treated him in the same demoralizing manner. *Consistency is key,* she thought to herself as she watched him fumble with the computer keyboard at his desk.

For a moment Laura wondered whether anybody at the station would connect her to the explosion. No, she'd been discreet.

"Hey, Mike, is Headline News interested in a feed?" she called out to another editor, before jumping out of her chair to hover over his desk. This could be big.

CHAPTER 2

Three Weeks Earlier, Friday, May 1

Ellen Anderson could see the fork in the road from her kitchen window. She watched as cars chose one route or the other. Some drivers were confused, swerving at the last minute as they made a choice. Many seemed to know exactly where they were going. Only a couple had smashed into the tree growing in the median.

That's me, she thought. *In the middle, smashing into the tree. Barren. Empty. Dead. Hungry.*

It was almost time for lunch. She stared out the window past the bright green carpet of grass at the acres of farm fields rolling behind her Victorian dream home. She expected her husband's red convertible Mercedes, top down, to burst around the back corner of the house any minute.

Michael's dark brown hair—thinning on top—would be tossed by the wind. He liked his hair like that—young, carefree.

His six-foot frame folded into the front seat, and even in a small sports car, he appeared in command of the road, his home, his life, and of course, his wife. With his sunglasses on and his face locked in a grin, his music cranked, he still looked the part of the fraternity social chair he was when they met. Glasses off, he had lines at the corners of his eyes, golf squint lines, defining his thirty-eight years.

She didn't see him yet. So Ellen waited. She'd been cooking all morning. It was her hobby, really her only passion these days, and now, with the Internet, she could find recipes for anything. Everything had a recipe. Except, of course, her life. She planned, thought she had all the ingredients, but always, something was missing. Having finished cooking, she waited.

An observer may have thought that, standing there on her tiptoes, silhouetted by sunlight piercing the leaded glass panes, Ellen looked like a bird about to take flight. Her shiny black hair was pulled up in a high ponytail. Her dark skin, a tribute to her Brazilian roots, made the perfect contrast to the white countertops and yellow and white walls of the kitchen.

As with most things in the house, the countertops were built too high for her, a bow to Michael's height and ultimate say on everything, even her kitchen. After thirty-three years of feeling small, whenever Ellen wanted to feel empowered, by habit, she would stand on her toes and lean forward.

The last time she had done so was earlier that morning, as Dr. Burnhardt, her fertility specialist, murmured there was nothing else he could do and handed her an adoption brochure. He didn't seem to understand adoption wasn't an option for Michael and, therefore, wasn't for her either. She'd endured years of tests and humiliating procedures. All in vain. The dream home she and Michael had completed the year before was a family home, with four extra bedrooms and a large nanny suite.

"I'm so very sorry, Ellen, dear," the doctor said. Listening, Ellen fell off her toes. Her last hope was gone; she felt deflated, subhuman. Women were supposed to get pregnant and have babies. Weren't they? It's supposed to be natural. Why had she worried about contraception all those years? Maybe it was the miscarriage, she thought, and shuddered.

"But, you know, I had, had—"

"Yes, you mentioned the miscarriage. I remember, dear. And while you were able to conceive then—I believe that was what, ten years ago, right?—your body changes, and conception is harder the older a woman is. It's a mystery. I wish we could control conception like we can contraception. I am sorry, Ellen," Dr. Burnhardt said again, sounding anxious to conclude the discussion and send his pitiful patient home.

Ellen thought she was about two months pregnant when she had lost the fetus. *I wonder if it was a boy or girl, and I wonder who the baby looked like.* The same questions floated through her subconscious often, never dislodged by the reality of a new fetus growing inside.

She was still dreaming of the baby she would never hold when she heard the sound of gravel rumbling outside. Michael had arrived home for lunch. They'd planned this date at home so she could fill him in on the results of her latest and final round of tests.

"Ellen, what did he say?" Michael asked quietly when he walked in the door behind her.

"We won't be having any children, Michael. I wish I could've kept our baby, the one we made," Ellen said, turning, tears streaming down her face.

"Maybe it'll still happen, Ellen. We need to get on with life. You know, maybe you should go back to work," Michael said, trying to be calm, be nice.

"What about adoption, Michael, please?" Ellen asked between sobs.

"I've told you my feelings on this. I'm just not going to raise a kid that isn't mine." Seeing her tears, he softened his tone. "It just wasn't meant to be, El. You know that. It's OK. You can start up your career, or do that garden club or whatever. That's why I put you through school. You'll be fine. We'll be fine."

"You're already fine, aren't you? Where were you last night?" Ellen asked, quietly. She wondered why, if he thought she was as pretty as he said, why she wasn't enough.

"Working."

She turned back to the window then, as Michael grabbed the sandwich from the plate on the table and said, "Have a nice day, and don't wait up. It'll be another late night at work." She heard the rumbling as his car pulled out on the gravel and then sped silently back down the winding driveway.

Ellen counted to twenty and then pushed the button to close the front gates.

****

"Well, I wanted a boy and we ended up with this scrawny thing," he said to his girlfriend, who moments before, in a final agonizing scream, delivered his fourth child. Her first. Delivered in a twelve-dollar hotel room so no one would know.

"She's pretty. Just give her time, you'll love her, you'll see," said the new mother, shaking as she cradled her newborn.

"I doubt it. I'll see you later; I have stuff to do." He left then. And he never came back. If the manager hadn't found them and called the ambulance, they both would've died.

Subsequently, instead of celebrating her birthday every year, her momma dreaded it. Dreaded the day and blamed her daughter for her aloneness. For their poverty. For being.

By her second birthday, she'd caught on. She knew how to be quiet, to be like a mouse. She didn't want to get a beating on her birthday. She didn't want anything except for her momma to love her.

****

Janet Jones was lost, a stranger in her own community. A spectacle in the suburbs. Suddenly life as she knew it was over, so she stood, watching the traffic drive by, her typically coifed white-gray hair blowing in the divergent directions of each passing car. Some honked. There were, she learned, two distinct types of honk. A short, light, beepish honk. Polite. Helpful. And the other. A firm, hard, blaring honk. Her presence near the street, in the gutter actually, upset the normal drive home for some people, resulting in an affront to their sensibilities and a loud honk.

"Oh, take another way home," she yelled, teeter-tottering on and off the curb.

She didn't know why she'd ended up here, on the road, at rush hour. Her yellow suit, from the best boutique in town, was wrinkled and dirty. If only she hadn't picked this day to come home early from work. So, so stupid. She'd surprise him at the showing, she had thought, and maybe they could go eat an early dinner. Yeah, what a surprise.

Janet noticed a car stopping next to the curb across the street. "Great, it's Maddie," she muttered. Her friend, Madeline Wilson, the city's gossip columnist to the rescue. *This is just what I need*, Janet thought.

"Don't move, I'm coming to get you," Maddie yelled to Janet as cars swooshed past between them. "It's going to be OK. You'll be all right. Don't worry."

Janet watched as Maddie darted—yes, she could dart at five foot four—across the street. Her brown highlighted hair and small build made her appear more like a burglar caught in a heist than a guardian angel friend. Once she'd crossed to Janet's side of the street, Janet noticed Maddie's trademark pin: today it was a southwestern Native American dream catcher in silver.

"Nice pin. Maybe all of this is just a bad dream," Janet said by way of greeting.

"Janet, please, come with me. I'll take you home, to my house. We'll talk."

"It's all over. He…he was fucking her in our duplex listing. There I was walking in like an idiot to surprise him, and he was having sex with our administrative assistant on our client's white couch. Surreal."

"You guys have been a real estate sales team and a couple forever. You're in shock. Let's get off the street, go have a cup of coffee or a drink. Come on," Maddie said, gently steering Janet across the street and helping her into her Jetta.

Janet had helped Maddie find her home, her condominium in German Village, a historic district downtown. It was the first place Janet showed her, and she made an offer immediately. Janet had been friends with Maddie's parents until her parents' divorce. At that point, Janet's husband remained friends with Maddie's dad. Maddie and her mom remained friends with Janet. Fifteen years older than Maddie, Janet was a perfect surrogate mom when Maddie needed a working-woman role model. They tried to have lunch at least once a month. Typically, Maddie needed Janet's advice.

Today, the opposite was true.

Looking in the visor mirror, Janet saw she looked terrible, like someone had poured just enough water on her face to force her makeup to slide down two inches. Her mascara, foundation, even her lipstick was low. Her chin-length hair looked like it'd been in a tornado, and her suit looked like a crumpled piece of paper.

"Where have you been all afternoon? The entire Grandville Real Estate office is out looking for you." Maddie clicked off the hazard lights and pulled out into the traffic. "I mean, by the time that receptionist called me, they were all at the end of their ropes. They've been looking for you since lunch. Luckily some freaked-out commuter recognized you, Janet, and called your office." Maddie punched in her lighter, waiting for it to get red-hot as she paused for Janet's answer.

Janet sat silent for a few minutes. She had been married to Chuck Jones for twenty years, and they were the top real estate sales team in the city for fifteen of those. A model of success in both work and home life. Parents of two boys, one in college, one building a life in Dallas.

Yet, out of the blue, her visit to the duplex had revealed the truth about the Joneses—Chuck was having an affair and Janet caught him in one of the homes they had listed. According to Maddie, a caller three hours later had informed the office Janet was roaming the streets of Grandville.

"I've been walking, I guess," Janet said finally, staring out the front windshield of the car but not seeing anything. "You know, it's funny, Chuck's always made fun of the fact I'm a Realtor, but I can't find my way across Grandville without getting lost, let alone Columbus. So today I just did what I'm best at: wandering. All of a sudden this town just seemed so small."

"Janet, you grew your business. You had the sense, the clients. Chuck learned everything from you. You are the face of the Joneses of Grandville Real Estate. Don't forget that," Maddie said, inhaling deeply.

"I did everything he ever asked me to do. Did you know I always let him drive, just to make him feel important? At first. Now I'm just used to it. Sitting. Supporting him. Oh my *God*, he was naked with *Angie*," Janet sobbed, dropping her head into her hands.

Maddie drove out of the suburbs and back downtown. She pushed in her lighter again. "Maybe being single in my mid-thirties isn't so bad after all," she said consolingly.

"I'd gone over to surprise him, you know, during his showing. I knew he was showing the Hamilton house and it's on a lockbox, still furnished. I heard sounds upstairs. I walked in and his butt was sticking up, you know. He was on top. It was so white, and his back had all that dark hair all over it and he was, disgusting. I couldn't even see her, just him. She said, 'It's Janet.' And I said, 'Angie? Chuck?' Like an idiot, I felt guilty at first, for interrupting them. Ha." Sniff, choke. "It was all in slow motion."

"I know, that's what your brain does when you are in shock. That happened to me, when I was in that armed bank robbery in Nice, France. Did I tell you about that?"

"He rolled off of her," Janet said, ignoring Maddie's blatant attempt at a change of subject. "And I could see his midlife midsection and her young, firm body, and I turned to the wall and threw up. Not pleasant, but all of this seemed to last an hour and I bet it was seconds. It was gut-wrenching, actually. And then I walked."

Maddie paused her parallel parking, shaking her head briskly, probably trying to erase the graphic scene from her mind. "Let's go inside, talk. Don't think about it anymore right now. OK?" Her voice was pleading.

"You're right, I could be sick just thinking about it again," Janet answered, opening the car door to follow Maddie into her condo. "I wouldn't want to make a mess of your carpet."

*****

Angie Brown, former personal assistant to the Joneses of Grandville Real Estate, stood leaning against the doorframe, halfway in and halfway out of the kitchen. The two women were the same age, but while Laura Mercer was driven, Angie was drifting. Laura's eyes glistened with life's promises, and Angie's were circled by life's experiences.

Laura poured a glass of wine for each of them, smiling, as the story unfolded.

"You're sick. You think this is funny, don't you?" Angie insisted. This wasn't funny; this was her life. *You're a complete bitch*, Angie thought, glaring at Laura.

"Not funny—how about mildly amusing? Anyway, you got what you wanted, didn't you? Good-bye nine-to-five, hello Grandville Country Club. No more waiting tables and answering phones at Grandville Real Estate. You'll be buying your own home now."

"Do you really think so? I think Chuck was a little shook up. Maybe he'll want to go back to the hag. She looked horrid today, like Big Bird or something. She was all in yellow, and you know it cost a fortune. On me, it would've looked great, but on her, that suit was stretched in all the wrong places," Angie said, hopefully. Married. Rich. It was all she ever dreamed of being, and Chuck could make it come true.

"You're screwing your boyfriend when his wife walks in on you, and you have time to check out her fashion statement? Now that's sick." Laura smiled her broadcast smile.

"You think Chuckie will call me? I mean, after he straightens things out?" Angie asked.

Laura made a strange face. She said, "Of course he will, dear. He's not going to blow it with you. He loves you, right? He told you he did. You're his—what does he call you? Peach? Pumpkin?"

"Puppy."

"Right, puppy dog. Everything will work out fine. Don't worry." Glancing at the clock, she said, "I've got to go. I'm emceeing one of those charity functions tonight. The anchor with the most community service hours wins at bonus time, they told me. See you tomorrow." Laura walked past Angie in the doorway, through the living room, and out the door.

"Thanks, as always, for the support, roomie," Angie said after she heard the door slam shut. Angie grabbed the glass of wine Laura had left on the counter for her and poured it down the kitchen sink drain. She picked up the bottle of gin from the cupboard under the counter, grabbed a glass from the kitchenette, and created her own type of martini to kill time until Chuckie called. *This may make her leave him, seeing the two of us together like that,* she thought. She chugged half of her drink and then shivered as the alcohol raced through her system.

So much for my career in real estate. She wandered into the small living room of the apartment, which was almost completely filled with an overstuffed orange velour sectional she'd found at a rummage sale. *I guess I'll be a professional waitress until Chuckie marries me.* She grabbed the TV controller and clicked on the movie of the week.

"Puppy" sat.

****

For once, Laura was glad she had a stupid charity event. It made for a perfect escape from the lame roommate. She hated Angie Brown, the waitress, and felt she deserved about as much attention as the mouse that also shared their apartment. In fact, Laura thought, Angie looked like a mouse. Pinched nose, white sallow skin, thin lips, and brownish blondish mousy hair. Skinny. Laura would live through living with Angie, just as she'd survived other things. The rent was cheap.

Arriving in town from Dayton, Laura was friendless and strapped for cash. The job in Columbus was a promotion, without the commensurate pay. Ah, but the glamour. She needed a roommate and perusing the want ads led her to Angie. She was fine for now.

****

This one, he was the worst, she thought.

In her four-year-old life, she'd seen a lot already. He definitely scared her from the moment he stepped foot inside their trailer. He smelled like hate, and monsters, and dinosaurs. And he looked like a spider—a hairy spider with black scratchy hair, scratchy hairy face, and hairy hands and arms.

Why does Momma like him more than me? Why does she like everybody, even Mr. Platz next door, better? I'm going to go collect some more rocks, *she thought.* Maybe I'll find a special one with shine on it for Momma.

"Beat it kid," he told her, with a grin.

"Just play outside right around the trailer. I don't want to have to come find you and beat you, you hear?"

"Yes, Momma," the little girl said and went out the door, listening for it to bang behind her. It did. She hoped the noise scared them, but knew they probably didn't even hear it.

****

An hour later, wearing a borrowed cotton pullover dress, with her hair combed and makeup redone, Janet popped her head into Maddie's kitchen. Maddie did a double take and smiled.

"I'm calling him now. Do you want to listen?" Janet asked.

"No, thanks, unless you need me. You look great, by the way. Let me know if you need me," Maddie said.

Janet walked down the hallway and back into the bedroom. She remembered the condo from showing it to Maddie. Janet never forgot floor plans. Sitting on the edge of Maddie's bed, she thought of her two boys, one in college, one finding life on his own in

Dallas. She'd talked with the cowboy just the other night. Told him how hard it was in the early twenties: deciding on your career, where to live, who you want to date and possibly marry. "Welcome to the real world," she had told him with a smile. She didn't add that life just kept getting more complicated from there.

Career, marriage, kids. I put everything else aside for those three things. First, I taught Chuck the real estate business—pricing a home to sell, staging it, holding buyers' and sellers' hands, and all of the other subtle and not-so-subtle tricks of our business—and then I had babies. Close together, one after the other. They had been fifteen months apart. *My beautiful baby boys. A month off with each of them, and then they went to day care and I went back to the business. The Jones Team, the number-one real estate sales partnership in the city. And our kids grew, and our business grew, and our relationship died.*

It had died. While they were busy living, working, caring for their children, their relationship ended. They went through the motions. Sex once every six months. *No wonder he found Angie so appealing. She's probably looking for a father figure. He's looking for sex. How stereotypical all of this is. Except I don't think the wife is supposed to catch you in the act.* The sick feeling in the pit of Janet's stomach became a sour taste in her mouth.

"Hello." It was a tentative Chuck. *What a strange voice for him,* she thought.

"It's me."

"Janet, oh my God, I'm so sorry, so very sorry. I don't love her. It was all a mistake. She's fired, of course, and I'm begging your forgiveness. Where are you? Can I come pick you up? Please, let's talk in person, get through this, for the boys' sake. Janet?"

"Chuck, I don't love you anymore. I just had a dawning. Suddenly, I don't care about you or our facade of a happy marriage."

"You don't know what you're saying—"

"Yes, I do. I'm saying you don't love me and I don't love you. We made a good business team, we raised a couple great kids, but we're through. I won't be embarrassed by a man I don't love. We're over. Don't make this ugly."

"Listen, I'll call you in the morning. You're in shock or something. You don't know what you're saying."

"Good night, Chuck. Sweet dreams."

Janet's next phone call was to her personal banker, Donna, telling her she needed all of the joint accounts frozen until the divorce papers were filed. She transferred the proceeds of the most recent closing into her own account, since he'd presumably pocket the cash if the duplex sold. "I guess now it has scandal appeal," she told Donna after finishing the story of her day. "I'll be by in the morning to finish up all the transactions. And thanks, Donna."

"No problem, Janet. What a jerk. I can't believe he did this to you."

"He did it to himself. Thanks for your help. I'll see you tomorrow."

Janet placed four more calls, to her travel agent, her mother in Pittsburgh, her favorite administrative assistant at the Grandville Real Estate office, and her brother, an attorney in Cleveland. With those four calls, her life was in order.

By the time she rejoined Maddie an hour later, her plans were made. Janet thought she looked refreshed, like a successful Realtor about to show a new client around town. It was 9:30 p.m. and Maddie smiled when she saw her.

"Are we going out or something?" Maddie asked.

"No, I just wanted to get cleaned up—you know, if you look good you feel good, that kind of thing," Janet answered as she plunked down on the dolphin-gray leather couch next to Maddie. She leaned back, allowing her head to rest on the couch.

"Did Chuck apologize?" Maddie asked.

"Of course he did," Janet said.

"And?"

"And I'm filing for divorce in the morning. Chuck's made his choice, and I've made mine. Did you ever think that choices are like a chain reaction? Your choice affects another person's, and so on."

"But divorce, Janet, are you sure? A lot of men wander, women put up with it. Right?" Maddie paused. "What am I saying? I sound archaic, don't I? " Maddie realized she would never live the life she advised Janet to lead. And it sounded stupid, crazy. Janet was watching her. "Maybe you should just take some time, think it over. Now I sound like the crazy person, don't I?"

Janet sighed, staring up at the ceiling. "Many of my friends do stay. And that's not all bad. Staying together for the sake of your family, your kids. The problem is—and mind you, I've been doing this myself for many years—in the end, everyone is happy and fulfilled except you," Janet added, "a career isn't the answer, and neither, probably, is motherhood, although a lot of women think one or the other or both can be. My husband had sex with his assistant in someone else's house and I walked in on them. It's a movie of the week. He made his choice. And I'm making mine."

"Janet, you've had a long day. Come eat. I saved you some dinner. The sheets on the bed in the guest room are clean, and I put some of my pj's on the chair in there for you."

"You know what, I am starving. It smells like fresh-baked bread in here, oh, and garlic. My goodness, what have you whipped up?"

"Just a small Italian feast," Maddie answered.

"Thanks, Mad, you're a class act. Unlike Chuckie, and, by association, me." Janet took the proffered glass of Chianti from Maddie's outstretched hand, lifted the glass in the air, and said, "Cheers. What I have now is time. I'm glad I've been saving my money all these years. Now, I can buy my fun and peace," Janet said, clinking her glass against Maddie's and drinking from the glass.

"Meaning?"

"Meaning, unfortunately, I waited for this inevitable outcome before taking charge of my life. Chuck and I were over long before Ms. Brown landed in bed with him. The business kept us together. That's not a life, though."

Janet paused, drinking deeply from the wine glass. "Would you be able to drive me to get my car in the morning? I have errands to run before beginning my life again. This time, I'm in the driver's seat—well, as soon as I get my car," she laughed, finishing her wine.

And there they sat, talking and drinking when Lyle Boardman, Maddie's most recent brooding artistic boyfriend, reluctantly walked in.

****

Lyle had taken the long way home. Driving was peaceful for him even though he was a classic aggressive driver. He was feeling old and tired and stressed. Driving with the bumper of his Jeep Wrangler almost touching the bumper of the guy's Lexus in front of him was fun. A release. Stupid rich jerk should be in the right lane.

People called him "sir" when he went to McDonald's now. Two weeks ago, he pulled the first gray hair out of his brown head of hair—at first he couldn't believe it—and then before he knew it, there was one growing in his pubic hair. Gray. Old. Shit. At work—he was a copywriter at the Martin Agency, a local advertising agency, until he could sell his screenplay or a blockbuster novel and then, of course, he'd be gone—he saw a group of interns at the coffee machine, hanging out. He asked them if they were new grads or seniors in college. Turned out they'd graduated seven years earlier.

Lyle decided he was old, then. He thought about that Frank Sinatra song: "When I was twenty-one, it was a very good year, it was a very good year..." In the song, the guy ages from seventeen to twenty-one to thirty-five, and then to it's all over, sonny. The end of life. The end. Shit.

Why won't that guy in the Civic get going? he thought, blaring the horn. "When I was twenty-one, it was a very good year," Lyle hummed. "It was a very good year for—" *I'll be buried and my tombstone will read, here's a damn dependable guy. Predictable. Almost artistic, a pseudoliterary genius. Stable. Sensitive. Oh, and, he almost sold a prize-winning screenplay.*

Today was one of those days Lyle wished he didn't have to be so damn dependable. He knew Janet was at his house, and he knew he'd have to help Maddie deal with the emotionally draining situation. Lyle didn't have an excess of emotion anyway. Physically, he didn't have an excess of anything either: no fat, skinny; no distinguishing features, pasty white skin; and a slow, languid gait that drove Maddie nuts.

In bed, though, he excelled, almost as if all of his energy was stored for exuberant lovemaking. Actions were easy in a relationship; the corresponding emotions were too tough to unlock. So he provided Great Sex. That was his forte, his hold over Madeline Wilson, at least for now.

In Maddie, he'd found a woman who loved words—as Lyle did—and didn't try to compete to be published. "She's an editor at the city's daily," Lyle proudly told his starving poet friends. So what if it was trivial shit she wrote? At least they paid her. He thought that was cool. He knew she cared about him and supported his dreams of the big time. Just as he knew tonight he'd be in trouble. He was late, and she'd know he was avoiding dealing with the Joneses.

Maddie had called him after picking Janet up out of the gutter. Stupid shit, this relationship stuff. He'd handled the soap opera all day long at work, a pleasant listener for whatever tearful young account executive had a crush on whichever young creative director. And now, the drama had invaded his home.

Like any place where young, attractive energetic people gather, the Martin Agency was a hotbed of sexual tension. Lyle had enough energy to follow the gossip but not enough to participate in the flirting frenzy. Therefore he'd become muse and advisor. As he parallel parked in front of Maddie's—well, their—condo, he pasted a smile on his face. He wasn't amused.

*****

"Hi, ladies," Lyle said too brightly as he shoved the door closed behind him. Maddie rolled her eyes, and Janet smiled. "How are you holding up, Janet?" he asked.

"Howdy, Lyle, so nice to see you," Janet said, standing up to give him a hug. Hugging him suddenly made her eyes well up, and she pulled away and carefully wiped her eyes. "It's just that hug felt, well. Sorry. I'll be fine once I have some distance."

"What are you talking about?" Lyle asked, plunking his laptop down on the rugged pine desk in the corner of the sitting room. The room was cluttered with an eclectic mix of Maddie's traditional dark-wood antiques and her favorite leather couch, and Lyle's light minimalistic Scandinavian pieces. The walls, a bright sky blue, were covered with contemporary paintings, gifts from Maddie's former live-in lover. Maddie suspected Lyle resented them.

Janet simply smiled, and Maddie said, "Lyle, your dinner's in the oven, if you're hungry."

Obviously sensing an easy escape, Lyle murmured, "Great. Hang in there, Janet," before walking out of the room. He had looked confused by and relieved at the relative calm he'd encountered.

"I think he expected to see me wailing and ruined," Janet said.

"It's good for him, to see strong women. You are strong, Janet, and you'll be all right," Maddie answered. At the same time, Maddie thought Janet was the confused one, that she didn't really mean to dump Chuck and start over. How could she? She was in shock, Maddie thought. Later, she understood Janet's future materialized the instant she discovered her husband's betrayal.

Choices are a chain reaction. Chuck's decision to have a fling with Angie Brown, once discovered, forced Janet to choose a response, Maddie thought. Acceptance and forgiveness—or not.

CHAPTER 3

Monday, May 4

Like a tropical hardwood tree deep in the rain forest, Ellen Lopez Anderson had strong roots. Today, she thought, driving her black Infiniti down the highway, was the day she'd test their strength out in the world. She'd left the security and isolation of her home in the country and was headed into town, traveling down I-70 like a regular commuter.

Ellen sensed she was a product of proud, fearless ancestors, because every once in a while, a flare-up of self-esteem ignited in her center. That's when the reality of her life made her sick. Deep in the heart of Brazil, there was a strong presence pushing her to be more, to do more. The tiny brown rain forest sea beans she wore in the sterling silver box around her neck signified her connection. Her hope. For a long time, that hope allowed her to believe Michael loved her, even if he wasn't faithful, and that they'd build a happy family together, with at least four giggling children. Babies with soft olive skin and sparkling eyes and a lifetime of smiles. But now, no kids. Ever.

But, I still have myself, and Michael, sort of, and more than half of my life to live, she thought. Ellen knew she needed a new pursuit. A new focus. Her inner spirit kept her willing to try; the question was, try what? Shopping and cooking were hobbies; they couldn't fill up a lifetime.

Why did everyone else seem so happy? Did they really have it all, or were they just acting? Did the obnoxious police captain seated at their table at Saturday's charity function think he was charming when he told Ellen and the other three women at the table not to listen to a story about a police raid? "You girls, married to successful men like us, with your lives, you should only worry about making it to your hairdressers. That's all my wife worries about, and you ladies, you're just so lucky. It's a whole other world out there, and it's just better that you don't know about it," he added with a smile.

What were they supposed to do? Plug their ears with their manicured fingers until he was finished? Ellen smiled at the condescending jerk. And she was supposed to feel, what, blessed, that she was one of them? Michael was laughing beside her, scarfing down lobster tails and shrimp. That's what a ten-thousand-dollar donation got you. Lobster tails and a fat pig as a dinner partner.

If only she were pregnant right now. Michael would be home with her, instead of roaming every night. That night at the charity dinner, she had admired the pregnant woman sitting at the next table over. Ellen had stared at the woman's stomach, in silhouette, until she felt someone watching her. The woman's eyes met her own, and Ellen looked away.

Now, as she had then, Ellen felt sick.

Sick of an absentee husband.

Sick of the other women looking at her at the grocery store because she could shop in peace, without little voices begging for

Pop-Tarts. She longed for somebody little to beg her for treats and snacks.

Sick of giving all her time to charitable causes and then having people ask her what she "did" for a living. *I guess nothing, since volunteering doesn't count as real work any more,* she would think.

Sick of shopping, and the guilt of buying, because Michael told her she didn't need anything. And really, she didn't.

So, Ellen had looked around at her life, and she decided to get a job.

Really, it was her strong, life-and-death surviving ancestors talking her into it. "You need to feel valued," the voice had told her. "Do something." Ellen knew that Lopez women in the past had to "do" to survive. They lived hard, physically stressful, backbreaking lives. Most women in the world still lived those lives. Most women still didn't have the choices she had. She had too many choices and opportunities, she realized. And what had she become? Stuck. Mired. Choiceless. A doormat on the walkway of life, only not quite as useful.

No more indecision. Ellen decided; until she could talk Michael into adoption, she would try to find a job. She had majored in history, much to Michael's dismay, but loved to write. Maybe, just maybe, she could get a job. At an ad agency? At the newspaper? She had made some phone calls, put together a résumé, and before her doubts could stop her, she'd mailed letters and placed calls to contacts her friends suggested.

And today was the first step. *It wouldn't work out,* she told herself and believed. But it was a start. They'd see right through her, she knew. She'd never even gone on a real job interview. She'd graduated as Mrs. Michael Anderson and hadn't looked back. Today, she'd become Ellen *Lopez* Anderson again.

She felt thrilled to be heading downtown, on the highway, with a purpose. She opened the sunroof and took a deep breath. The black of the car and the road matched her hair and her eyes.

For years, she'd driven past all the office buildings she now longed to work inside on her way to charity events. After hours. Today she'd be part of the bustle. It all started when she'd casually mentioned to Laura Mercer, the TV celebrity, she'd like to find a job in the newsroom. Laura said she'd ask around. They'd attended so many charity functions together, they were on a first-name basis. Ellen as the planner, organizer, and facilitator—Laura as the treasured special guest. *Imagine. Little ol' me, working in a newsroom,* Ellen thought with a smile. Madeline Wilson was a newspaper columnist who also was a frequent guest at Ellen's functions, writing about the events and the dollars raised. Casually, at the end of a successful function, Madeline had asked for some inside scoop about one of the honorees, and after furnishing it, Ellen asked Madeline if there were job openings at the newspaper. At another event, Ellen had asked an acquaintance, Francis Hall, who worked at the top advertising agency in town if there were any positions available. There had to be something out there.

And there was. An empty parking spot.

That's a good sign. She quickly parallel parked in front of her destination, the Martin Agency. Directly across the street: WCOL-TV5, the local NBC affiliate. Both operations were housed in rehabilitated, turn-of-the-century brick brewery buildings. The brick streets added to the charm. She was in the heart of downtown, in the brick-street, funky rehabbed warehouse district. And she'd found a parking spot. This was good.

She was interviewing at *the* advertising agency in town, and the gleaming glass entrance was like a beacon and a threat. Alluring and frightening, like a strong summer storm. Cars rumbled by her, some slowing to see if she was relinquishing her spot, but she wasn't going anywhere. She was going to get a job at one of these places.

Laura Mercer had told her the television station didn't have any openings right now.

Strike one.

But during the same phone call, Laura convinced her to apply at the daily newspaper and at the Martin Agency, telling Ellen to use her name as a reference.

Ron Martin, president of the Martin Agency, had by then heard about Ellen from Maddie's boyfriend, Lyle, and from Francis. Ron called Ellen, who was shocked at the prospect of a job interview. She would be interviewing for a copywriter position at his advertising agency, he explained. Was she interested? he asked. "Of course," she'd said. So here she was. She hadn't even used Laura's name yet.

Suddenly, the pearl choker elegantly adorning her neck felt as if it was living up to its name. Her throat was tight. Her resolve began to crumble. *I'm a facade. A farce. They'll see right through me.* She looked at her eyes in the rearview mirror then and saw the dark fear staring back. Her underarms began to feel sticky; her hands shook on the steering wheel as she sat idling at the meter. *I must go in. I have an interview.*

Maybe I should just leave. It won't work out, she counseled herself, but that was OK. *I'll drive back home. Nothing would change, no one would know.* She only saw Laura four times a year, if that, and considered her merely an acquaintance. No one would know and nothing would be different.

That, of course, was the problem. She'd pictured her life as a suburban housewife and it was a life as a mom, a good mom. A cross between Florence Nightingale and Florence Henderson. The life she could never have, now. So now, she would work. Find a new purpose.

Michael wouldn't approve; in fact, he'd be shocked she'd ventured downtown alone. He liked to think she'd only dress up when he was escorting her to some charity function where he needed his spouse as a date. If he could see her now, he'd be mad. She did, she reasoned, look good.

This was all Maddie's fault. Down to earth, practical, the paper's style editor, Madeline Wilson talked Ellen out of a newspaper research job, telling her to go for the ad agency position. Maddie's boyfriend du jour—Lyle Boardman—worked at the Martin Agency, in the creative department, and he had told Maddie they needed people. Maddie had asked Lyle to tell Ron Martin. Maddie told her to dress with confidence, and the job would be hers. Ellen had listened for some reason.

All at once the whole thing felt stupid. Stupid. What did dressing with confidence mean? Why did she buy a pistachio suit? It was supposed to be the color this summer, but was her skirt too short? OK, it might be a little short, but Ellen could still be sexy. She deserved it. Her dark hair, swept up into an elegant knot at the base of her neck, shimmered in the sunlight pouring through the sunroof. Her rings tossed off sparks of light that danced inside her Infiniti.

She looked sophisticated, suburban, sleek. She felt like an impostor. *They'll see right through me*, she thought. Maddie said most of the people at the agency were OK, not exactly friendly, but polite. Lyle had a couple friends from the shop they would go to dinner with occasionally. Maddie had asked him to drop off the homeless shelter's annual brochure, written and conceived—pro bono—by Ellen. The accompanying note was penned by Maddie, of course. *But surely, a shelter brochure can't impress a big agency exec*, Ellen reasoned.

She glanced at the clock. It was time to go in. Climbing out of her car, she breathed in the hustle of downtown, so different from her life in the country only twenty miles away. She fed the meter—how long would it take for them to see her as she really was? *An hour should do it*, she thought—and hustled inside.

"Please, have a seat," said the intimidatingly friendly receptionist who sat behind the huge half-moon mahogany desk. "Mr.

Martin will be right with you." *You poor little imposter,* she didn't need to add. Ellen knew.

Ellen sat in awe. Awards glistened on shelves; the downtown skyline shimmered in the summer heat. She leaned forward on the soft leather chair and pointed her toes. *Maybe I should just leave now,* she thought, when the glass doors behind the receptionist opened and a beautiful young woman said, "Mrs. Anderson, please come with me."

Following the model/secretary down a marble and carpet hall-way, suddenly Ellen found herself inside a dream office—exposed brick on three walls, a wall of glass for the fourth—with elegant antiques throughout. Ron Martin extended his hand, and she walked forward to accept a firm handshake. Ellen flushed. She quickly sat in a fat gray leather chair, looking down at the floor to hide her red face.

I'm going to faint, she thought. Glancing up, Ellen realized she was face-to-face with the world's most beautiful man. Taller than Michael, more striking than Michael. More blond, dimpled on both cheeks, broad shoulders, and a huge smile. *His eyes are green,* she thought. His cream silk golf shirt moved as languidly as he did. She was stunned, speechless. *Why didn't Maddie tell me he's gorgeous?* she wondered. *If I live through this, I'm going to kill her.*

"It's nice to meet you Ellen," Ron was saying, "And I very much enjoyed reading your copy. Do all the clips in your portfolio carry the same tone?"

Oh, no. It's happening, I don't even have a portfolio. The World's Most Beautiful Man will now know I'm a fraud. This is a crush. This is ridiculous. Speak, Ellen.

"Well, I guess—" Ellen began, but before the words reached his desk, his office door flew open and a blur of a forty-something woman, wearing flashing gold jewelry, just the right amount of perfume, and what seemed like a sophisticated suit, stormed in and stopped, hands on hips, lodged between Ellen and Ron.

The model/secretary/centerfold followed in her wake, trying to stop the blur woman and spewing apologies until Ron shooed her away with a wave. "It's OK, Danielle. We'll be fine."

The blur stood frozen with her back to Ellen, but Ron smiled and came forward to perch on top of the antique banker's desk, closer to her. Ellen noticed the woman's stylish auburn hair, short but not boring, with many waves and depth. *Not many women have great hair in the back...why am I thinking about another woman's hair?* she thought suddenly. *Probably to keep myself from obsessing about Ron Martin.*

Finally, the nameless intruder began to speak: "Here's the deal, Ron. The spokesperson can't be somebody negative because soap is clean. Squeaky Clean better change its name if you're going to approve of a bisexual, cross-dressing basketball player as a spokesperson. If you want a basketball-shaped soap, fine. But he's not the one to introduce it." And then, turning to look over her left shoulder, she said to Ellen, "Sorry to interrupt, but this is vitally important."

Ellen, eyes wide, simply nodded.

****

It was morning. Francis wasn't a morning person. She'd had a fight with her ex-husband on the phone last night, and now, this. She wasn't in the mood to fight with Ronald Langly Martin. She was right, period. Unfortunately, Ron was her boss.

As she had known he would, however, Ron smiled, first at Francis, and then at the nervous-looking woman perched in the corner of his office, who exhaled and then slowly smiled back. Francis thought the other woman looked great in a crisp suit, and she was mature, which meant at least she wasn't twelve like most of the people he hired these days. But she also looked scared—of her. Francis felt guilty for intruding, but she had a point to make with Ron.

"Strong woman. Stubborn as a mule, she is," Ron said to his guest, smiling. "Et tu, Brute? What do you think?"

Turning to fully face the frightened woman, Francis answered for her, "Of course she agrees with me. We're the customers, not you, remember?" Francis was accustomed to changing Ron's mind. She trusted her instincts and so did Ron. Typically, she used a little more tact. But it had been a rotten morning. Francis knew she'd won. She usually did.

As the woman continued to look a little stunned, Francis finally put her finger on who she was. "By the way, I'm Francis Hall, senior account supervisor and soon to be vice president of the Martin Agency. Been with him almost since he opened the shop. Sorry about this." Francis extended her right hand to shake Ellen's. "You must be Ellen? I'm a friend of Maddie and Lyle's. We've met before, at a charity thingy, right?"

As Ellen stammered her answer, Francis glanced back at Ron. She had had a crush on Ron since spotting him in the grocery store. She'd almost proven her worth enough that she could—maybe— start flirting with him. At one time, she had thought he was interested too.

But now, back to business, she reminded herself as she uncrossed her arms and looked straight at Ron. One of the women in a business book she'd read told her to take that stance when she felt weak. Crossing your arms over your chest holds in all of your power, concentrates it or something, she remembered.

She waited expectantly. After all, Squeaky Clean was her baby, and Ron wasn't going to mess it up. The advertising campaign had been an overnight success. The soap, once a regionally known brand, was suddenly appearing on lists as one of the nation's megabrands, right up there with Dial and Ivory. It was Francis's passion, and she guarded the message that went out to the consumers as such.

Squeaky Clean changed shapes with the seasons: a leaf for fall, a seashell for summer. Celebrities selected to appear in the commercials represented the seasons or the shape. A football player with a football-shaped soap. Each TV commercial or webisode showed the hand of a famous person, up close, reaching for the bar of relevantly shaped soap. Ten seconds later, the celebrity and his or her soap were revealed. Moms loved it; kids loved it. Francis loved it.

****

Ron wondered if he should take another chance. He knew a little about Ellen Anderson, knew she was smart and beautiful, and had never worked in an office before. His question about the portfolio was designed to measure her sense of self. Was she insecure about her lack of a career path or proud of being a star volunteer?

Now, with Fran's interruption, he'd lost the element of surprise. But he'd already decided Ellen had talent. He sensed it. And he liked the copy he'd read. Anyone he asked spoke highly of the slight, shy woman sitting stunned in his chair. *Yep.* Ron had to be honest; he had sold himself on hiring Ellen before meeting her. The fact he found her an exotically attractive woman closed the deal. She didn't fit the typical Midwestern housewife stereotype.

Besides, hiring Ellen wouldn't be that big a risk for the consummate risk taker. He'd taken a risk hiring Francis—and it had paid off. Sales of Squeaky Clean, once sagging and in decline, skyrocketed from the moment Francis had been assigned to the account. The owners loved her, the creative team respected her, and together, they had repositioned the product. Francis's campaign reached for the next generation, making Squeaky the soap of choice in every mom's grocery cart—because their children put it in there.

Ron had met Francis in a grocery store. His friends had laughed: hiring a forty-something divorcée and handing her one of his biggest accounts? Come on—just because she made some interesting observations about soap in the grocery aisle? What was he thinking? they teased. He wasn't. Advertising was an art, a passion. Francis was right. Period.

If Francis represented one of Ron's many trademark leaps of faith, Ellen would be another, maybe a more peaceful, quieter leap of faith. An exotic and overwhelmed leap, whose wide brown eyes watched the conflict unfold in front of her.

But first, he needed to answer Francis, who wasn't about to give in. Hands on hips, solid stance, Francis looked elegantly stubborn. As she waited for his answer, she massaged her neck with her left hand. Ron knew Francis suffered from tension headaches. He felt guilty, suddenly, for causing another one.

"I know what you're saying, OK. It was just an idea. I'm golfing with old man Drummand tomorrow and I wanted to get his thoughts on potential spokesmen...ah...spokespersons. You'll need to steer me in the right direction. I guess that's why we need some help, huh, to work on the top twenty market localization project?"

"You've got it, boss," Francis said, smiling. "I knew you'd agree."

"Like I had a choice. Uh, by the way, Ellen—may I call you Ellen?" Ron asked.

"Of course," she answered, looking stunned again.

"Do you think you could speak, say anything? I just want to be sure you're not letting Francis put words in your mouth. We need independent thinkers, of course, just not quite as independent as this one," he added, cocking his head in Francis's direction.

"Yes, I think she's right. I'm fascinated by this whole industry, your exchange. I'd love to work here," Ellen answered.

Ron believed each person had a mental age almost from birth. His was twenty-eight, he felt, although the face in the mirror—currently thirty-nine—kept getting older each year. The problem he had with most adults, even young ones, was they were mentally already fifty-five. Ron hated that.

He made it a point to hire people with panache. He was still waiting for Lyle Boardman to come out of his shell. Ron knew there was excitement in there somewhere. He had known Francis had spunk the moment he met her. Ellen's eyes said she did too.

"Well, welcome aboard. Let's start with a project, see how you do. Sound good?" Ron said, as Ellen's face flushed and broke into a beautiful smile. "An unconventional interview, alas, but I'll let you two work out the details. Francis'll fill me in later."

"If you'd give Ellen and me the rest of today, we'll have a list of celebrities for you to take with you tomorrow," Francis said. "And thanks, boss. I can always use help with *my* client."

Ron loved the idea of making a utilitarian product fun on a massive scale. Squeaky's owner, Mr. Drummand, skeptical at first but with nothing to lose, took a chance and now loved the profits. Ron protected Francis from her client's doubts and gave her the freedom to implement the campaign in her terms. Now he'd watch as Ellen added her own touch of creativity to the soap.

*****

Two years ago, Francis had been a fairly conventional wife and mother of one sparkling teenage daughter, living in upper-middle-class Grandville. Her husband's note, left in their bathroom, telling her he was leaving after twenty-one years together, was her first inkling something was wrong in her marriage. Very wrong. The job at the Martin Agency saved her life. Francis was sure she would've become a closet alcoholic, or worse, without it.

Ever since she was a little girl, watching Darrin Stevens on *Bewitched*, she had wanted to be in advertising. While most little girls dreamed of being Tabitha or Samantha, she wanted to be Derwood. Every time she saw a bad ad, it bugged her. She knew she could help them do better at least. After reading the Dear Francis letter, she walked back into her bedroom and clicked on the TV. A stupid, condescendingly typical commercial targeted at housewives.

Clicking the television back off, she decided to go grocery shopping. That's where fate came in and she met Ron Martin in the soap aisle. After one conversation, she had a new life, in addition to community volunteerism and what motherhood her almost-grown daughter would allow her.

Ron had offered her a job that day. Not sure if he was serious, she called his office the next morning, at 8:35 a.m. He took the call, and she was ecstatic because it was his voice, the grocery store voice. She told him she'd be in for work the next day. And that's when the second half of her life began.

Since then, Francis learned the ropes in the advertising business, while guiding her client to unheard-of profits. Fortunately, her bonus measured up to her client's success, because her departing husband left town, and she had no idea where he was. Her daughter's college tuition was paid, and while Ohio State University wasn't quite Stanford, where her daughter had applied and been accepted, at least she could go to school.

Francis smiled. She'd come a long way, she reminded herself. "Let's get to work, Ellen. Come with me and I'll show you my office and a cubicle you can use while you're here. We're actually pretty close to the creatives—you know, Lyle's department," Francis said.

As the women turned to leave his office, Ron asked, "Francis, Ellen, do you two want to join us on the course? It's supposed to be a great day and Drummand loves you."

"He just likes to have women around to lust after. Besides, Ellen and I wouldn't want to outshoot both of you; that's not good for client-agency relations," Francis joked.

"Well, at least you're listening to a few of the things I've been teaching you."

"I've learned so much, don't minimize it. You know I love working here. Except for those young AEs and copywriters walking around in short skirts and stiletto heels. Ellen'll fit right in," she joked, making Ellen blush, self-consciously looking down at her short, pistachio skirt.

"Despite the fact you can't walk in high heels, Franny, you're a natural at this business. You know it is an art and a science. You had the art all along; we've just been refining it since you've been here. So, can I take you ladies to lunch?"

"I'm meeting Sophie—my daughter," Francis added for Ellen's sake. "She's a sophomore in college. Calls this morning, says she wants to drop psychology. Says it's too depressing—dysfunctional families are the first subject. 'Been there, done that,' she tells me on the phone. Ellen, you should take him up on it."

Francis didn't think anything of her frequent lunches with Ron. They were great friends; she wasn't ready for anything more, yet. During their frequent working lunches, over salad (her) and club sandwiches (him), they brainstormed and talked business. Besides, if she didn't eat with him, she usually ate alone at her desk. The majority of the female staffers steered clear of the strange housewife who had catapulted over them into a senior position with seemingly no experience. The fact that the Squeaky Soap campaign was an unmitigated success didn't convince the grapevine of Francis's worth. Nothing ever would, really. She wasn't even sure if her assistant liked her. Nor would her assistant approve of Ellen once she met her. The fact that her assistant and just about every other woman at the office felt that Francis hadn't paid her dues left Francis with few friends at the agency. Ron Martin was one. And Lyle Boardman, who had the energy of a snail but the calm warmth of a true friend. In Ellen, Francis recognized a younger version of her own empty sadness. If they didn't depress each other, they'd be great friends.

※※※※

Ron told Ellen they should celebrate, and for lunch, he drove them to Lindey's, a small Italian bistro a few brick-covered blocks away. He ordered a bottle of Chianti for her, surprising Ellen, who was about to ask for a Diet Coke. Once the hostess left the table, he raised his glass of sparkling water and said, "Cheers and welcome aboard."

"You know, if you treat every new employee like this, you can't be making any money," Ellen said, in awe of her day. She wondered if Michael would agree this was wonderful but realized she no longer cared.

"Not every new employee is so elegant, beautiful, and intriguing. Usually, they're fresh out of college," Ron answered, smiling, holding eye contact until Ellen broke it to look down at her menu. *I think he's flirting with me. No. Well, maybe?* It had been so long since she'd shared a meal, alone, with a man. She decided to concentrate on the menu and rubbed the box holding her lucky beans again to be sure she wasn't dreaming. Emotions she thought were gone with her twenties were stirring inside her as everything and everyone except Ron Martin receded and dissolved into elevator music.

"Hi, my name is Angie, and I'll be your server today. Are you ready to hear about the specials?" asked their waitress. Had Ellen not been so infatuated, she might have connected their waitress with an item in Maddie's column the other day, naming the young woman caught with Janet Jones's husband in a seedy affair. Today, only three days later, the item still was the talk of the town. But

Ellen's day had been far too overwhelming to focus on anything except her new boss across the table.

****

Meanwhile, on the other side of the Lindey's terrace, Laura Mercer grinned. She could spot an affair in the making a mile away. She made it a hobby to observe bored husbands and place bets. It was like a day at the racetrack. Almost. Since her move to Columbus, with her high-profile charity celebrity appearances, there hadn't been much time for stray husband watching, although she tried to squeeze it in whenever possible. This was a twist, however. Ellen—she knew—was the married one. Ron she also knew—far too well.

Today, for lunch, Laura looked the part of an elegant suburban woman. Composed. Graceful. It was a sudsy pink look she tried to achieve whenever she was in the public eye: a light pink Dior suit, just a touch of makeup. Of course, several men had noticed her as she waited for her lunch date. But so had women. She'd been equally nice to all. That's how Martha Stewart would act if she were a local television celebrity, Laura had decided. She needed to appear to understand these people's bland existence. Once she hit the big time—soon, very soon—she'd ditch the conservative image and become ultrahip. Then, she'd fly over this boring middle-American nightmare between LA and the Big Apple.

Laura was waiting for her stand-in father figure, the restaurant reviewer she'd met at the Lindey's bar during her early days in town. It had become her habit to go there after the late news to sit at the bar and unwind from the newscast. It was a challenge. To get the names of the streets right, to pronounce well-known community leaders' names. To use the correct adjectives on live stand-ups. It mattered. Especially if she wanted to move up and out.

It hadn't taken long for the Dashing Diner—what most people called Dixon Crane—to work his way over to the bar, pulling up a barstool next to Laura's. Lindey's was one of his favorite haunts too. Dixon was the city's beloved food critic, a fixture in the daily newspaper who also had guest spots on the Channel 5 news. Discovering she was on-air and on the same station, he began to assume a paternal role. He even had her as a guest on some of his on-air restaurant reviews, legitimizing her arrival in the market.

Today, when he showed up, she smiled broadly at him and he said, "I'm glad you remember me. I thought you'd become such a big famous person, you'd never give me the time of day." After uttering this greeting, he pulled out a chair and leaned his cane against the table, smiling as he sat down. He looked like an old-time sailor—white beard and hair, lined face, and perpetual tan—but he'd never set foot on a boat. It was a look, though, and people definitely noticed, pointing at him as he settled in. They were both celebrities in a top twenty-five market. For Dixon, that was enough. For Laura, it wasn't.

"It's good to see you, Sugar," he said. He'd called her Sugar ever since her first guest appearance on one of his television segments. They reviewed a pastry shop and ate a cream puff at the end of the taping. Thankfully, he didn't call her Puff.

"You too, Dixon. How's my favorite restaurant reviewer?"

"A lot better than Ron Martin, from the looks of it," he said, snorting and sniffing, and Laura turned in time to watch Martin's "date" fleeing down the bistro's back stairs.

"How interesting," Laura said, swirling her water glass and watching Ron. "He's single, I know, because he works across the street. We've known each other awhile. Hey, maybe he offered her a job. I know she's looking. Bored at home and all. No kids, you know. It looks like he's giving her a job and she's stealing his heart. What d'ya think?" Laura asked with a smile. "She's the married one, you know. I love it when women play. Although, it's dangerous to play with Ron—unless you know what you want, what you're doing."

"That's Ellen Anderson. Once living grandly on Grandville's Berkshire Road, huge house, all that, and now a country bumpkin living in Field City for some unknown reason. Who would live out there?" Dixon asked, with a snort.

"I know who she is, duh. She's a regular on the charity circuit," Laura said, laughing because she spent her first year in Columbus absorbing everything Dixon told her about everybody who was anybody. Now she didn't need any coaching. "I don't care where she lives, I just wonder what happened. Maybe just a potty break. She needs a job and he needs a date. I thought it looked like a wonderful affair in progress. Anyway, back to us. I have a favor."

"I guessed that, Sugar. First, you don't call for nearly a year— just e-mail me occasionally—"

"I believe you have my number, too," Laura said, cutting him off. "Anyway, one of the women in town who has made me so popular as a celebrity emcee and who really has gotten me incredible exposure is opening a restaurant. It's a breakfast and lunch place, called the Good Egg or the Happy Chicken or something. She's not really a friend, more an acquaintance, but I sort of told her you and I would cohost the grand opening celebration. It benefits Action for Children. Don't say no. Please, please," Laura begged, knowing he typically didn't appear at restaurant openings. The woman had ties to New York. With the right people, people in media. "Please, Dixon."

"Fine, Sugar. I'm sure whatever you want from her will be worth it," Dixon mused, guffawing, snorting, and then chuckling. His beard twitched. His eyes opened wide and then squinted when he was deep in thought. Laura thought, it was as if you could watch as he processed information, watch it sink in on his face. Finally, the twitching stopped. "Which reminds me, what about you, Sugar? You're not getting any younger. When are you moving on?"

"They promise within the next year. Oh, look, she's back. And she looks put together—happy, even smiling. Hmm, he's such a charmer," Laura said, nodding toward Ron and Ellen's table. "And she still hasn't spotted me. Ellen told me she can't have kids and that's all she ever wanted. Maybe she really is getting a job at the Martin Agency. She said she wanted to start a career. I offered to help her, you know. I checked, and there's nothing at the station right now." *Actually, that's a lie,* Laura admitted to herself, taking a sip of her iced tea. She didn't want Ellen in her newsroom—*it's not good for the society set in town to discover how bitchy you are at work,* she thought. To be a prima donna, you had to act like one, after all.

"She's pretty. I'm surprised you'd even pretend to help her."

"Very funny, Dixon. Yes, she's gorgeous, in that third-world country, Latin American, mysterious way. Exotic. Not a threat, though, unless she's in the broadcast media business, you know."

"She's married to a louse?" Dixon asked, twitching and then pulling on his white beard.

"Yep. Michael Anderson. He doesn't mingle much at the events Ellen hosts. I've met him a couple of times and he seems like a jerk. I hear he's an entrepreneur who's always on the verge of the world's greatest invention. What he's done well is meet the needs of The Limited and its women's accessories divisions. When bow barrettes were in, he made them faster and cheaper and won the contract to supply them. Tortoiseshell accessories, same idea. Weathered, torn baseball hats. That was him. He's a hustler, that's for sure." *I'd also love to meet him, conquer him myself,* Laura thought, but figured she wouldn't be in town long enough to play that scene out.

"OK. I'll come to the opening of the Egg and Chicken place, if it means so much to you," Dixon said, changing the subject. "But which came first?"

"Who cares? And thanks. Now what can I do for you?" Laura asked.

"Order a bottle of wine and try this, this entrée"—he said pointing to the linguine and clams special on the menu. "I need to get the review filed this afternoon. Here—" he said, sliding a thin reporter's notebook her way. "Remember, you have to write down everything: smell, taste—"

"It hasn't been that long, Dixon." Laura smiled, grabbing the notepad.

"No, but I was afraid those big ratings were going to your head. You up for a guest spot on next Sunday's show, Sugar?"

"Where? No more pastries."

"No, ice cream. It'll be easy. Isaacs in the Village. We'll have the shot all set up. All you need to do is smile, and lick," Dixon said, flashing her a devilish grin as he dove into his Caesar salad. "I'll have my girl call you to set a time."

"How is everything here?" Angie asked, smiling.

"Everything is fine, Angie," Laura said, in her best snooty tone, dismissing her with a wave of her hand, as if brushing away a fly.

"Did you really need to shoo her away?" Dixon asked.

"You can flirt with her after I'm gone. I need to run. Thanks for the salad. I wrote that the pasta was fabulous, although a bit heavy on the garlic for lunch crowds. And please, don't forget the restaurant opening. I'll be looking forward to our ice cream date. And one last thing, don't call me Sugar or I won't do your guest spots anymore. I hate that nickname." And with a peck on his whiskery, bumpy cheek, Laura was gone.

*****

As Laura swept by, Angie heard Dixon say, "I know you hate it, Sugar," snorting.

Angie swooped in to keep Dixon company. She had been on her best behavior through the whole meal, since she was serving the Dashing Diner dick. She couldn't give a shit about impressing her roommate, but she decided to be nice. Plus, she had a splitting headache. She'd waited all weekend for the call from Chuckie and she couldn't sleep. But it never came. Laura hadn't come home all weekend either. Not until late Sunday night, actually. Angie felt like asking her where she was, in front of the restaurant reviewer guy. Just to rattle her a little. But she didn't.

Once Laura was gone, Angie sucked up to Dixon, letting him flirt with her, until he finally paid the bill. *Figures—15 percent.*

Angie was having a truly shitty day.

She thought Chuckie loved her, but he didn't. She had gotten a call from the real estate company; the bitch receptionist Becky told her she'd been fired, for insubordination. *Ha*, she thought. After Becky hung up, "I'm a model employee," she said to no one.

That evening, she was counting her tips, sitting at a table in the corner of the bistro's kitchen. Not bad money today. She'd pulled a double and was about to punch out when one of the other servers handed her a note.

Inside, she found a man's name and hotel room number in elegant handwriting. *Please join me at The Hyatt bar for a nightcap*, the note read. She remembered him. He'd been at table twenty at lunchtime. Cute. No wedding ring, which didn't mean anything. Nice clothes. Polished shoes. Angie always checked out their shoes. Rich guys always had shiny shoes. It was one of her secret ways of telling the good from the bad. Almost always, she was right.

She hadn't been to the Hyatt for drinks for a while. It was early—only 10 p.m.—and she didn't want to go home. Laura would make fun of her again for being busted by Chuckie's wife, and then she'd have to tell her he never called. She had better go to the Hyatt. Free drinks with a stranger was better than facing Laura.

While primping in the bistro's bathroom, taking down her ponytail and enjoying her shift drink, Angie wondered who Laura was dating these days. He was married, for sure, because those were the only guys Laura wanted. Angie had been afraid she'd try to steal Chuckie, but Laura said she hated fat ones. Chuckie wasn't fat, just a little pudgy. Well, maybe he was fat after all. Suddenly, Angie hated Chuckie too.

Waiting at a stoplight, she thought, maybe the Hyatt guy was really from Columbus and just got a room for them to have a romantic romp. Maybe he had a crush on her for months and it was finally time to consummate it. He'd leave his wife and kids, kick them out of the mansion, and buy Angie a convertible Porsche. That's what she wanted. He'd wrap his arms around her, secretly reach into his back pocket, pull out a diamond necklace for her, matching the nine-carat ring in his other pocket, and propose. He'd have her strip and, when she was naked, he'd put the necklace on her and slide the ring on her finger and run his fingers, lightly, down her body, between her breasts and then kiss her all over.

He'd be good, and gentle, and pick her up; then, he would tell her she was beautiful. And when he put his penis in her mouth later, on the bed, she'd swallow. She'd do anything for him because he'd make her dreams come true. And he loved her. And he was rich. Somebody behind her was honking and Angie looked up, realizing the light had turned green during her dream.

She hated the valet parkers at the Hyatt, she thought, pulling her Dodge Plymouth into the circle. They made her feel like she didn't belong. Looking her up and down unabashed. *Jerks.* She never tipped them. As she rode the escalator up to the bar, she decided she needed to find out who Laura's new guy was, so when Laura was tired of him, maybe she'd get him. Unless ol' shiny shoes Hyatt was the one.

CHAPTER 4

Tuesday, May 5

Maddie Wilson asked a bewildered Angie Brown, "OK, tell me all about it. Tell me the story of you and Chuck Jones. Don't you think it's time your side of the story was told?" Maddie tried to keep her expression neutral as she checked out the young tramp who wore her white blouse unbuttoned one button too far, her khaki pants tighter than all the other servers. Angie wore more makeup than most would wear waitressing while Maddie wore almost none. It would be hard to keep the disdain out of her voice.

"Who are you?" Angie asked, looking around at her other tables, making sure nobody was listening. The restaurant was getting busy, the beginning of the lunch rush.

"I'm Madeline Wilson. I do that column, you know, in the *Journal*. I just thought you'd like to tell me your side of the story,"

Maddie said in her most soothing tone. She'd dropped Janet off on Friday morning to get her car and hadn't heard from her since. Janet told her she was going to the airport and she'd write or call. Maddie didn't know when she'd be back or where she was going. She did know, though, where the slut worked, and so she'd decided to dig a little.

"I'm not talking to you. Are you ordering, or should I have my manager ask you to leave?"

"Bring me a half-order of angel hair pasta, and some sort of answer as to why you would sleep with a married man. Why would you betray a woman who helped you get into the real estate business? That's all I need," Maddie said, smiling sweetly at the bimbo, who looked a little shaken for a minute, like her worst nightmare was coming true, and then looked mad.

"Chuckie loves me. He said he did. Janet's old and boring and—I don't have to talk to you," she added rushing away. Maddie actually felt a little sorry for her, then. The young woman seemed frightened as a mouse. And really, not all there. *I wonder what her story is*, Maddie thought, as she made note of Angie's brief response. Maddie still wasn't sure how or if she'd write the follow-up piece. She'd decide after lunch.

Janet had told her to write something, whatever she wanted. Maddie did just that, not concealing her disdain for Chuck Jones and his indiscretion, naming Angie, "the waitress/real estate assistant," and providing a few details. She'd skewer them again in her next column. Maddie's society/gossip column was one of the most popular features in the daily newspaper.

Maddie had decided a while back that she was living vicariously through her column. Announcing engagements, births, and celebrations of the important people all over the city. The only thing was, she'd really like to join in some day, her way. She just couldn't seem to decide how.

It wasn't a money thing. Maddie grew up in Grandville. Her parents had had money and still did. Separately, of course, since they were divorced. But what Maddie had trouble picturing was that husband-children-house-in-the-suburbs stuff. She was getting to the age where people always asked. Why was she still living downtown? Dating starving artists? Treating her cats—two of them—as if they were her kids?

Who knows? Maddie twirled her pasta—served to her by a new waitress, Melony or Melon Ball or something—and thought. Her dream of a career in New York City wasn't going to come true. She'd pretty much accepted that fact. She did want kids. Two girls. Lyle, like her other boyfriends before him, thought marriage and kids were bourgeois and too demanding, interfering with narcissism and perfect sex.

But—hey—at least she didn't need to worry about divorce. Her parents stayed together twenty years and let a bimbo break them up. Somebody like Angie Brown. She may keep choosing men who were commitment phobic, Maddie reasoned, but at least she knew they wouldn't break her heart in the end. They did from the start.

When Melon Ball tried to remove her pasta bowl, Maddie said, "No, I'm not finished yet, thanks. More bread, please."

Maddie's metabolism would stop one day, she knew, and she'd blow up into a square. At five foot four, she wasn't a line like Angie Brown, but she wasn't plump either. Just right, as Lyle kept saying. But Maddie's mom was a square, and she estimated it happened at about age thirty-seven. The metabolism stopped. That meant she only had two more years of eating freedom. She would make sure she enjoyed it. Food and cigarettes.

As she lit one of her trademark Marlboros and leaned against the outside wall of the restaurant waiting for the valet to bring her car, she smiled again at the simple pleasure of summer. Winters were hell for smokers who wanted to enjoy a cigarette after a meal. Spring and summer were smoking season, even though a couple of suburbanite women gave her the stink eye as they joined her in the car valet line, before realizing who she was. She smiled at them. They quickly smiled and then looked away, intimidated. Maddie knew she could rattle almost anyone, wearing her signature all black—an accidental rut she hadn't been able to break. With the only color in her entire ensemble a pin on her lapel depicting sunglasses, she knew she looked tough and powerful.

In her car, on the way back to the newspaper, Maddie called Lyle. While on hold, she stopped at a light, and pulled a comb through her dark-brown-with-red-highlights hair, which she wore in a short, edgy cut. She hooked on her pink breast cancer awareness pin next to the sunglasses on the lapel of her jacket. *Fashion with a purpose*, she mused. The light turned green right when Lyle picked up the phone.

When she launched into the Jones saga, Lyle grunted. "The problem with the story is that it's tragic and gross all at the same time. I'm just not sure what you can do with it that's tasteful," he said. "Maybe you should just let it go."

"Let me worry about that, the writing, OK? Did you know Chuckie's paramour, Angie, is the roommate of that anchor Laura Mercer? That's a nice little item." Maddie was proud of that scoop.

"I think we're all so tired of these predictable midlife crises. I think you have enough to write about without this stuff," Lyle said. He was ruining her day, and her story. She wished she hadn't called him. "How about running a thing about Squeaky Soap and Ellen's new position on the account? That's better, Mad. By the way, where did Janet go? I know she left town. When is she coming back?" Lyle asked.

"Oh my God. Was that actually a question about one of my friends? I'm shocked. Honestly, I don't know where she went. I hope it has a beach and lots of great-looking eligible men who aren't commitment-phobic," Maddie said. "I'm going for a long visit."

"Yeah, yeah. I need to get back to work. See you tonight," Lyle said, hanging up.

Maddie hung up and pulled into her reserved parking space next to the newspaper's hundred-year-old building. The building was charming, in its asbestos-ridden, huge crown molding, dirty, newsprint way. She walked into the lobby, smiled at Earl the guard, and got into the elevator, punching the button for the fourth floor. She was still deep in thought, and mad at Lyle, as she crossed the center of the busy newsroom.

Sitting behind her fake wood desk, Maddie stared at her phone. Should she call the cheater? Or should she just write a scathing column with the facts? Her assistant buzzed. A Mr. Chuck Jones was calling.

Perfect, she thought. *Another case of inaction providing somebody else with the opportunity to take action.* Just like her last boyfriend. She'd let him have the chance to think about marriage. She gave him space. Lance the painter ultimately decided marriage was out and so was she. Finally, she'd purchased her own downtown condo. Soon afterward she met Percy, her Costa Rican tropical hardwood tree farmer. The thought of tall, dark, and handsome Percy—nose ring, and all—still made her tingle with desire. Percy's subsequent disappearance led to reliable Lyle. But even though she'd been with Lyle for almost a year, when Maddie dreamed at night lately, she dreamed about Percy.

"This is all a terrible mistake," the frantic voice at the other end of the line blurted. "Believe me when I tell you I never meant for this to happen. She didn't mean anything to me, and I know you're friends with Janet's friends, and if you could just not write about the incident again, you're ruining my life, please it would—"

"Listen, Chuck," Maddie said, allowing attitude to flow over the phone line. She pictured Percy as he walked out of her life, and got mad. "You made your bed, or actually somebody else's bed, big guy. So are you marrying the nymph?"

"God, no. Are you kidding?"

"No? That's what the rumor mill is saying, and the poor little thing thinks that. I tend to write about what I hear. Have a nice day, Chuckie."

Shit. She pulled up the front page, already filed in the system. She was late. She quickly typed a scathing blurb in her column. Entitled "Chuckie's in Love?" the short piece talked about Janet and Chuck's years of marriage and partnership in business, pointing out how Janet taught him everything he knew about real estate. The boys weren't mentioned. The affair was. So, too, was Angie Brown's quote about Chuckie loving her, not his wife. Feeling Janet was sufficiently vindicated, Maddie filed the column. It was then that she had a chance to read the front page, appearing on her computer screen.

How'd she miss this story all day? Tracking down the Chuckie story, that's how. As she read, she really wanted a cigarette.

Abduction Leaves City Stunned
All Local and Statewide Authorities on the Lookout

Special to the Journal

According to police investigators, as bystanders looked on, a young mother and her two children were carjacked by two masked gunmen as they waited in the car for their husband and father, who was inside the Grandville Ohio Savings Bank branch withdrawing cash for the family's planned trip to King's Island amusement park.

Unaware a robbery was in progress, 34-year-old William Parks was forced to the floor with eight other customers, three tellers, and the branch manager. As one of the armed gunmen cleaned out the teller's drawers, the other held the customers at gunpoint.

Finished, the men fled out the front door of the bank and jumped into the car with the 32-year-old mother and her children, ages 2 and 3, and sped away down Lane Avenue, headed toward State Route 315. Some witnesses say the car headed north. Others said south.

According to eyewitnesses, one suspect jumped into the back of the car while the other sat in the passenger seat. Several onlookers placed 911 calls from cell phones at the scene, but none attempted to intercede.

The car—a white Lexus—has Ohio license plate number MFL 654. The suspects, who wore ski masks throughout the bank robbery, are described as white and of average height and build. The surveillance camera footage is below.

Local FBI Bureau Chief Sam Mallard said the perpetrators of this crime will be caught. Columbus Police Chief, Grandville Police, and the State Troopers have joined in the search for the woman and children. If you have any information concerning this crime, please call the Columbus Police Department or the FBI.

There's fate, Maddie thought. *Choices. One minute, you're playing hooky from work and taking your kids to the amusement park; the next you're sucked into a violent crime.* Maddie had to know who the woman and children were. She felt sure she knew them. She had a premonition. Growing up in Grandville as she had, she knew most of the young families who lived there now. *Life happens to everybody,* she thought sadly.

"Bruce, who's the woman? Is it Melissa Parks?" Maddie yelled to the city editor, whose desk was across the newsroom.

"Maddie, it's confidential!" he yelled back.

"Please. Off the record, confidential," Maddie said once she'd reached his desk.

"Yes, the missing woman is Melissa Parks," he answered quietly.

"I feel like I know everybody," Maddie answered while saying a silent prayer for her grade-school friend Melissa and her children.

※※※※

Across town, television sets were tuned, anxiously awaiting the eleven o'clock news.

Alone in her sprawling Field City home, Ellen paced. Michael, out of town as usual, wasn't available when she called him in his hotel room. *Probably on a date*, she thought. She walked around the entire house—too large and too obviously belonging to someone wealthy—checking windows and doors and rechecking the alarm. Outside, she heard the sounds of summer: cicadas, birds, all oblivious to the drama unfolding in the quiet suburb a few miles away. Ellen had been in Junior League with Melissa Parks.

The phone rang. It was Ron. They hadn't seen each other since lunch two days earlier.

"Are you alone? I was worried," Ron said. "I like to make sure all of my employees are safe," he added with an awkward laugh.

"Do you think you could come over?" Ellen asked.

Half an hour later, her boss, lunch mate, and new friend was at her door.

****

When the little girl was three, she wet her bed for the first time, sending her momma into a tizzy. No water or anything to drink before bedtime, she told her girl. Nothing to drink before bed became the mother's rule. The little girl, when she became thirsty in the middle of the night, decided the only thing to drink was in the bathroom. Turning on the faucet would wake up her momma.

The little girl drank out of the toilet. She had to drink out of the toilet, she got so thirsty. And she had to drink out of the toilet without her momma seeing her. She never wet her bed again, though.

The mother's favorite punishment was forcing the girl to stand behind the trailer, outside, all night, on a square board. She couldn't sleep and couldn't even sit. All night. One time, she fell asleep. The mother decided to teach her a lesson. With a tea kettle of boiling water, she went outside and woke up her daughter by pouring the liquid over her daughter's leg. The girl was four.

The first thing she remembered feeling was a point of heat pushed into her hand. It was a lit cigarette, but at the time, she thought it was a really hot pencil. And she remembered the yellings. The yellings kept getting worse. By the age of five, she knew when the yellings would come and when they wouldn't. Momma brought her to the emergency room three times that she could remember by then. The doctors would ask her what happened and she'd tell them she was clumsy and fell down the stairs again. They didn't have "stairs" in the trailer. Nobody cared enough to check.

Then kindergarten came and she felt safer. She got to leave home all morning, and Mrs. Berryderry loved her and talked to her, and she got to color, and she even had a friend, Katie. But then the bad thing happened to her. It was Momma's new guy. He told her to say she fell down the stairs. She really fell into the wall, and the dresser, and his fist.

Mrs. Berryderry knew she didn't have any stairs. She didn't believe her, or the story. When she started to cry, Mrs. Berryderry picked her up and carried her to the principal's office. So what was she supposed to do? The principal smelled really nice. And now they asked again what happened, and they knew she was lying, and lying was sin, and she thought she might go to hell. And then she told them it was her momma's friend. And then she cried. And they called the police. And somebody from something called children's services, who opened a file.

And she told them she didn't want her momma in trouble, and inside she wondered again what she'd done to make her momma so mad at her all the time. Was she bad? Why do they hate me? *It got worse when they moved to the country.*

*****

Ellen and Ron sat on the couch, the small velvet one in the otherwise looming family room, staring at the oversized television set. As the Channel 5 news theme music began, Ron reached over and held Ellen's hand. Unlike at lunch, when his touch had sent her running to the restroom in shock, this time Ellen returned the squeeze.

After the Squeaky Clean commercial ended, Laura Mercer appeared and stared at the teleprompter with a tight smile. Her purple suit, tailored to fit snugly, was a perfect complement to her expensive jewelry glistening in the bright lights of the studio.

"Good evening. I'm Laura Mercer, News Channel 5. We have breaking news for you tonight. Good breaking news, right John? John Taylor is live at a rest area on Route 33, near Lancaster. John?"

"Great news, Laura. I'm told by authorities this is the place where the kidnapped Grandville woman, Melissa Parks, and her two young children were found just ten minutes ago. The three had been abducted by two armed bank robbers fleeing the scene of the holdup at the Ohio Savings Bank in Grandville. We understand the hostages were tied up together and left in the back seat of their Lexus. The robbers apparently carjacked another vehicle at the rest stop, forcing the driver out of the driver's seat and onto the on-ramp of the highway. The man walked back to the rest area to call for help, spotted the Parks family, and freed them. All three were treated and released from University Hospital. The unidentified man who was the second victim was treated for cuts and scrapes.

"Police in a five-state area are on the lookout now for his vehicle, a white Honda Accord, Ohio license plate number MNH 254. And that's all we have from here at the scene, Laura. A lot of relief for the Parks family of Grandville and on the part of police, since at least the robbers have only a car now and no hostages. Back to you, Laura."

Ellen squeezed Ron's hand, so relieved a family she didn't know, but whose lives she could relate to, was safe and reunited. Ron squeezed her hand in return and slowly put his arm around her shoulder, pulling her close. She felt warm, and cared for; she felt worthwhile.

"Thanks for that report, John. Authorities would like us to remind you, these men are to be considered armed and quite dangerous. Just call authorities if you spot them; do not try to intercede.

"And now onto the rest of today's news..."

Ron gave Ellen half a bear hug with his right arm. A friendly, friend hug while using his left hand to find the controller and zap off the TV.

"You really never know what's going to happen, do you?" Ellen asked rhetorically, resting her head on the back of the couch, staring up at the ceiling fan languidly twisting above them. She sensed him then. His essence. The man inside him, not just the advertising guy. The caring, charming man who really seemed interested in her. He smelled like fall leaves after they were raked into a pile. A fun, breezy, solid smell. "Thanks so much for coming over. It's the nicest thing anybody's done in—well—in a really long time."

"Is that a tear? For goodness sakes, Ellen, I'm happy to be there for you," Ron said. "I can't believe Michael's not here for you. Where is he?"

"I'm used to it. We've been married thirteen years. We married a year after we met. I was...infatuated. He seemed so, well, established. I was twenty. He paid for my classes at OSU. He was older. Graduated. Started his own company." Ellen still stared up at the ceiling, arms folded across her chest. "Yes, it was romantic, and it felt real. Michael promised to take care of me. I didn't mind taking care of him in return. Have you been married?" she asked.

"No. The right woman just hasn't come along yet," Ron answered, smiling at her. "What's so interesting up there?"

"Sorry," Ellen answered, and then, making eye contact, said, "It's amazing, really. One choice. One double shift. I was working the concierge floor at the Hyatt. Michael was wheeling and dealing at a convention in the ballroom. He came up to the private lounge, ordered scotch and water, and we started talking. I wasn't even supposed to be working that night, the night we met."

"To a certain extent, you can make choices, but so can everyone else around you. It's where those choices collide that things happen," Ron said, standing then. He held out his hand, she put hers into it, and he pulled her to standing.

"In advertising, we try to influence the choices. That's really what it comes down to, in the end. Making choices. You can't predict life, but you can do your darndest to make it the best it can be."

As he leaned over to kiss her, Ellen held her breath. It'd been so long, so long since a man had longed to kiss her. She knew the kiss would be a beginning. But there, standing by the couch that night, it was right. She didn't care if Michael walked through the door, didn't care about anything.

Ron gently pulled Ellen to him and asked if she was OK. She nodded her answer and he covered her mouth with his once more. His lips were sweet and soft and full. She began to get excited and he pulled away.

"Ron?" she whispered. She was breathing fast, he could hear it.

"We're not going to move too fast with this," he said, stroking her face with his finger. "I should go. I wouldn't want my newest employee too tired to work tomorrow. The bad guys are gone and the Parks family is OK. And you, you're a great kisser. Lock up," he added, kissing her on the head and walking toward the door.

"You are too," she said softly, reluctantly standing and following him to the front door. "Sleep well."

I'll be dreaming of you, she didn't tell him, but it was true.

****

As Ellen closed the door behind him, Ron wondered if she realized how gorgeous she was. It had been a long time since he felt this way about a woman. He wanted to take care of her. He needed to go slowly, he knew. She seemed so vulnerable. But she also was very married.

Ron knew Michael Anderson, had since high school. Anderson was an opportunistic jerk then—and nothing had changed. Whenever they saw each other by chance, at the Columbus Country Club's stag bar, they were backslapping euchre-playing friends. Ron would never turn his back to Michael, who'd stab it at the first chance. Perhaps Ron could return the favor.

CHAPTER 5

Thursday May 7

"Don't you just love Phoenix?" Michael Anderson asked the beautiful brunette seated next to him. Her plunging neckline and lack of a wedding ring excited him. But she seemed familiar, somehow. He hoped they hadn't done it. He tried to remember.

"Actually, I've never been," she said, turning back to her *Cosmopolitan* magazine. She bit her ring finger fingernail.

"You look familiar. I'm Michael Anderson," he said, offering his hand.

"What? Oh, Laura Mercer, Channel 5 News." She smiled at him.

Thank God, he thought. That's why she looked familiar. She was on TV every night. *She's even better looking in person,* Michael thought, smiling back. Her soft skin begged to be touched. He put his arm on the shared armrest between them, sliding it over so his bare forearm could nudge hers. He felt a tingle. That was his sign, he decided, that he'd like to get to know her better. He'd never had a TV anchor. *Anchors away,* he thought smugly.

Michael knew he was infatuated with the brunette. It wasn't love, it was a need. A conquest. When he saw Ellen for the first time, through his haze of scotch and small talk, he had thought it was love. Only after he married her, promised to care for her, promised to love her, did he realize what he thought was love had been infatuation. Infatuation, unlike love, is impossible to sustain, but he had tried, he liked to remind himself.

Suddenly, a memory flashed into his conscious, of his own mother, waiting for and on his father. Sad. Alone. A shell of a person by the time she died. *That's not Ellen,* he reminded himself. *Hell, she has it all. Money, a great house.* Well, she did want kids, but he wasn't adopting some kid whose parents were trash as part of his family. No adoption, no sir. Not an option. He'd tried to get her pregnant.

At one time he thought a kid or two would help him sustain some interest in their relationship. Well, it just wasn't meant to be. They tried every month, at the right time. Unfortunately, that had been a bust. But they tried. He did his part and even that failed. And hell, she could leave him if she wanted. It was a free country. But she wouldn't, couldn't. She was a dependent little tropical bird in a gilded cage, who also happened to make a mean dinner. They both had their eyes wide open, didn't they? He smiled over at the conquest next to him then, proving just how wide open his eyes were.

And then he felt it. That stab, like heartburn in the center of his being. He recognized it, classified it as guilt, and made the necessary note to himself to bring Ellen back a gift from the desert. If he thought nice thoughts, the feeling would pass. Sometimes when he really felt alone, in between one-nighters, on a long flight or a sleepless hotel-room night, he'd catch a glimpse of himself in the mirror and it would frighten him. The wrinkles.

Had he become a pathetic cheater like his father had been? he would wonder. How could he avoid becoming just that? The answer was Ellen. A wife and a home were the anchors he needed, the feigned stability, there for his twilight years to make him respectable. To make him unlike Michael Anderson Sr. in the end: a pathetic, lonely alcoholic. An embarrassment. A disgrace. *No, that won't be my fate,* he assured himself.

"Miss, another please," he said to the flight attendant, and then, shaking his head to get rid of the darker thoughts, he struck up another conversation with the anchorwoman. She'd be fun, he decided, turning on the charm.

****

Two hours and three glasses of champagne later, Laura was anxious to see the desert. Michael had been her visionary tour guide. They had discovered both were flying to Phoenix for a convention. Accessories and gadget manufacturers for him; broadcasters for her. Coincidentally, they were booked at the same hotel, deep in the heart of the Sonoran Desert.

Poor Ellen, Laura thought. *This guy couldn't be faithful if he wanted to be—and he's probably great in the sack, with all that practice.* He played the role of the consummate gentleman perfectly. Yes, a skillful, well-traveled, articulate chameleon.

Probably does make a lousy husband, though, she thought, when he reached under the blue airline blanket covering her lap and gently rubbed her thigh.

She was glad she wasn't wearing pants. She'd seen a television show saying women should never wear skirts or shorts or open-toed shoes on an airplane because if there was an emergency, they'd be less equipped to escape. She had a love-hate relationship with flying. So she compromised. She still wore skirts, but now traded her sky-high heels for flats on airplanes and knew where the closest emergency exits were located.

For this flight, she was doubly glad she wasn't wearing pants, she thought, trying to suppress a moan as he gently placed his fingers inside her.

****

The first time she ran away, she didn't get very far. She thought the way out was across the cornfields. It was early spring and there was only dirt, no plants. She could run and run until she reached the busy road. She was seven years old. She had been stuck in the country ever since her kindergarten teacher tried to help. By the time the nice people at the school came to talk to Momma, they were gone. To the country where they'd breathe fresh air, her momma told the little girl.

It always smelled like poopy. Chickens were mean, and the boys who had the farm next door were meaner. The trailers in the park stood like freight cars in a line between two rich farms—a pool of labor for them, and a dusty, meager living for the trailer dwellers. But still, better than where Momma grew up. Much better.

She decided the busy road must have more people driving on it like Mrs. Berryderry than like Momma's man. She decided this was the day and put some Cheez-Its into her pockets. She waited for Momma to take her nap and then tiptoed outside.

The field seemed to go on forever. In the heat, steam mixed with dust to blur the horizon. She got a little scared. Blinked. She ran. Then she walked fast, and then she was so tired she sat on the dirt, halfway to the busy road. She ate three crackers and stood up again. Just keep going, *she told herself.*

She didn't hear the tractor behind her until it was too late. Momma's man stopped the big contraption just before running over her. She was almost to the busy road. She could see the prickly fence. She didn't know there was a fence.

When he beat her, she imagined him using the prickly fence wires, because that's what it felt like on her back.

****

"Here's your first project," Francis said to Ellen when she walked into her office. "We're launching the new Squeaky Clean local campaign—you know, giving college scholarships to high school seniors with clean images and community service. We're asking for user-generated video, and we've already received more than five thousand videos. Anyway, I need you to review them and narrow it down to twenty finalists. We'll have a contest, where consumers can visit the Squeaky Clean website and vote for the winner. I suggested you for the project this morning at the department head meeting and Ron agreed. What do you say?"

"Wow, really?" Ellen said, sounding twelve and feeling as transparent as plastic wrap. The mention of his name made her skin tingle. *This is crazy,* she thought. *In a week, my life has turned upside down. First, I find out I can't have children. Next, I find a job. And now my first crush since high school.*

"Ellen? Earth to Ellen."

"Oh, I'm so sorry. I'm just so grateful to you and Ron. Yes. I'd love the project," Ellen said.

"Great. How long do you think it will take you to weed through all of the submissions?" Francis asked.

"I've got nothing but time. Give me a deadline and I'll meet it," Ellen answered.

"I like your style. I think we'll make a great team," Francis said.

Ellen walked slowly down the hall to her cubicle, hoping, as she had since arriving that morning, she'd catch a glimpse of Ron. She didn't want to talk to him. Just see him without him seeing her. No luck. Reluctantly, then, she sat down at her desk. She blinked as she opened her laptop and found a note inside.

Ellen:

Can we see each other again, soon? Please let me know if you're interested. I'll handle the rest.

—Ron

Michael might not want her anymore, but she was sure he wouldn't want anyone else to have her. Didn't she really just want a job, to keep her busy until she talked Michael into adoption? Why did life need to get confusing—why did she hate it when it was boring? Why was she feeling these sensations deep inside at the mere mention of his name? Why did a secret note make her feel alive, undead as a woman for the first time since she'd married Michael?

But more than anything, Ellen wanted to see Ron. And so, opening her e-mail, she typed him back with a one-word subject line: YES.

CHAPTER 6

Friday, May 8

Laura stretched and opened her eyes a crack. Was it always sunny here? she wondered. Rolling over to ask Michael what time the sun rose, she came face to face with a hand-sized black spider, complete with shaggy black hair.

Michael flung open the bathroom door, naked and dripping, looking around until he spotted Laura cowering naked on top of the table in the corner of the room, where she had sprung.

"Get—it—now!" she screamed, pointing to the bed. He dashed back into the bathroom, grabbed a plastic drinking cup, scooped the creature off his pillow, and dashed out the bedroom and into the bathroom, quickly flushing the offender down the toilet.

By the time he came back into the room, Laura had managed to stand up, although she was still frozen in the corner.

"They grow big bugs in the desert, dear," he said. "Come here. It's OK. I'll protect you." And as he gave her a big hug, Laura was shocked to find herself needing it. Needing a man, instead of using him. She tried to shake it off, but the feeling, the caring was nice.

"Let's go to Sedona today, Michael. I'd like to blow off the seminars. I've already heard the network propaganda too many times."

"Sounds like a great idea to me. But first, I think you need a nice warm relaxing shower. Allow me to join you. A massage is on the house," he said, steering her into the bathroom and into the shower. The water was still running from before the spider sighting.

An hour later, they were off on an adventure. It was hot, riding in a convertible, but Laura didn't care. They were free. The scenery was so different and so spectacular. Wild. Laura wore a sleeveless silk blouse in vivid peach and her dark brunette hair up high in a ponytail, with a wide headband keeping stray hair from her eyes. Behind her tortoiseshell glasses, her dark brown eyes sparkled with mischief as she listened to Michael's running commentary.

"Did I tell you those cactus—those with the arms and the flowers on top—are called saguaros? They grow an inch a year, and they're protected. You have to transplant them if you want to build something where one is growing."

"Why would you want to build anywhere out here?" Laura asked, still reeling from her eight-legged encounter. She watched Michael, wondering why he was able to keep a pretty wife at home and still have as many flings as he'd like on the side. He was handsome, in a heading toward middle-age way. Still firm in the middle, hair thinning on top, but beginning to look distinguished, he definitely had a look. He exuded confidence.

"Kip, the concierge, says just as many people are desert people as beach people or mountain people. There aren't any nuisance bugs—just huge ones. Sorry. And the sunsets are spectacular and the climate is perfect. I could live here," Michael said dreamily.

"I'll take the manicured scenery of a penthouse in a big city. Room service. Dry cleaning. A masseuse. A maid, driver. You know. Look at that beautiful rock formation," Laura said, catching the fever even though she tried not to, as they began to drive through Red Rock Country.

"See? You may like it here after all. Kip said in all the years he's lived out here, he's only had positive animal encounters—whatever the hell that means. No rattlesnakes, no scorpions. He couldn't believe our spider sighting."

"Yeah, right. If you believe that, I've got a lot in the desert I'd like to sell you for two hundred and fifty grand," Laura joked.

"Did I tell you the cab driver said one of his cousins got killed out in the desert?"

"By a rattlesnake or a scorpion?"

"No. By a cactus. Seems he was hunting and wasn't having much luck, so he decided to pump a few rounds into a saguaro. The thing fell over on him," Michael said.

"Wow, kind of poetic justice or something. Do you believe in fate?" Laura asked.

"Like us hitting it off and both having a meeting out here?"

"No. More, well, global. Like all of your life has a master plan. I do. And, you know what's strange, even though I'm having a riot with you, something is telling me to stay away. It's weird."

"It's just that spider—it's got you nervous. Relax. Enjoy the ride."

Lunch was along the banks of Oak Creek in Sedona at L'Auberge, a country French restaurant and inn. Sharing a bottle of pinot grigio and a pâté-and-cheese plate, they watched a bride and groom host a reception for their family and friends.

"She's beautiful, and they look so in love," Laura said, dreaming of the day she, too, would wear all white and wed the man of her dreams. She knew her wedding would be the talk of the town, of New York or Chicago or LA—whichever major market she landed in next. To make it to the network, she'd need to be married, to look stable. To make it just below that level, she'd need to keep sleeping her way up the ladder.

Thus her disappointment when nobody new from New York had materialized at the meetings in Phoenix. So she had found Michael, her airplane mate a few hours before, who was finishing up his own cocktail reception under the setting sun on Carefree's patio bar. They made eye contact, left together for dinner, and spent the night together. It amused her, being with him, because he was married, and because he was married to one of her few Columbus friends.

Taking a sip of pinot grigio, Laura asked, "Don't you feel guilty? About Ellen?" turning her attention back to Michael. "I mean, you know I know her, and it's just such a small world. She must know about you and your wanderings. You promised to love and cherish and cling only to her, or something like that. Just like that young couple. It was your choice. Your pledge. And now…"

He ran his fingers up her thigh, slowly, and answered, "No, I don't feel guilty. Ellen's happy. She even got a job. She can't have kids. I've given her everything she needs. I'm all she's got. She came from nothing, you know. I paid for school for her. Gave her some class and some cash. Her mom was a maid or something, and so she really likes to cook and clean, which works out fine. But enough about me. Would you like to see our room? I reserved the inn's honeymoon suite, to celebrate us."

"You are naughty. Very naughty. But fun. Definitely fun." Laura smiled and finished her wine. Today was their last day in the desert together. They both left in the morning. He had business in California. She was heading back to Columbus. She hoped he didn't plan on seeing her when they got back. They walked hand in hand up the stairs to the old-fashioned incline that would take them to the top of the mountain and to their suite. Halfway up the hillside, in the jiggling two-person cab, Michael stood and pushed the stop button.

"Aren't we supposed to be hiking up the mountain for exercise?" Laura asked when he leaned over to kiss her.

"Not if I can burn some calories this way," he answered, sitting down on the wooden slat seat and pulling her onto him. "I'm inclined to do it on an incline. What do you think?"

"Sounds good. And new," she answered. The rickety cab shook on its track as they frantically found each other. As with the night before, they came simultaneously, just as the incline resumed its slow lurching movement up the mountain, called to the top by another couple. Michael yanked his pants up, and stood in the doorway, giving Laura an extra moment to zip up. Finally, he stepped aside and she walked out, a mess, but smiling.

"Hello," Michael said to the couple waiting to board the incline. All four shared an embarrassed chuckle.

"Nice evening," the other man said.

"We almost got caught with our proverbial pants down," Michael said as they walked down the open-air corridor in search of the honeymoon suite. "This, my dear, is our room."

Inside, the Mexican tile floor blended well with the red rock scenery outside the large windows. The view was breathtaking, and the bed, king-size.

"Michael, you've thought of everything," Laura said, noticing the champagne cooling in a silver bucket next to the bed. "We can watch the sunset from bed." She took his hand then, leading him to the bed and pushing him backward. Taking charge. Michael, probably unaccustomed to a woman taking charge, was thrown off.

"Easy honey," he said.

"You take it easy, babe. I'm on top this time," Laura said. And she was. She teased him for a long time, trying to make him give in to her control. He wouldn't, and he kept trying to roll her over. They ended up on their sides, facing each other, and Laura began to laugh. She couldn't stop. She decided to take a shower. Lovemaking wasn't supposed to be a war, she thought, realizing she was over Michael Anderson.

"Let's head back to Carefree, shall we?" Laura said, walking back into the honeymoon suite after a long, hot shower.

"Why not stay the night? Drive back in the morning?" Michael asked.

"I'd rather not," Laura said, getting dressed and then towel-drying her hair. She remained standing as Michael lounged in the bed. "My flight's pretty early, and I have a cab scheduled already."

"Too bad," he said, not moving from his spot. "I don't feel like driving tonight. Relax. I'll get you back in time in the morning. I'm taking a nap. You missed a glorious sunset," he mumbled, and then rolled over onto his left side, placing a pillow over his right ear.

Laura was furious. After gathering her few things from the room, she stomped out, letting the door slam behind her. Instead of riding down on the incline, she hiked down the mountain to the lobby of the hotel. Once inside, an enraged "Mrs. Smith," as she was listed on the guest registry, persuaded a helpful concierge named Ben to drive her back to Phoenix—her spontaneous nuptials, she told Ben, were a terrible mistake.

"I'm so sorry, Mrs. Smith," he said, trying to comfort the distraught bride-to-be who wasn't. They didn't talk during their late-night ride through the desert. When they pulled into the hotel entrance, Ben again told her he was sorry.

ALL THE DIFFERENCE | 71

"I'll be fine. And it's Ms. Mercer. Thank you so much for the ride," she added, slipping him a fifty-dollar bill she'd taken out of Michael's wallet.

Laura knew Michael was one of *them* once she saw his attitude in the honeymoon suite. She hated guys who always wanted to be in control, who thought there was more to their relationship, who thought there would be more. There wouldn't be, ever. He was psycho.

CHAPTER 7

One Week Later: Friday, May 15

Angie banged on the bathroom door. "He left five messages on the stupid machine. If you don't call him back soon, I'm gonna do it," she yelled through the door to her roommate. "His name is Michael Anderson. Says he had a great time in Sedona, whatever that is, and wants to know why you won't return the call. He's called every day for a week. Would ya just call him already?"

Angie wondered if the guy had shiny shoes. He sounded like it. He also sounded like he was lusting after the ice maiden. Poor guy, the desperation in his voice made Angie's heart ache. Laura couldn't care less about him, Angie knew. *Maybe he needs me,* she began thinking. She'd just watched a daytime talk show about what guys need. They just need respect, the experts said. That and routine. That's why they needed women. *I could be like that,* she thought, watching the show. *You know, dependable, wearing an apron, growing flowers.* They really didn't want superwomen, guys didn't. Not really. They just wanted a wife and a good mom for their kids. Simple.

"He's flying back from the coast today," Angie yelled.

"Fine. I heard you. Fine," Laura yelled back.

The coast, that guy had said, "the coast." Wow. Angie pictured a Hollywood hunk, a movie-star-type guy in a casual California-cool suit. Dark sunglasses. Muscles. He must work in the entertainment industry, she imagined. Next time he called, she'd call him back if the bitch didn't.

Finished with her shower, Laura opened the bathroom door. Angie was still in the hall. "Angie, he's a jerk. He's married, treats his wife like dirt, and thinks he's God's gift to women. If he keeps calling, I'll get the number changed. I'm not calling him back. Got it?" Laura demanded, standing in the doorway, one thick white towel wrapped around her head, another wrapped around her body.

"Whatever. I'm outta here before I'm late for work," Angie said, turning and huffing out the door. *She's so stupid. Playing around with married men. It could really get you hurt. At least fired,* she thought, and then laughed at her own little joke.

*****

The driver's seat. She'd sneak into her momma's clunker car and pretend she was driving away. Far away. In her make-believe world, she'd drive a big car up to a big house and there'd be lots of toys and cookies and air conditioning and Barbie dolls.

If only I could drive, *the girl thought. No longer little, but not really big, she attended a country school, where bruises and scrapes and other accidents were a way of life on the farm. Not unusual. An expected result of chores. That hers were from beatings and not from milking a stubborn cow didn't cross anybody's mind. The effort to survive was more important than a little girl's somewhat messy appearance.*

Her momma always looked worse. Later on, after she ran away, she'd hear a song on the radio about mothers and daughters or something and it would make her cry. Her momma was so pathetic. She really didn't care about anything anymore. The caring had been taken out of her a few men before.

The girl still cared. She'd make it. It was almost time. Almost. At age eleven, she had a plan. She'd execute the plan as soon as she could.

****

The speakerphone on Maddie's desk said, "I'm out of time," in a woman's voice. Realizing it was Janet, she picked up the phone.

"What's that supposed to mean?" Maddie asked, worry mixing with relief. It was the first she'd heard from Janet since the day after the gutter, more than two weeks ago.

"No, not like my hourglass is empty, or that my time is up, just that I've become timeless. For the first time in my life, I have no external structure. I can choose when to wake up, when to sleep, when to eat. It's strange and wonderful all at the same time," Janet said, a smile audible in her voice.

"OK, now that I know you aren't suicidal, where the hell have you been? I've been worried sick. Everyone has," Maddie said, worry converting to anger. "It's irresponsible. Selfish. That's what it is. I was about to file a missing person report with Pete over in homicide. He owes me. He can find anybody. You've been gone more than two weeks."

"Well, now I'm found, Maddie. I'm so sorry to have worried you. I just needed to disappear. Why don't you come see me? It'd probably do you a lot of good to be timeless for a few days. And by the way, my boys know where to find me."

"Chuck doesn't. He's been driving all your friends crazy trying to find you. Do you care?"

"Not in the least. I'll text you my new landline and you can call me when you'd like to visit. Cell service is a bit spotty here. Oh, and you'll need a bathing suit, a carton of your cancer sticks, and that's about it," Janet said mysteriously. "And, if any of your friends need a trip out of time, invite them along. Girls only."

"A trip where?" Maddie asked, amused Janet had read her mind. How did Janet know Maddie had been dreaming of a getaway from Lyle? Space, that's all she needed.

"You'll see. Come visit. It's amazing the insights you achieve with distance. That's why age is a wonderful perspective; it's just too bad we don't take advantage of it very often."

"So you're becoming my voice of wisdom, is that it?" Maddie teased.

"No, dear. Only you can do that for yourself. It's just that I wish I had stepped out of time when I was younger. I might not have wasted those years being busy. Doing instead of being. Do you understand?"

"I guess so, but while you were busy doing, you built quite a career and raised two great kids. That's being, too, isn't it?"

"No. That's outside me. My marriage was failing and I lost myself. My dreams didn't originally have anything to do with real estate, Maddie. That career choice set my fate. One thing led to another. Suddenly, I'm driving the big flashy car, wearing the big jewelry and fancy clothes, and I'd lost my soul," Janet said. "I'm finding it again, now."

"But your career? I mean sure, we all compromise. That's not bad, it's just reality. What else would you be, Janet?"

"Take some time and come see me. I'll fill you in," Janet said, mysteriously. "And while you're pondering this conversation, don't read too much into it. That forces inaction, I think."

"What are you talking about?" Maddie asked, frustrated.

"Come visit me, Madeline, and maybe you'll understand."

*****

She's somewhere in South Carolina, for heaven's sake, Maddie thought as she drove home. After her cryptic conversation with Janet, the text arrived with Janet's new landline number. Maddie had Googled the area code and found Janet's location. She'd pack warm-weather clothes.

Next, she'd called the Martin Agency, where suddenly virtually everyone she liked worked. She asked for Lyle, Ellen, or Francis. She got Lyle.

"Lyle, Janet called."

"Cool. Is she OK?"

"She's fine."

"So great. I'm sort of in the middle of something, um, do you want me to call you back later or—"

Maddie hung up on him, imagining him turning his attention back to whatever it was that was more important than her.

*****

"Lyle has the depth of a rock. A flat skipping rock," Maddie said to Ellen, who answered Francis's line.

"Forget about Lyle. Tell me more about Janet. When did she call you? Are you sure she wants more than just a visit?" Ellen asked. Following Maddie's write-ups about the Jones mess made Ellen realize she and the high-power Realtor had more in common than she'd known. Maybe talking with Janet in person would give Ellen the answers she needed, the answers about what to do about her loveless marriage, and her growing romance with Ron. But first, she needed to forge some real friendships. And she'd start with Maddie. She couldn't believe she'd just been invited on a girls' trip the following weekend.

"Thank you so much for including me! I'd love to go somewhere, anywhere. I'll ask Francis if she'd like to go, too, but I bet Ron needs her," Ellen said. *For work. Is that all there is between them? Of course it is. What about me? Does he need me for life?* Ellen wondered.

"Go for it," Maddie had told her, talking about a girls' trip. And she would. Her plans were coming together. Michael envisioned no life for Ellen beyond himself. She was an extension of his plans and dreams. Until now. This would be her first trip without him, ever. He wouldn't say no. He'd just be surprised. Madeline and Janet didn't need to know that. No, it was enough they invited her. It was more than enough. It was perfect.

Meanwhile, her slowly unfolding relationship with Ron was exciting. They had met after work twice, at out-of-the-way places where no one would recognize them. They'd kissed and held hands, but that was all. Ron wanted to take it slowly, he'd told her. But the more time she spent with Ron, the more she was drawn to him. Their e-mail exchanges kept her going—sometimes twenty different exchanges a day now.

A weekend away from Ron would be tough. But with Michael in town for once, Ellen looked forward to her chance to be away.

****

Looking across the bar, Angie decided the man wasn't too sappy looking, and he had very shiny shoes. The top of his head was covered with a thin smattering of brown hair. She fought an urge to go over and rub the top of his head, give him a noogie. He had a nifty suit on. But he looked sad, she decided. Maybe he didn't feel good. And why was he alone on a Friday night?

He'd walked into Lindey's ten minutes earlier, plunked down at the bar, and asked Ed the bartender to put it on Channel 5, so he could watch the eleven o'clock news.

Angie was leaning against the bar, waiting for her last table to pay the bill, and sporadically chatting with Ed. After watching the sad, cuddly guy for a few minutes, Angie begged Ed to go talk to him, find out the scoop. Ed rolled his eyes at her, but he was bored, so he sauntered down to the other end of the bar to talk with the guy.

While she waited down at the other end, Angie remembered when the restaurant first opened. It was the hot spot. Nobody would've dared ask for a TV to be turned on. *Was there even a TV in here before this year?* she wondered. *Restaurants, like people, only have a set time to shine,* she thought. Some people peak in high school, others, during college. *Some, like me,* she thought, *peak later, once they get money.* She needed to hurry. She was getting old, she told herself.

Maybe this one's the guy, the one. While Ed talked with him, Angie decided to check on her one remaining table, a four-top of businessmen she'd been respectfully flirting with all evening. They seemed like expense-report types, middle management. They'd leave a respectable 20 percent. Not like small business owners, CEOs, and those guys, who—if they looked her in the eyes when they ordered—would leave Angie at least 23 percent. No eye contact—cheapos, 15 percent if she was lucky.

The bald one in the blue suit looked her in the eye and said, "Check, Miss." He didn't smile. He'd give her 17 percent, she guessed. At least they were leaving so she could focus on the mystery man.

"You're not going to believe this, but he's pining for your room-mate," Ed snickered when she returned to her perch at the end of the bar.

I bet it's the California guy, Angie thought. "Did he say anything else?"

"Just that babes didn't usually get to him but she did. It's pathetic. The idiot's married—at least he's wearing a ring—and here he sits staring at the television...Angie?"

She barely heard him, already heading for the fool at the other end of the bar.

****

Maddie rummaged through her dresser drawers in search of the flattering bathing suit. She had one she liked. When she yanked the suitcase out from under the bed and opened it to pack, she instantly created a new spot for the two cats to curl up in and snooze.

Even though she'd been writing about fashion for years, she didn't keep up. The latest runway ideas would flow from her eyes to her computer and out through the written words in her column, none of the information retained in long-term memory. It just wasn't important when all she wore was black. The notion of a vacation, though, was throwing her off. She needed to find out what "resort wear" she needed to buy, versus what she could scrape by with wearing again. It'd been awhile since her last vacation in the sun. A long while.

"Shoo, you two, you're gonna make my clothes all hairy. Go," she yelled lifting up one side of the hard-sided, beat-up black case. Hobson, her twenty-pound black and white cat, simply dug his claws into the soft insides of the case. Bosworth plunked to the floor, feet first, orange hair flying.

"Maddie, chill. They'll get out once you've filled it with stuff," Lyle said. He was parked in a yellow beanbag on the floor just inside their bedroom.

"Uhhh," Maddie said, but left the suitcase and returned to rummaging through a drawer.

"I'm getting you some wine. I'll be back," Lyle said. By the time he returned, Maddie's face was streaked with tears.

"I'll make 'em move. It's not worth crying over," Lyle said. "You have a whole week to pack."

"It's not the cats. It's this. A stupid family photo. God, I hate these. It's from the church directory. I think it's our last photo as a family." Maddie sniffed and shoved the photo back into the drawer where she'd found it.

"Sorry. I didn't know it still bugged you that much, Mad. You can hang out with the Boardmans, you know. We're just a normally dysfunctional group. They really like you too."

"That's not the same. When Dad decided to leave Mom for his secretary, he declared his life up until that point had been miserable. He had to, of course, make his past a mistake to make his new decision OK, you know?" Maddie sniffed again. "He told me, you know, after he'd moved into his condo love pad, that he hadn't been happy for a decade. To a sixteen-year-old girl, that means all but six years of your life your father says he's been miserable. I remember thinking, *Excuse me, that's my life you're smearing with shit too.* He didn't care, of course, because, as he explained it, he'd found his soul mate," Maddie said, pausing to take a drink of her wine. Lyle was still sprawled on the beanbag on the floor, staring up at the ceiling, letting her vent.

Crossing the room, she grabbed a smoke out of the pack, lit it, inhaled deeply, and blew smoke up to the ceiling. With her left hand, she stroked Hobson and Bosworth, who were both back inside the suitcase. Bosworth got up, stretched, and went to sit on Lyle.

"I know you have a point to all this, besides your family was dysfunctional like 99 percent of all families—" Lyle interjected.

"Here's the point. I tried to explain it to Ellen when we were chatting the other day. I had to let go of it all, or else it would ruin me. Most of the time, I do a pretty good job of it. Of letting go. I told Ellen, if you won't tell Michael good-bye, at least give yourself a try. Decide to make your own way. Natalie Merchant said it: 'She'll make her way.' My favorite song, as you both know," Maddie said, adding, "Life's too short to ride shotgun."

"And did she listen?" Lyle asked, stroking Bosworth.

"She's still working for your ad agency, so yes, I think she's listening. And Francis seems to think Ellen and Ron Martin are becoming an item. Don't you repeat that."

"Great," Lyle said, sighing. "Let's go to bed, my dear. Not to sleep, to bed." He stood then, tossing Bosworth back into the open suitcase. He took the cigarette out of Maddie's hand, crushed it out in the ashtray, and led her down the hall to the couch in the living room.

It was dark outside and inside, and she could see an almost full moon through the window. *Maybe I'm not meant to get married,* Maddie thought. *This is actually working out pretty well. Unconventional. But no disappointments, or not as many at least. Can you still be classified as being in a dysfunctional relationship if you're living together?* she wondered. *Yes, and you can still get hurt just as bad.*

Maddie pushed back from Lyle, who was trying to kiss her. "Lyle, thanks for listening. I know it's hard for you," she said, meaning it. "I don't want to end up like that."

"Hey, I know, Maddie. Everything'll work out. No more talking," Lyle said, unbuttoning her black blouse.

****

Momma got fed up, *the little girl thought happily. It wasn't like she took charge or anything, but she didn't stop the little girl.*

Really, Momma was just tired. Too tired to fight.

This time, we'll really leave, *the girl knew it. Her momma lost her eye. The doctor told her momma next time she would die. Guaranteed it. Said it to the girl, now fourteen. Said, "Get your momma and go. Go far away. Tonight."*

He gave them five hundred-dollar bills. More money than the girl had ever seen. And finally, they left. They left from the emergency room. Went to the Greyhound station. Bought two one-way tickets to Dayton, Ohio. The girl picked the place, and her momma simply nodded. She liked the name. Day-ton. Daylight. Happiness. Probably not. But at least they could live. She knew he wouldn't follow them. Wouldn't have the money to and couldn't stay sober long enough. He'd rather buy a new pair of shoes than spend money on his girls. Like they belonged to him or something. Shiny new shoes and fancy new clothes were always more important to him than food for us, *the girl thought.*

As the bus rolled through the night, she thought her momma slept. By the first light of the morning, the girl thought she saw the tears flowing from her momma's remaining eye, tears for the man she left behind. Because, although he tried to kill her again, she loved him. She heard her momma pray for the man's forgiveness, and her momma prayed he would find them.

The little girl hated her momma then. Hated her more than anything or anyone in the world.

CHAPTER 8

One week later: Friday, May 22

"You can't miss it. I live in the only pink house on the island," Janet told Maddie gleefully when she called to say she was coming and bringing Ellen. Francis had decided to stay behind, saying she had too much to do.

Ellen and Maddie flew to Savannah, Georgia, then hailed a taxi and headed for a dock on the Savannah River and waited for a man named Bud.

So far, Maddie had enjoyed the trip with Ellen. They weren't that close, more social acquaintances than friends. Ellen was funny, she'd discovered—and she told great inside stories about the ad agency during the flight. Sporting oversized sunglasses and a bright yellow sundress, Ellen had become the perfect sunny balance to Maddie's more skeptical demeanor. Looking at her, Maddie wondered why she found it so hard to be happy. Why couldn't she just be content with what she had, who she was with? Why couldn't she be more Ellen-like, she wondered. *Because, Ellen's clueless,* she reminded herself.

"Y'all visitin' the lady in the pink house?" called a suntanned, fiftiesish man in the smallest boat Maddie had ever seen.

"Are you Bud?" Maddie asked, hoping he wasn't. *Surely he isn't taking us across the Savannah River and into the Atlantic Ocean in that...that dinghy.*

He was. And before they had time to object, Ellen, Maddie, and Bud were off to visit "the lady in the pink house."

"Now that Janet, she's some lady," Bud said, navigating his tiny boat across the huge and mysterious Savannah River. Barges bigger than Maddie's office building in Columbus seemed just a stone's throw away, waiting to pull them under in their wakes. "Fortunately for you ladies—and excuse me if this surprises y'all—but I killed a rattler on my way over to get you, and if you all don't mind, I'd like to pick it up to bring home for the boys to make a belt with. They'll be so jazzed. Don't worry, I cleaned up all the blood earlier."

Bud smiled. Maddie kept her eyes focused on the huge tanker looming too close. "Sure, Bud, go on and get it. Where'd you leave him?" she asked.

"Right over there, on that buoy," he answered. As he captained the boat over to the orange buoy bobbing in the water, the women could see the huge snake draped over the drum. Its rattler still twitched. "Don't worry, y'all, the tail twitches after it dies. But it's dead." Bud used a stick with a hook on the end to grab his snake, then dropped it into a burlap sack, pushed the throttle of the boat, and said, "Now, fine ladies, without further delay, I'll deliver you to your friend and mine, Janet Jones."

"Just another good argument for life in the city," Maddie mumbled.

"What d'ya say, ma'am?" Bud asked.

"Nothing," she answered, wondering just how out of time Janet was.

As they were docking the rickety snake-infested boat, Maddie discovered they still had a bus ride to reach Janet. This, after a flight to Savannah and a taxi ride to the dock.

"You know, I'm not sure we're really going anywhere. It's some type of transportation nightmare. What's next? A train I guess," Maddie said.

"A golf cart, actually, Miss," Bud said, eyes twinkling.

"I think it's wonderful and romantic and exciting," Ellen said.

After enduring a bumpy school-bus ride on a dirt road, the women entered the gates of Melrose, a plantation on the island, well-groomed, peaceful, car-free, and stretching out along the ocean. A golf cart transported them the final leg to Janet Jones's pink shingled beach house standing on stilts at the edge of the world.

"It *is* pink!" Ellen exclaimed with childish delight as she and Maddie climbed out of the golf cart. "Easter egg pink!"

"Welcome, you guys," Janet called, dashing down the white wood steps, grabbing Maddie, and hugging her tight.

"What's with the pink?" Maddie asked as a way of disengaging. She hated overt displays of affection, and this one was all she could take after her day of traveling adventures.

"Oh, Janet, I love it," Ellen said, hugging the older woman. "You look so, so rested. And happy."

"I am. You know, girls, this was just about the best decision of my life—besides having my babies. Oh, sorry Ellen," Janet added, looking at a loss for words.

"It's fine. Really," Ellen answered. "I'm just so happy to be here. Thank you for including me."

"Of course! I'm sure you're hungry, so come on in and let me show you your rooms and then we'll head over to the oyster roast. Come on. They'll have your luggage over in a minute."

****

Even though they'd done it on their first date a week ago, Angie liked pretending this would be the first time. She'd taken off work. They'd be spending two nights together at his huge house. He promised that someday, it would all be hers. He'd told her to pack her bags, and he would pick her up. He also told her not to chew bubble gum anymore and so she'd tried giving it up. For him. She had a stash in her overnight bag, just in case.

She told him not to come by her apartment. She would meet him at the restaurant. *No Laura messing this scene up,* Angie decided. No, she had better be safe. She had told Michael how awful her roommate was, how she just used men and really just wanted to move to New York and get out of this cow town. But he might still harbor a flame for the ice maiden. One Angie hadn't doused yet, although she would.

And Angie knew how. "By the end of this weekend," she told her smiling image in the restroom mirror, "I'll be a shoo-in for Mrs. Michael Anderson." She dreamed of a big ring, a matching convertible Mercedes. She didn't even mind that little bald spot on the top of his head. She thought it was cute. And she still wanted to rub it, but she hadn't. He seemed a little sensitive about it, always pushing his hair over it and stuff.

He said maybe, since she was young, she could help him with his business. They could be partners. She needed to help him spot trends. Tell him what was hot with teens and the twenty-something crowd. It was all just unbelievable. A dream. Michael was her dreamboat. Everything was perfect, except meddling Ed, the bartender.

As soon as she sat down at the bar, Ed had asked her if she would be sticking around to watch the Channel 5 news—resulting in dagger eye stares and stony silence. "Fuck off, Ed," she finally said, and resumed her daydreams.

Michael told her she was unbelievable in bed. They'd done it three times so far, but she'd used her best sex performance. At least an A plus.

And another plus, Angie knew from looking through Michael's wallet while he was sleeping, was that she resembled his wife, a younger version of his wife. That was good. She was his type. More natural than Laura Mercer. More real.

Angie began trying to make herself into a young Ellen Anderson lookalike. Ellen's skin looked darker in the pictures she'd seen, but Angie was working on a tan. All in all, she felt really good about this one. And maybe it would make Laura jealous…

"Hi, beautiful. Ready for our weekend of love?" he whispered into her ear, coming up behind her, placing his hands on her shoulders.

"You kids have big plans this weekend, I take it?" asked Ed, rhetorically.

"Just a weekend alone together, getting to know each other. Right, Pumpkin?" Michael said.

"Right. Bug off, Ed. Have a nice working weekend." Angie smiled and got up.

"You too, Ange, you too," Ed called, laughing when Angie flipped her middle finger at him.

Michael tossed Angie's suitcase in the trunk of his car, which he had left idling right outside the restaurant door under the guard of the valet parking attendants. As they sped off, Angie couldn't believe she was sitting in the passenger seat of a Mercedes convertible driven by a wealthy, successful, and attractive businessman who couldn't keep his hands off of her. Once they were on the highway, he began teasing her, rubbing her, and he wanted to stick his finger inside her. She looked at him, he smiled, and she decided, *What the heck. So what if it's two in the afternoon?* She'd excite a few truckers on the way to Michael's house.

She parted her legs, stretching the clingy miniskirt even tighter. It was Laura's—she'd swiped it a couple months earlier. As he discovered, she wasn't wearing underwear. She couldn't have unsightly panty lines with a classy guy like Mike. Uh, Michael. He hated when she called him Mike. She moaned, squirmed lower into the seat, and reached for his shorts.

She'd never seen a house so big. They had finally turned off the highway, followed a series of rolling hill roads, and turned into his driveway. He punched in a code, opened the huge gate, and followed a winding drive past a pond. They glided into the four-car garage.

"I probably should carry you in the front door, but this is my favorite entrance and, well, it's not like you're my wife," Michael said.

"When I am your wife, you can carry me," Angie said, smiling sweetly, as he opened her car door.

"Whatever you'd like, doll," he answered.

*****

She was cute, Michael thought. Not a knockout like her roommate. But cute. Fun. Eager to please. That was good.

He wondered if he was promising too much. He needed to use Angie to get to Laura. He knew Laura was the jealous type and that the two women hated each other. He'd make sure Angie would have fun, though. He'd make her feel good while he was using her. That would be OK for everybody.

*****

"Is she throwing up again?" Janet asked Maddie. Maddie nodded, making a face.

Maddie was glad to be back at the pink cottage on the ocean after enjoying a fabulous dinner in a one-room restaurant, called Marsh-Side-Mamma's, which was actually the converted living room of an island native's house. The house overlooked the marsh and sound. The smoked oysters were fabulous and Maddie had made a pig of herself. Meanwhile, both Janet and Maddie watched as Ellen seemed to look sicker and sicker. Greener and greener.

"Yes, she's praying to the porcelain god again, poor thing," Maddie said. "But I don't get it. One glass of wine isn't going to do that—and she didn't touch an oyster. Just had soup. Could it be like time-delayed seasickness? Is there such a thing?"

"I think some people's equilibrium is thrown off pretty easily. I don't know, but I hope she's over it soon. I have so much to show you tomorrow. Maybe she's just unwinding. She's had a tough few weeks of change."

"So have you, but you seem to be adjusting quite nicely. She'll be fine. Maybe she needs sleep." Maddie was reclining on the pink-and-white-striped second-floor porch with white wicker furniture. "I adore this porch, overlooking the ocean. We're at the very edge of the world." To her left, the lights of the big city—Hilton Head Island—glistened, and the Harbor Town Lighthouse beckoned. To her right, the Atlantic Ocean. Incredible. Peaceful.

"So have you talked to good ol' Chuckie since I skewered him in my column?" Maddie asked.

"Not once. Probably won't. When he and I visited this place—it had to be ten years ago—I fell in love. He went crazy. Too slow. Nothing to do. But I have kept in touch with a few people—and, well, I knew when the time was right, I'd live here. I've been offered a teaching position at the island's adult training program, and I'll probably dabble in real estate. That will be enough. For now. I'm really content."

"Is content enough?" Ellen asked, joining the women on the porch. "Sorry about my poor company. I guess I'm seasick?" She stopped, looking around. "God, this is beautiful, Janet, I never dreamed I'd have a chance to stay at a place this magical."

"Now you know why I'm never leaving, and why, at least for now, content is enough," Janet said, leaning back, curled like a sleepy cat within a white wicker womb. "I need to start over on my own terms. When I read the real estate listing for this place, I knew it was perfect. The ad for this place read something like, 'Need a retreat and a place to make you smile? Need sunshine in the mornings and salt air throughout the day? Then my pink paradise is just for you.' It was very romantic and freeing, and immediately I knew I'd found my new home."

"But it's so isolated. I mean, you don't see a soul, and it's so quiet. It sorta makes me nervous. Are you safe?" Maddie asked, enjoying the crashing ocean as she looked out into the dark abyss the sunset had created. Would she be able to live in an isolated place like this? The thought gave her the chills. "It's just that I feel like I'm on the edge of the world—ah, not that there's anything wrong with that. Can I have another glass of sangria?"

"Of course. Ellen?" Janet asked, reaching for the pitcher.

"Thanks, Janet, but I better pass. Once my stomach settles down, I'll be right there with you guys," Ellen said, staring out into the void.

"So what is your charming husband going to do with himself this weekend without you?" Maddie asked, lighting a cigarette.

"The same as usual. He'll just do it at home," Ellen answered. "Oh, shoot, excuse me," she said. She covered her mouth and ran inside.

"Strange. This better pass or we're leaving her behind tomorrow. I have a bunch of exploring planned. It'll be my first chance to show off my new island home. A woman can't live by just thinking alone," Janet said. "By the way, I'm writing a book."

"No way. About what?" Maddie asked, surprised. "I never pictured you as a writer. I never knew you were even interested."

"I've always dreamed of it. Not that I'll be any good, but I'm gonna try. I blocked out that part of me, the striving, learning part. Was satisfied with the money from real estate, with being a mom. Now I need to make up for lost time," Janet said. "Don't ask me, 'cause I'm not telling you what it's about. Not yet."

"Fine, be that way. I'll wait. But do you really think you lost time, Janet? I mean, raising two kids, that's a lot of accomplishment," Maddie asked. "And a full-time, successful career. You've been a role model, a working-woman trendsetter. We all look up to you."

"That's nice. I love my boys and I loved my life, but I lost me. I was doing, not thinking. Do you understand the difference? I chose to block out my other, deeper desires because it was the easy way out. We depended on my income to live a certain way. Chuck and I were a team; at least at the office, he needed me. Heck, that's what we women do. We become selfless. Other-focused. Others' time and needs matter more than our own. And it doesn't matter whether we work at home, work at an office, or do a little of both.

"But enough about me," Janet said finally. "Are you following your dreams, Madeline?"

Maddie didn't answer. She lit a cigarette and asked Janet to tell her more about the island. And for the rest of the night, until Maddie's eyes couldn't stay open any longer, Janet shared her stories about island life.

Ellen never returned to the porch.

CHAPTER 9

Friday, May 23

With hot, penetrating sunshine filling the pink house, despite hangovers and little sleep, Janet and Maddie said they were ready to explore. Ellen felt great.

The good-morning text messages from Ron had been just what she needed to start her day. Ellen had transformed from a person who usually forgot her cell phone into one who checked it constantly because of Ron. They talked often throughout the day. They also e-mailed each other and texted like schoolkids. And while they'd agreed not to talk while she was visiting Janet, the text message was a wonderful surprise. Ellen was amazed by how close they had gotten in such a short amount of time. Like it was meant to be, all of it.

Ellen didn't expect happiness like this to find her. She'd almost given up on feeling needed, loved. She wished she could share more about Ron with Janet and Maddie—explain to them the love she'd found. But she couldn't. Not yet. She and Ron had agreed to wait for the right time, after she'd had a chance to confront Michael and address their dead relationship. She'd need courage for that, and she hadn't gotten there yet.

Ellen had followed behind Janet and Maddie during a leisurely morning of strolling on the deserted beaches, jumping over driftwood stumps, and watching the dolphins frolic.

After the long beach walk, Janet loaded them into her custom golf cart—pink and white to match her house—and drove them all over the island. She even showed them the one-room schoolhouse where she'd be teaching adults two evenings a week. Maddie and Ellen were enchanted by the island and shocked by Janet's complete transformation. Listening to Janet's joy, Ellen couldn't help but imagine starting a new life of her own, one with Ron. A new start. Everything would be OK.

"What did you do with all of your expensive suits? You spent a fortune at Clothes the Loop," Maddie asked suddenly, as they whizzed past yet another beautiful marsh water scene.

"I gave them all away. All of them. I figure if I do show property on the island, I'll dress the way islanders do. Khaki shorts, white shirt—you know, kind of like I look right now," Janet answered.

"I'm so inspired by you, Janet," Ellen said, turning to face the front of the golf cart from her backseat spot. "Thanks to both of you, for including me."

"Well, thanks, honey," Janet said, giving Ellen's hand a pat.

"Did I tell you I had a miscarriage?" Ellen added suddenly, surprising herself. She never shared her heartache.

"No, Ellen. When?" Maddie asked, turning to face her.

"Well, it's just that I did, a very long time ago, and now, I think, maybe that caused me not to be able to be pregnant again. And then, sometimes, I dream about that baby, the baby who would be sixteen or so years old. And, well, I was just wondering," Ellen continued in a rush of words, giving voice to the guilt and pain she had harbored inside for so long.

"I don't think a miscarriage could affect your ability to conceive," Janet said.

"I know, that's what the fertility specialist said too. I just feel like there's some connection there. Well, anyway, enough about that," Ellen added, embarrassed she'd shared.

"Oh, you poor thing," Maddie said, reaching back to pat Ellen's knee. Ellen kept her arms crossed and stared out of the golf cart. "I'm sure your doctor told you that had nothing to do with your, ah, infertility or whatever. What about Michael?"

"The doctor said everything is fine with him," Ellen said, her voice trailing off.

Janet chimed in, "I think you've come a long way since I left town, Ellen. Just think. You have a job. You're more confident, independent. You can't change the past, but you're doing a great job with your future. Will it include Michael?"

"You know, it's funny," Ellen answered. "For so long, I couldn't imagine life without him. But I honestly think I'm beginning to hate him. Actually, I do hate him. But I love him too."

"So what are you going to do?" Maddie asked.

"I'm going to start taking care of myself, like Janet said. I've decided that much." All three women fell silent.

Janet stopped the cart in front of her favorite island restaurant, only open for lunch. As they walked through the swinging screen door, half the people in the restaurant began calling hello to Janet. Eric, apparently the seafood wholesaler based on the smiling fish logo on his T-shirt, came up to give her a hug. The restaurant air was thick with the smell of Cajun spices and boiling seafood.

"Look at that little tyke." Eric pointed to a table where a mother, a father, and a toddler boy sat enjoying their lunch. "That little one's eating grouper. That's what I like to see. He's a customer for life." The four of them shared a laugh, and Eric tipped his baseball cap as a good-bye to Janet and ducked into the restaurant's kitchen.

Ellen's stomach began churning as she followed her friends to a corner table. She hoped there was something besides seafood on the menu and was relieved to be able to order from the kids' menu.

After they'd ordered, Maddie said, "Eric's cute, Janet."

"I hadn't noticed, Mad," Janet answered and then smiled. "OK, maybe I have noticed, but I'm not ready yet. I'm not even divorced yet. Ellen, it's nice to see you eating, even if it's just peanut butter and jelly. What is it with you? They have the best hamburgers. Grilled. Just like in your own backyard, if seafood is sounding bad."

"Actually, I'm fine. Just fine," Ellen answered, although she was beginning to feel not so fine at all, and she could feel her face drain of color. "I'm just not sure what's getting to me. I'll be fine. Just fine," she said again, trying to convince herself.

*****

"When the sky looked like that, my mom always told me it was gonna rain," Angie told Michael. She was standing in the bay window, looking out at the backyard—in Ellen's favorite spot.

"It's going to rain—'going to,' not 'gonna'—and it's going to be fine. Just a spring shower, if anything, cutie," Michael answered.

Things just have a tendency to work out, he thought to himself as he checked inside the huge Sub-Zero refrigerator and found his wife had left all the makings of a complete gourmet weekend. She'd even labeled the shelves. The one he'd taken their dinner from last night said "PICNIC." On the shelf just above, a sign said "GRILL." The assorted chicken breasts had been marinating; the vegetables were cleaned and placed on a skewer. They were all ready for a gourmet barbecue. There was enough food on each shelf for four adults. *Four?* Michael chuckled. "I'm good, but not that good, honey," he said aloud, closing the refrigerator door. He was surprised to find Angie standing there.

"What did you say, Lamb Chop?" she asked, sliding one of her scrawny hands into his back pocket. She had reminded him of Ellen, the first time he saw her. That was it. That was the strong attraction. But now she was getting on his nerves. She popped her gum.

Ellen had seemed much more mature at a much younger age than this creature. In fact, Michael knew he had to have Ellen the moment he saw her. So vulnerable. So different. So willing to serve him. To make him comfortable. And desperate, yes desperate, to be someone. To please a man. With her little superstitions and shy sexuality. She was born to clean and cook and care for a man. Service a man. And he loved the fact she was a virgin. Well, almost a virgin. She'd been raped, she told him. But that didn't count.

So, when did he get bored, exactly? He wasn't sure.

And now that Laura Mercer bitch wouldn't even return his calls. He wondered, briefly, if he was losing his touch. Of course not...

"Earth to Lamb Chop, come in—or just come," Angie said too loudly into his ear.

"Why are you calling me Lamb Chop anyway?" Michael asked, angry that it was Angie's hand in his pocket, not Laura's.

"You remember—it was the first time we did it and you called me cutie and the first thing that popped into my head was Lamb Chop. I love lamb chops. Show me around the rest of the house, please. Last night, I really just saw the bedroom," Angie said, and begrudgingly, Michael threw himself into his role as roommate seducer.

"Fine. Spit out the gum," he said. "Please." And she did.

They meandered through the huge home; all the while, Michael tried to figure out a graceful, subtle way to ask about Laura.

"So, how's your roomie?" he asked finally, stupidly, as they arrived back in the master bedroom.

"The ice maiden is fine. I'd tell her you asked, but she hates you more than dirt," Angie said, the anger contorting her face into fine points. "More than the fuzz hanging on a speck of dirt. So don't ask about her again, or you're gonna have a really long bachelor's weekend, if you get my drift. I didn't take off all those shifts to sit around talking about her. OK?"

"Got it. Chill. I won't mention her again," Michael said, calmly. *No, I'll just dream about her.* "I have a wonderful dinner planned for tonight. Last night's picnic out in the pasture will be surpassed by a romantic barbeque. Would you prefer steak or chicken, my dear?"

Turning around and smiling, for a moment, Angie looked victorious. "Steak sounds perfect. I can help you grill out, Lamb—ah—Mikey."

****

Freedom definitely has its ups and downs, *the woman decided.* No stupid jerks at all times of the day and night, and no more of Momma's crying. *She thought she and her momma would find the freedom together, in Dayton, but it hadn't worked out. Momma missed the jerk. Left to go back to the jerk as soon as she made enough money at the Holiday Inn to leave. Momma had worked the night clerk job. They got a room in the back, in exchange. When Momma left, she left a note saying sorry. And twenty dollars. And the little girl, now a woman, was alone at sixteen. So she worked the desk at night, in exchange for the room, and went to school.*

She loved school. Ever since Mrs. Berryderry. It was a haven. Her haven. She dreamed of finding Mrs. Berryderry, but she didn't know what city she had lived in back then. So she just dreamed about her. It made her happy. Although she didn't have any friends, she smiled at everyone at school, and many smiled back. It wasn't like that in the real world. She loved school, so nobody noticed that the girl with circles under her eyes slept during lunch after putting all of her food from the cafeteria tray in a bag. That would be dinner. She got a free lunch because the manager lied for her. Said he was her guardian and that she didn't have money. It was almost all true.

She begged the hotel manager not to tell anyone. To let her work for money and a room. If they were full, she said, she'd move to a couch. She'd be quiet, helpful. And she'd clean if they needed it or cook or anything. If only he'd sign her forms and not turn her in.

And he didn't. He seemed to agree with her that it was right that she be there, at his hotel, and not in a foster home. She didn't belong in a home. She belonged in room 218 and that's where she stayed, quietly, because that was their deal—no visitors. Period. She stayed there until she graduated and then, she was gone.

****

Angie thought she was dreaming when she woke up from their afternoon nap.

She blinked, twice, but she was still in an all-white room, under a white canopy, looking out a floor-to-ceiling bay window that faced nothing but a huge green expanse and the woods beyond. Next to her, the owner of the dream. A man with as much sexual experience as Angie—and the money to fill in the picture. *This is heaven*, she thought.

Climbing out of the bed slowly, careful not to disturb Michael, she decided to get their barbecue dinner ready. She wanted it to be elegant, like the house. Like him. So formal. So proper. So married—yet here she was, sharing their bed. It was dangerous and exciting, appealing to both of them. On the edge. Even he said he was turned on by fucking her in his wife's bed, that he'd never done it before because she never left home.

Yes, she'd make him forget about his wife and Laura. She just did it for two hours. And she still had tonight and tomorrow morning to make him love her. They'd made love long into the night Friday night. After the house tour and an early morning horseback ride, they'd eaten lunch and then hopped back in the sack. *This guy just can't get enough of me*, Angie thought. *And even though he's kinda cranky sometimes, it's all right, 'cause he's old*, she told herself.

Suddenly he began to stir, so she hurried toward the bedroom door, fleeing the room before he caught her awake. She might be young, but she needed a break already.

Angie glided down the spiral staircase, pretending she was in a TV commercial when the wealthy star descends slowly, smelling the coffee below. The television commercial ends with the lady sitting at her antique kitchen table drinking steaming coffee from a really expensive china cup, smiling as the sun rises over her estate.

She realized, self-consciously, she should be wearing a long silk robe instead of Mikey's T-shirt. She'd seen a yellow one up in the huge master closet. His wife had more clothes than Laura. More clothes than Angie had ever seen, except in a store. Angie decided to rummage around in the wife's closet for tonight. The wife would never know anything was missing, she had so much.

She grabbed a piece of Bazooka bubble gum and read the fortune. "Don't lie or you'll get caught," it said. She tossed it in the trash. Angie looked at the clock above the stove and couldn't believe it was almost five o'clock. They'd slept three hours.

"Yep, that's me, the lady of the house," she whispered, bopping around the kitchen, finding the coffee, and quickly making a pot. "OK, now for the challenging part." Angie was committed to making Michael dinner, a great one, one he'd never forget. They'd begin with food and end with sex. What more could a guy want, she reasoned, and opened the refrigerator door. She'd know what to make when she saw it, she thought, and then realized a whole shelf was labeled for grilling. He really had prepared. She emptied its contents onto the counter.

****

"What the hell are you doing, Angie?" Michael bellowed as he walked into the disaster that was formerly a spotless kitchen. She was really beginning to get on his nerves.

"Oh hi, sweetie, I'm making you dinner, but you're supposed to be in bed," Angie answered. "Are you upset? What's wrong?"

"I thought you were tearing the house down, that's what," he answered, huffing to the coffeepot and silently taking the mug Angie offered him. After a couple sips, he looked up and saw her crying.

"Sorry, Angie. I'm not mad. It's just that I was really looking forward to grilling for you, remember? Impressing you with my cooking prowess. I went to all the trouble of marinating the chicken and steak and all." Michael said.

She looked up and sniffed. "All I was doing was getting it out for you. Sorry if I made you mad."

"That's OK. You go on upstairs. Take a shower and all. Get dressed. Get cute for me, and then we'll have a special dinner from Chef Michael. Candles and all. OK? Atta girl," he added, patting her on the butt. What was he thinking? A whole weekend with this twit?

What a mess. Laura probably didn't even know they were together, Ellen would probably find out, and Angie, well, poor kid—she'd already gotten the wrong idea. Oh well, he'd make the most of it, he thought, feeling his erection. Then he grabbed the fixings—steaks, chicken breasts, potatoes, asparagus, tomatoes, vegetable skewers—all ready to toss on the grill. Heading into the garage, he went out the side door to the patio and over to his huge built-in restaurant-grade gas grill. *The last bastion of cave manliness,* he thought to himself. *Why is it that cooking is a woman's job, but grilling is considered manly? Funny,* he thought.

He heard a knock on the window. *Couldn't she just leave him alone?* he thought but had forced a smile by the time he turned around. "Yes?" he yelled, and Angie opened the window.

"Can I borrow something of your wife's?" Angie yelled back.

"Sure, whatever. Take your time and then come on outside—sweetie," he called. *Leave me alone,* he thought, reaching for the electric ignitor to turn on the grill.

"I'll be right there. I'm going to change," she yelled back, before turning to hurry away.

Then Michael pushed the button.

****

The force of the blast shattered the huge bay window in back and the large stained glass window over the front door, sending a shower of colored glass down on Angie just as she reached the top of the spiral stairs. She dropped to her knees and shielded her head, fortunate the largest shards had fallen past her to the ground. In shock, she stood, walking back down the stairs, crunching through the shattered glass in her bare feet. She tripped on a step and fell, banging her head on the railing as she slid down the rest of the stairs. She didn't notice she was bleeding everywhere.

She struggled to her feet at the bottom of the stairs and raced through the family room and kitchen, toward what had been the picture window overlooking the backyard. A gaping hole in the wall gave her a better view than any window.

****

Ellen thought she was dreaming when she woke up.

She heard the crashing waves and the music of crickets. She looked up at the white ceiling fan slowly turning, turning, and then realized she was in Janet's pink cottage, sleeping on a thick mattress with a down-filled duvet, chilled by the air conditioning. Her room boasted painted white wood floors and sky blue walls. She could stay in this room, dreaming of Ron, all day. Except she shouldn't. She'd kept the peanut butter and jelly down. Had endured a cart ride of questions on the way back from lunch and then excused herself for a nap.

She grabbed her watch off of the whitewashed bedside table and saw it was almost five o'clock. Dinnertime. Her heart pumped wildly for a moment and then calmed. She'd get dressed and go find Maddie and Janet. They were eating in tonight. Boiling shrimp. Drinking wine. She hoped she'd feel better.

*****

By the time the flames subsided enough for Angie to run toward the spot where Michael had been standing, all she saw was black. He was black, burned, still.

She threw up then and then everything went black.

When she woke up in the hospital, a bandage covered her right eye and she screamed. The nurse came running, said her eye was fine, that it was just for the stitches to heal. And then, the nurse told her about the explosion. Angie went back to sleep.

*****

Dixon Crane heard the bulletin on his car radio. He was on his way to be a celebrity judge in the city's annual and prestigious chili cook-off. *The ChiliFest folks will have to wait*, the Dashing Diner thought to himself as he smelled a story. *Not a restaurant story per se, but hell, when a gas grill goes kaboom as a prelude to a cookout,* he figured, *it's my beat.* And he was close to the scene.

So, with that rationale in mind, Dixon pulled into the berm of the freeway, placed a call to the *Journal* newsroom to tell the metro editor he'd cover the story, and hung up before the young punk could sound off an objection. Next, he floored the gas pedal on his mint-green Honda Accord, found an illegal U-turn spot in the median, and was on his way to Field City.

The Andersons were a wealthy family and community leaders in this part of town. After his lunch with Laura Mercer, he'd even called Ellen Anderson, saying he'd heard she needed work, and she told him she got a spot at the Martin Agency. She was nice, appreciated the call. He told her he'd ask her to help him with a downtown review some day, maybe lunch. She told him sure. Dixon hoped it wasn't too late to have her as Mrs. Crane du jour, as he referred to all of his beautiful and helpful lady reviewers.

Dixon loved his job. Young waitresses to intimidate. Great wine. Great food. Power of the pen and all. And through it all, he and the real Mrs. Crane, Caroline, had been happily married for thirty years. She stayed in the background of his public life. When he wasn't being "the reviewer," they spent every spare moment together. His life would end with hers and vice versa.

"Look out, Metro desk, this one's mine," he said aloud, snorting and snuffling with allergies while gunning his Honda and checking his map. Dixon loved his car, created in the only shade of green Honda made back then. He laughed when a hip young travel reporter informed him that green was now the hot color in trendy places like South Beach and Rodeo Drive.

As he turned off the highway onto a two-lane country road leading into the small community, a dark cloud descended on his adventure in the form of a Volvo station wagon with "Practice

Random Acts of Kindness and Senseless Beauty" bumper sticker right next to an "Abortion is Murder" sticker. *It's one of those optimistic God-fearing Volvo-driving housewives,* he thought. He exhaled and then inhaled deeply. He floored the accelerator, passing the Volvo with ease.

Tuning in to the all-news radio station, he tried to gather some more facts. *The broadcast folks don't know any more than us lowly print reporters,* he decided, listening to a report from John Murray that basically said there was an explosion at Michael and Ellen Anderson's home in Field City. The cause of the explosion was the gas grill.

A minivan with the license plate MY3SONZ cut in front of him, and Dixon honked at the jerk. As he continued to press the gas pedal to the floor, Dixon dialed Laura Mercer's private line at the station.

"Sugar, tell me what you know, and I'll feed you the scoop when I get it," he said.

"Dixon, you aren't there on the scene, are you?" Laura asked, incredulously. "You know, they think it was the gas grill. It's kind of sick that a food critic and restaurant reviewer would be on the scene."

"The special of the day is Anderson flambé, I guess," Dixon said, sniffing.

Ignoring this, Laura said, "Try to find out who the woman was, the one who was injured. We don't think it was the wife, based on the family photos around here. She's too young, doesn't look like the pictures. And call me, and only me, when you know something. I'll stay right here. We'll send the crew if you get the scoop."

"Send 'em. I'll get it," Dixon said, hanging up. Most likely, he'd be relegated to writing a column about the dangers of grilling, he thought, since he was a newspaper reporter. He loved being on camera, and there was a slim chance they'd let him. Either way,

Laura would owe him. And so would the Metro section guys at the paper. All in all, he liked how things were turning out.

Much better for him than for poor Michael Anderson, he thought, pulling into the driveway of the estate. A young cop tried to flag him down, so Dixon pulled out his press credentials, waved them in the air, and said, "Outta my way, son." Glancing in the rearview mirror, Dixon chuckled. *It's that old act like you know what you're doing principle,* he thought. Then he wondered what he'd do when he reached the grown-up cops. He'd work it.

As he drove inside the estate, Dixon thought about how the Andersons had caused a stir moving to the boondocks from graceful suburban life in Grandville. He hoped Ellen was OK. He liked her. Saw her at charity events. Dixon thought about her husband; during those charity events, typically, Michael was on his best husbandly behavior while Dixon upped his lecherous act at those same events. *Ironic,* Dixon thought. Since talking to Laura, Dixon had heard Anderson stalked most of the young women in town. *What a jerk. And he had a beautiful, devoted wife.*

Dixon spotted Detective Pete Moore among the official-looking officials in the crowd. He parked at the edge of the driveway, nosing his Honda up to the yellow police tape. Ignoring the arm-raising suit-wearing lawyer type, Dixon made a beeline for the detective. Moore was in the investigations bureau of the Columbus police, Dixon knew. Homicide Squad.

"Pete, come here a minute," he yelled. Pete turned, saw Dixon, and shook his head, but he walked over to him anyway. Dixon met him halfway, on the official side of the police tape.

In a voice loud enough for the rest of the homicide cops, the Field City sheriff, and his deputies to hear, Pete said, "Dixon, we don't know anything, OK? I can't help you out." In a more normal voice, he said, "The three TV stations already reported on the explosion, but they didn't have anything else, no other details.

Besides, you're a food guy. This is, well, a grilling catastrophe. A terrible accident, probably, but definitely, not a food item." He added, "A strange one, this case. Do you know them?"

"A bit, I served on a charity board or two with Ellen. Tell me something, Pete. It's all off the record. It's not like I'm covering it for the *Journal* or anything."

"Yeah, right, Dixon," Pete said, sounding like he didn't quite believe him. Dixon felt hopeful, however—he gave Pete free certificates to restaurants sometimes. Pete removed his glasses and began wiping them on his pants leg, his trademark thinking gesture. Sighing, he said, "The wife wasn't here, OK, and she's still not. She's out of town, at the beach or something. And you're writing about this," Pete said.

"But you're blind without those specks on, Moore," Dixon said, startled Pete had caught him taking notes.

"Yeah, but I'm a good detective. I heard your pen. Remember, I'm on to you, Dixon, OK? And Mrs. Anderson's attorneys even beat me to the scene, so trust me, that's all the information you're gonna get from me. The scene's secure. Now scram, before I get in trouble for talking to the media."

"You always talk to the media, Pete, thank goodness. But who's the female victim, then?" Dixon asked. "And are you still running the scene materials by the coroner's office and the FBI?"

"Dixon, we don't think it was a homicide. And we really don't know who the female victim is. She's young, name is Angie Brown. I'll tell you that. All we know is the guy is Michael Anderson. He decided to grill out, and now he's in critical condition. Hopefully he'll live. The woman's not as bad off. She'll pull through. Scary, you know, the force of the thing. I just fired mine up last weekend. Just tossed on some brats. Didn't think twice about it. Seems like that's what he was doing, and then kaboom."

"They should've eaten out," Dixon said, looking up to catch Pete's reaction.

"You're nasty, Dixon. This blast is going to scare a lot of us with grills. Doesn't it give you the creeps?" Pete asked, flexing his biceps as he spoke.

"No, but it is strange though. The whole incident seems, well, especially wasteful," Dixon remarked, pulling on his beard.

"You need to get outta here, Mr. Crane. Go on. Now," Pete said in his tough cop voice when several of the other officers began approaching them.

"See ya, Petie. You're the best," Dixon said, turning to find his car in the dimming light. It was surrounded by cop cars. *Fine. I'll go four-wheeling,* he thought. He needed to get back to the gate at the base of the driveway and find the Channel 5 camera crew for a live feed.

"Sugar, are they here yet?" Dixon asked into the cell phone as he finagled his way out of the swarm of cop cars. *They thought they had me,* he chuckled, freeing himself by driving on the grass around the large man-made pond and back to the driveway on the other side.

"Yes, they're waiting for you. What the hell are you doing?"

"Just a little four-wheeling. Tell 'em I'll be there, on the inside side of the gate, in two minutes. Their job is to bust me out so I can do the stand-up, got it?"

"I think getting you out will be the easy part. I'm tossing the live shot to you, so be serious. This is a big one. No 'Sugar.' And by the way, who was the woman?"

"You should watch Channel 5 news for that exclusive," Dixon said, laughing as he pushed "End" on his cell phone.

****

"If he calls me 'Sugar' on the feed, cut his mic," Laura said to the sound booth ten minutes later. This had to be professional, like big-city stuff. When the general manager asked her to do the news bulletin cut-in, it was her big chance. Ironically, her big break now depended on whatever information a restaurant reviewer had come up with on the scene.

"We now interrupt our programming for a Channel 5 special report: grilling tips from the Dashing Diner coming right up," a voice from the sound booth said, and everyone except Laura burst into giggles.

"You're all sick," she said, clipping on her microphone, smiling at Rob, reassuring him he could laugh, and then sneering up at the sound booth hovering in the space above her.

"Ready and, three, two, one, music..."

"We interrupt our regular programming to bring you a special news bulletin from WCOL-TV5." Suddenly, Laura's face popped into the middle of *Law & Order*, prompting another round of angry calls from *Law & Order* addicts.

"This is Laura Mercer, News Channel 5 with a special bulletin," she read from the teleprompter. "During our last news update, we told Channel 5 viewers about the tragic explosion of unidentified causes that ripped through a large home in Field City, five miles northwest of Grandville. Sources on the scene tell News 5 the two adult victims were airlifted to area hospitals in critical condition. Now, doing whatever it takes to bring you the news first, Channel 5 is the first station to bring you a live report from the scene, from a seasoned reporter who actually made it behind the police tape to bring you the story: Dixon Crane, of the *Daily Journal*. Dixon, can you tell us the latest?"

"Yes, Laura, this is a scene of carnage out here in Field City. I'm standing in front of the beautiful Anderson mansion, home to one of the most community-oriented couples I've met in my years, and now sadly home to tragedy as well. If not for the fading light, you'd see the large pond, carefully groomed shrubs, and the rest of the fabulous grounds of the Victorian estate. As it is," Dixon said, pausing for effect, "the grounds are as dark as the events that happened here."

"Uh, Dixon, who were the two victims—have you been able to get that information from the police?" Laura asked, a smile belying her impatience. He sounded like Edgar Allan Poe.

"Yes, my dear. The victims include the homeowner, Mr. Michael Anderson, who is in very bad condition, and his young niece, Angela Browning, who was visiting at an unfortunate time. Ellen Anderson is unharmed," Dixon added. "It's a dark day for all of us, a sad, sad day for backyard grillers everywhere." Dixon stared into the camera until the red light went out.

On-screen, Laura was motionless. Her mouth was frozen, in shock. *It was Angie?* In her ear, a voice screamed, *"That's all for now,"* say, *"That's all for now,"* and finally, Laura Mercer said just that.

"This is Laura Mercer. We now return to *Law & Order*, already in progress," the voice of Channel 5 said.

"And, we're out. Nice job, people," Dave's voice boomed from the control booth above the studio. "What happened, Sunshine? You froze, and you never freeze."

"Leave me alone, you jerk," Laura screamed after removing her microphone, and she stormed out of the studio. "You are such an ass, Dave," she added as she slammed the studio door behind her.

Dixon Crane called her private line just as she sat down at her desk. "So, Sugar, how'd I do from the scene?"

"The woman, it was my roommate—it was Angie Brown, the waitress, right?" she demanded, knowing the answer.

"Right," Dixon answered. "Covering for her was the right thing to do. The "ing" on Brown was brilliant, don't you think?"

*****

They'd just watched a beautiful sunset. A beautiful yellow-orange-red sky lit up the pink and white porch. Ellen was relaxed, happy. At peace. She was enjoying her second glass of wine when Janet's phone trilled, an odd, old-fashioned sound, which vibrated out onto the porch. It startled them all, and instantly, Janet looked worried.

"No one knows this number," Janet said, looking at her two guests.

"I didn't even give it to Lyle, so don't look at me," Maddie said, defensively.

"Um, Ron is the only person I gave it to," Ellen said, staring back at Janet.

Janet answered the phone. She covered her mouth with her right hand as she nodded into the receiver. Her eyes filled with tears as she looked over to Ellen and said, "Yes, Mrs. Anderson is here." Janet's hand shook as she held out the receiver to Ellen.

With her left hand, Ellen touched the good luck beads in her pocket while she reached out her right hand for the phone. Exactly what the sheriff had told her was a blur. Something about an accident. After she hung up, the phone rang again. Ellen, answering it mechanically, discovered it was Ron. He was murmuring things in her ear, that he'd take care of her, that everything would be fine. Ellen thanked him for calling and wrote down the flight information he provided, and then she hung up the phone again.

She sat staring through Janet and Maddie, not seeing them, as she told them there had been an explosion at home. That Michael was dead. That Ron was sending a plane to take her home. Maddie and Janet hustled Ellen upstairs, packed her clothes as she sat, watching but not seeing. Ellen didn't cry. Not at all.

When Ellen noticed Maddie was packing her things too, she said, "No, please, Maddie, I need to be alone." A horn blared outside, the golf cart that would drive Ellen to the small airstrip on the island.

On the private jet Ron had sent to bring her back home, Ellen tried to remember just what the sheriff had said. She didn't know why it mattered, but it did. He said Michael didn't suffer, that he was unconscious and died almost immediately upon arrival at the hospital. That was good. She had loved Michael so much, in the beginning and for a long time afterward. He cared for her and about her then. Helped give her the self-confidence to finish school and follow her dreams. Stood by her. Gave her the freedom and the money to dream. Only later did he dash those dreams with his affairs. But she loved him. She did.

She awoke as the jet landed on the runway at the executive airport. The pilot opened the door and asked if she needed help getting down the stairs. Ellen nodded. Her legs didn't seem to be working, and her stomach was queasy again. The pilot hustled down the stairs in front of them as the copilot wrapped a strong arm around Ellen's waist and almost carried her down the stairs.

The limousine smelled of old smoke, leather, and cologne. She sneezed three times. And suddenly, the memory of Michael's cologne overwhelmed her senses, musty and sweet, like the smell of your clothes after rolling in a field of corn. They'd done that once, she remembered with a smile.

He'd made her promise not to peek, blindfolded her just to be sure, and escorted her outside and into his convertible. After what seemed like a long drive, the car came to a stop. The air was thick with silence and the smell of freshly cut grass.

"Michael, where are we?" she asked, fumbling to remove the blindfold.

"We're sitting in our new living room," he exclaimed, guiding her out of the car and handing her sunglasses. They stood in the middle of a field of corn whose stalks nearly reached Ellen's chin.

"Picture this, El. First, no corn. Next, the Victorian home of your dreams, with all the bells and whistles. Then, in the morning you awake to birds chirping and grasshoppers hopping and whatever, instead of BMWs warming up and front doors slamming and all those other suburban sounds. This is God's country, El!"

Ellen felt like a scarecrow. Limp and out of context in Michael's field of dreams. She hated the country. Hated open spaces. Her head began pounding. She sneezed. She was allergic to all she could see.

"Michael, I had no idea this was your…your dream? I thought you were happy. I love our house in Grandville," she said, and did. A white-brick colonial, complete with four graceful two-story columns, surrounded by a well-landscaped yard, located on one of the best streets in Grandville, the best suburb in the city—what wasn't there to like? Her neighbors were perfect, unobtrusive. A dual-income, childless couple in the stone home to the left, an older couple who spent at least six months of the year traveling on the other. Her gardens were beautiful and low-maintenance. Her kitchen—rehabbed to her specifications when they moved in just after their wedding—was her love. Mexican tile covered the floor, and granite, in a soft tan, graced the counters. The cherry cabinetry and commercial-grade kitchen equipment in gleaming stainless steel completed the ensemble. She loved her home.

"El, of course you knew we'd be moving up—bigger and better, remember honey?"

Ellen sneezed and said, "Yes, I remember that. But I thought you meant buying a bigger house on Berkshire—THE street in Grandville—not building a house in the boondocks. No, Michael, this wasn't ever part of our dream," Ellen said, leaning into the convertible in search of a tissue. She was miserable. The blades of grass growing between the stalks made her legs itch.

"Well, honey, it's all ours now. We break ground tomorrow," Michael said, patting her bottom as he held the door open. Fait accompli. Done deal. And then he kissed her, in that passionate you're-the-only-woman-in-the-world full-attention manner, and she'd melted. Even in the allergy zone. And they made slow, passionate love in the field. The fact she was sneezing and on cortisone for days afterward didn't matter. It was a romantic time in that field, and when she saw corn, a field of corn, she always smiled.

Back then, she didn't. By the time they arrived home in Grandville, sans blindfold, she saw there was a for sale sign in their yard. Janet Jones had the listing. Ellen burst into tears. She cried herself to sleep that night. Michael went out. In the morning, she decided she'd make the best of things she couldn't change, and create another dream kitchen. And a dream master suite and tons of indoor space for her, since she wouldn't be able to breathe outdoors. But it had been OK. She'd made the new house a home.

He meant well, she thought then. And still, she loved him. Loved him for what he was to her and for what he couldn't ever be. For being there in the beginning. And that lasted for a long time. Isolated and alone in the country in the house of his dreams, she was finally convinced by her friends, who made her see he was having sex with other women across the city and the country. And still, she loved him. She learned to be alone.

Later, alone, in her room at the Park Suites Hotel, she wondered if having your spouse die really made you strong. *That's a farewell, not just a good-bye.* And then, finally, a sob shook her and the tears fell. Good-bye, suddenly, had become a luxury for the living. Tomorrow, she'd face the dead.

Reaching up to turn off the hotel light, she noticed, for the first time, the single lavender rosebud in a crystal vase on a small table in the corner of the room. A white card leaned against the vase. Slowly, she climbed out of the bed and made her way across the room. She peered through her tears and saw the thick white envelope said "Ellen" in black pen. Inside, the note said, "I am deeply sorry for your loss and will be here for you, whatever you need. Ron."

Ellen burst into tears. Confusion and exhaustion came crashing in on her as she hurried back into the strange bed and fell into a dreamless sleep.

****

She was a survivor. She knew that. She'd lived through any number of terrible, terrible things. This, of course, could be the end of everything.

I graduated. I did it. Only to die. It's not fair.

She had needed a ride. She'd gotten a full scholarship. She had an interview. He looked nice enough. Was driving a respectable car, going her way. He'd even stayed at the hotel a couple times. No trouble. Always polite. Said he'd give her a lift. They left at seven, when he finished work. He drove her here, to this deserted place, and now, he told her he would rape her. If she screamed, he'd kill her. In fact, if she just cooperated, she'd be fine, he whispered.

He'd put something into her Diet Coke. She didn't remember being here, tied up like this. Now, she refused to die like this. Not here. Not now.

So she nodded. And he untied her legs and pulled off her shorts and raped her. And when he was finished, he told her he was sorry. Pulled her shorts back on her. Tied her ankles again, tossed her backpack on the ground next to her, and told her good-bye.

She lived. The farmer came and found her. She couldn't describe the man to the police, so they gave her a ride to a hotel, put her up for the night, and told her not to hitchhike.

It wasn't a smart girl's choice of transportation, one of the elderly-looking highway patrolmen told her. And she seemed to be a pretty smart girl.

CHAPTER 10

Two Months Later—Monday, July 15

Nipples.

Such incredibly amazing components of a woman's body, Ron thought, watching Ellen sleep, her chest rising and falling with the deep breathing of an exhausted sleep. He'd pulled down the sheets to watch her nipples. He loved nipples. Some sort of childhood yearning he supposed. He loved his wife's nipples. His wife.

Making love tonight, he thought he tasted milk. Something honey-sweet and warm. He kept sucking and sucking until Ellen finally cried out in pain. He didn't mean to hurt her; he'd just become focused, lost in thought. Not sexual, just warm.

He was married, he thought suddenly. He couldn't stand the thought of Ellen as a widow. From the day of the accident, the day of the explosion, Ron knew he couldn't picture beautiful fragile Ellen as a widow. A beautiful woman, smart, funny, and a great cook. A creative woman. She deserved to be a bride, not a widow. She loved piddling around her house, adding warm, feminine touches. She'd even made suggestions in his home. Nothing pushy or anything. Just right. Warm. And she was proud of his career—and she got it, man—she really got advertising and promotion, learning from life, not books. That had been his teacher too.

Ron Martin chose his life, step by step, creating the sophisticated advertising executive he had become out of the shell of a poor Southern boy from rural Louisiana. Nobody in his family—none of his brothers, neither of his parents—would become anything. Gus was a used car salesman, the last time he checked. Davey and his wife were essentially migrant workers. His mom still did other folks' laundry. He sent her checks, because she was his mom. The rest he disowned as soon as he could.

From a young age, he knew he'd grow beyond them. Recreate himself to escape his past, his genes. By fourteen, Ron Martin was the number-one money-making weight guesser on the state fair circuit, spending his summers traveling around the deep South, guessing weights and ages and screwing lemon shake-up girls.

"Hey, honey, do you have a permit to haul that trailer?" he'd bark at a heavy woman walking by his stand on the midway. Of course, drawing attention to himself while humiliating her ensured a steady stream of customers willing to lose a dollar. And they would lose, unless he wanted them to win.

Even today, thirty years later, Ron could guess the weight of anybody in a conference room within ten pounds. He hated fat. After studying the human form and considering body types from a young age, he hated pear-shaped people and anyone who was over his or her ideal weight. In fact, a casual tour of the Martin Agency would reveal no body fat. Ron had subtly informed the human resources director of his desire. He didn't care what color their skin was, whether they were male or female, straight or gay, but he wasn't going to look at a fatso. Period. And it was, by God, his company.

He had made a nice living for himself, guessing weights, and he got to leave home all summer. When fall came, after the Texas State Fair was a wrap, he'd go back home and back to high school, where he did enough to get by and spent the rest of his time getting stoned. For some reason, his college counselor saw talent in Ron that he didn't see himself, and when the SAT scores came out, Ron was offered a full ride to Louisiana State. He'd be the first in his family to go to college, so he tossed his graduation cap in the air, grabbed his favorite gal who was already stoned, and partied the night away before heading back to the weight-guessing road.

He'd go to Louisiana State in the fall, paying his own expenses with the proceeds of the summer and, with enough cash to spare, open a college bar. He was, he explained to his fellow carnies during teardown and setup, going to be rich. A self-made man. A classy man. While they laughed at his joke, he kept planning and screwing the balloon dart girl.

Ellen was gaining weight, he thought absently, returning to the present and staring once again at her full breasts. Maybe she was one of those binge eaters, who swallow their sorrow with fudge and stuff. The vision of Ellen chowing down made him feel sick to his stomach. No, more likely she was puffy. She'd been inactive since the funeral. She had quit the project at the agency, unable to concentrate on both Squeaky Clean and her grief. Then she'd been planning the wedding. It was a small wedding. Just the two of them and the minister, but Ellen made it special and perfect. They'd spent a weekend at a bed and breakfast an hour outside Field City for the honeymoon. He smiled at the memory of their first night of lovemaking. But since then, it seemed, she was always tired. Too tired to work. Too tired for much of anything.

Ron never slept. He needed four hours maximum—any more sleep, and he felt sluggish. At Louisiana State, he'd go to his classes, taking a full load, and then run his bar all night. He was there until last call, and sometimes later, if he had a date. Then he'd show up on time for his 8 a.m. business class. And he learned. And he changed.

First, he excised cusswords from his vocabulary and cut his shoulder-length sandy blond hair to a preppy length. He spent some money on cheap clothes that looked like good clothes: khakis, white button-down shirts. He looked the part of an emerging Southern gentleman and he never pushed his Southern good-girl dates for sex. Always dated sorority girls, good girls. Learned from them. Watched the frat guys in his bar. Becoming friends with the party animals in each frat house. They needed him not to card their pledges; he, in turn, became an honorary member. For free. During the school year he was learning, in school and out.

Summers he made up for what he'd missed. He'd fuck the first girl who flashed him her tits. It happened all the time. He'd be sweating, standing under the sliver of shade his scale provided him, barking at the throngs of losers and lowlifes walking past him—and suddenly, boobs. If he liked the looks of the rest of the body—no fat, nice nipples—he'd smile. If not, he'd heckle her: "Put those away, that's indecent exposure. Each one of those probably weighs thirty pounds; no wonder ya need that backside to keep em up."

The ones he smiled at who smiled back, the young and firm ones, he directed to the secret entrance for the band's roadies and the carnies. They'd have wild, fast sex inside one of the closed midway games, listening to whatever regional country and western band was playing a rendition of "Sweet Home Alabama" and other songs of Southern pride and longing.

At graduation, he made a decision. Advertising was his future. He could sell, and he could think, but he couldn't guess weights for a living anymore. So he told the guys no more fairs, sold his bar, and went to work as an intern for an advertising agency in Cleveland. The rest, as they say, is history.

"Ron," Ellen said again. "Hello." Coming to, he saw her propped up on one arm, the sheet pulled up under her chin, looking rested and happy.

"Sorry, just daydreaming," he answered, looking out the window at the sun rising through the fields and woods in the distance. "It really is like being somewhere else, here, in this house in the country. I guess we could make our life here, if you still want to—it's your decision. But I am starting to get used to it out here, not missing Grandville so much. It's just that I don't want Michael's ghost to haunt us or anything."

"Michael died a happy man. He'd just made love to another woman and presumably was about to grill their dinner. Tragic accident, but all in all, he lived a full life. This is our house now." Ellen smiled and rolled onto her stomach to cuddle closer to him. "You make me feel special and safe. Everything is just so right."

****

From the moment Ellen arrived back in Columbus from Daufuskie Island, to claim Michael's charred body and plan for his funeral, Ron had been quietly at Ellen's side. When she woke up from a deep, dark sleep, that first night back at the hotel, the message light was flashing on the phone next to the bed. She remembered, suddenly, watching the light, that Michael was dead.

She called the hotel operator for her messages. The voice on the message was Ron's, offering to drive her around town, to help make the arrangements. She hung up and called him, and they'd been inseparable since.

Except for work—since Ellen never returned but Ron had to—they were together. And, to anyone who saw them, even as Ron helped Ellen plan her husband's burial, they seemed like a perfect couple. Ron called his friend who owned the city's top funeral home, coordinated the printing of the death announcement, and personally handled the media frenzy instead of turning it over to his agency's media relations team. Ron instructed her interior designer and builder to put the house back together, to make the decisions, to get rid of the ruined furnishings and to make the home look perfect again.

When she cried on his shoulder, he hadn't tried to kiss her. He was just there. When she called him at home, a week after the funeral, to come, to be with her, Ron arrived twenty minutes later. Since her house was under construction and repair, Ellen was still living in the hotel room.

"Now what?" she had asked, staring into his bright blue eyes.

"Now we have us," Ron answered, smiling, stroking her hair. He always had an answer, a solution, for everything.

"Forever?"

"As long as you'll put up with me. Will you marry me, Ellen?" Ron asked. "I know it seems sudden and fast and all, but I can't imagine not marrying you, and I've never imagined being married to anyone before I met you. You don't have to answer tonight. I'll go home if you'd like."

"Marriage?"

"Marriage. You know, husband and wife. I know it's fast, but it just seems right...I'm really hanging myself out to dry now, aren't I?" Ron said, sounding self-conscious. But he dropped to his knees anyway, in front of Ellen, who was sitting on the edge of the hotel room bed. He pulled a five-carat diamond and platinum ring from his pocket.

"This feels like a dream. Yes, I'll marry you.," Ellen answered, tears flowing down her cheeks. Ron placed the ring on her finger, the same finger she'd removed her wedding band from a week earlier. She'd had that diamond made into a choker. "It's beautiful, Ron. Thank you."

As Ellen stared at the dazzling engagement ring on her finger, Ron said, "And now, my beautiful wife-to-be, time to relax." Ron pushed her back onto the bed and gently removed her shirt. "Now roll over, my dear," he instructed, and once she had she turned over onto her stomach, Ron sat carefully at the base of her spine to rub her back. Ron, so caring, so kind, so—

Ellen suddenly had déjà vu, of the night he kept her company when the Parks family was carjacked. It seemed so long ago. And now, he was caring for her again. Gently rubbing her back, whispering about how beautiful her body was. A traditional sentiment in an extraordinary affair.

"Ron, this all just feels so right," Ellen had told him, as he massaged her shoulders. It had only been two weeks since Michael's death, and yet being inseparable had become the norm.

"Remember, I'm not proposing just because you're about to get all that insurance money, although I could use some new office furniture," he teased.

"Ron, honestly," Ellen said, popping her head up and trying to knock him off her back.

"Take it easy, Mrs. Martin-to-be. I loved you before you were independently wealthy, remember? The fact you're rich just cinched the deal," he teased, still rubbing her shoulders.

"Oh, brother. You better keep rubbing buddy, to get yourself out of this one," Ellen said, smiling.

"You know I'm teasing. Let's keep the wedding simple, just us, if that's all right with you. I made reservations at a wonderful bed and breakfast for the weekend. Tonight please let me rub your worries away. You need your beauty sleep." And, Ron had massaged her until she fell asleep.

****

Now, as she cuddled him, Ron realized his new bride was indeed gaining weight, and he needed to tell her somehow. This was his worst nightmare of marriage coming true. *You marry a beautiful princess and end up with an ugly toad. Shit.*

He watched as Ellen walked across the bedroom to the bathroom for a shower.

She's getting fat, he thought, as he smiled back at her smile before she closed the bathroom door.

****

In the shower, Ellen was still beaming. She was pregnant. She was still trying to decide when to break the news to Ron. She'd conceived during their affair, although she didn't realize it for three months, explaining her morning sickness during her getaway to Daufuskie Island. That doctor had told her she was infertile. Having given up on the possibility of conceiving again, Ellen was unaware of the changes happening to her body at first. Now she smiled as she rubbed her swelling breasts and stomach with Squeaky Clean soap, realizing her lifelong dream would come true.

She wanted to think up a creative way to tell Ron. Her intelligent, sophisticated husband was about to discover, at age forty-two, it wasn't too late to have it all. Ellen was sure he wanted a family, too, even though they'd never discussed it. It hadn't been an issue, since she was supposedly infertile.

Infertile.

A week after Micheal's funeral, she was engaged. Another week and they had eloped. And then, she was sick. For a month. The same sickness she had attributed to the sea in Daufuskie Island. But it couldn't be seasickness in the middle of Ohio, the Urgent Care doctor had told her, and it wasn't her equilibrium. She hadn't been on a cruise. A blood test was ordered, to rule out all possible causes.

Ten minutes later, as she sat in the examining room, the nurse came in and told her she was pregnant. She was pregnant? Ellen had told the young nurse it couldn't be. That she was infertile. That her fertility specialist Dr. Burnhardt had tried everything.

Dr. Burnhardt, the nurse told her, was wrong.

"Congratulations," the nurse had said. "It's quite a miracle. You deserve all the happiness you can have. You better make an appointment with your obstetrician right away." *This woman knows me,* Ellen thought, *knows who I am because of Michael's death. Everybody knows me now. Maddie and that column. But who cares, I'm pregnant. Pregnant!*

"Yes, it is a miracle," Ellen stammered.

Once she was in her car, she called Dr. Burnhardt and he asked her to come into his office. His nurse had drawn blood, much like they had done at her general practitioner's office. "This'll confirm their findings, Mrs. Anderson—ah, I mean, Mrs. Martin. Let's hope they're right, shall we?"

Ellen couldn't quite believe she was pregnant, yet she knew she felt terrible. Her dream, was it coming true? she wondered. She sat in the green plastic chair in the drab exam room, refusing to climb back onto the examining table where she'd suffered so many demeaning and painful fertility procedures. Dr. Burnhardt entered the room, looking down at the floor. He confirmed her pregnancy.

"I thought you said it was impossible for me to get pregnant," Ellen stammered.

"I know, Ellen. In fact—and I feel terrible telling you this now, when I should've told you sooner—the problem wasn't you all along. It was, in fact, Michael, God bless his soul," Dr. Burnhardt said, studying his shoes.

"What?"

"He didn't want me to be the one to tell you he was infertile. He told me he'd tell you, God rest his soul. I'd known him and his family since he was a kid and—I was wrong. It was wrong, I know."

Frozen in shock and disbelief, Ellen simply stared at the man she'd trusted with her dreams. He didn't look at her as she searched his face.

"You can sue me or something, although I am about to retire. I am sorry. I hope the fact of your pregnancy will make up for some of your heartache, Ellen. Michael's secret will remain with me, as it has until now. I am so sorry for lying to you," he added, walking out the door.

Pregnant.

At another time, her anger would've overcome her joy. Thoughts of revenge glimmered at the back of her mind, but quickly, anger was replaced by the realization she'd have a baby. Ellen Lopez Anderson Martin. *Ellen Martin is pregnant,* she thought. She'd name her baby Adele and call her Addy for short, like the top awards in Ron's advertising business. He'd be so proud, Ellen dreamed.

Addy could've been conceived, she knew, on the first night they made love. Ron had needed to stop by the office, to check on things and pick up a few memos. They'd walked hand in hand through the gleaming glass doors that had once intimidated her. Ron used his special card key to enter the executive suites after hours. Ellen was glad nobody was there, working late at the agency.

Once inside Ron's office, he stroked her arm and they both quickly forgot about work. A moment later, they were undressed, and Ellen was lying on her back on top of his glass-top banker's desk. The glass felt smooth and cool on her bare back and buttocks. Her entire body was alive, eager for his touch. Ron dimmed the lights to a twinkle. With the drapes open, bright lights from the nightclub and restaurants across the street danced across the ceiling in an explosion of color. And Ron, naked and firm, toned and young looking, slowly entered her, moaning, and it was perfect and forbidden and wonderful—and Ellen was sure they had created a baby that night.

As she stood in her towel, drying off just inside the door of the bathroom, she watched Ron in the morning light, lying in Michael's old spot in the king-size bed, lost in his thoughts as she had been in the shower.

Finally, Ellen decided she couldn't keep the blessed news to herself any longer, and she said, "Ron, I've got a wonderful secret to share with you."

The word secret always caught Ron's attention.

****

"So, did you have a blast in the hospital?" Laura asked Angie when Angie walked through the front door of their apartment.

"Shove it," Angie answered, glaring and stomping down the narrow hall to her bedroom.

"Now, that's not very nice, after all the presents I brought you in the hospital to help make you comfy," Laura said, smiling and following the mouse down the hallway.

"That's only 'cause you want me to talk on camera, and I'm not gonna do it. No way. Leave me alone."

"Do you still think he was murdered, Angie?" Laura asked. Angie had mumbled something about murder while she was on pain medicine at the hospital. The accident had been ruled just that. An accident. Laura wanted the story; she wanted Angie to tell the world what it felt like to almost blow up.

Laura also wondered how Angie and Michael ended up together. She wasn't jealous. Just glad she'd broken it off. *Dating a married man can certainly be dangerous,* Laura thought, cracking herself up.

She also needed the mouse for a separate undercover investigation. Laura Mercer Target 5 Investigations were feared in Columbus. She typically targeted large companies, big business taking advantage of the little guys, the consumers. This case was no different.

This time, Laura was out to expose the big lie—or lye—as she and her producer had taken to calling it. "Operation Lye" was focused on an unscrupulous soap manufacturer. While marketing its product to women, the company, Drummand Industries, systematically subjected female employees to sexual harassment and gender discrimination. Not one salesperson at the company was female—even qualified women held only menial positions. The privately held company regularly used prostitutes for entertainment at corporate functions, treated male employees to all-expense-paid trips around the world, and gave them bonuses for nothing. No female employees ever received a bonus or a promotion above the ranks of administrative assistant.

Fed up, one of the female employees had called Laura. After listening to her story, Laura told the woman she could help her, told her to do nothing to draw suspicion to herself, and Target 5 would equip her with a hidden camera. Together, they would expose the company. No one had ever caught a sexual harasser on camera, Laura later excitedly explained to her producer.

"We'll get national attention for this. We'll interview the president of the company, who will of course deny everything. Then, we'll replay the interview with my source and other women talking about what goes on there, but instead of showing their faces again, it'll be actual footage of real honest-to-goodness sexual harassment.

Hell, Marty," Laura added, "A lot of people don't even believe this shit goes on. It'll be groundbreaking television. Nobody, not even the network folks, has been able to actually *show* harassment in the workplace. We'll do it." After the meeting, Laura could barely concentrate on the evening's newscast.

The next morning, the woman employee had called to tell Laura she'd been fired. The woman said she couldn't recommend anyone else; they were all too frightened. She suggested using one of the outside vendors—the insurance people, the auditors, the law firm—to gain secret access but said she could be of no further help. The woman hung up.

Laura was crushed—until she realized Ron Martin's advertising agency handled the Squeaky Clean account, one of Drummand's most popular subsidiaries. *When I'm finished, they'll be known as the Filthy Soap Company,* she thought, *and everyone who profits by doing business with them will suffer too.*

Her producers said she couldn't use her intern to pretend to apply for a job at the Martin Agency.

"We walk a very tight ethical and legal line with hidden camera reports, Laura," Dave said in his most superior get-lost language. She knew he hated her more every day—even as he had to watch her pull the station's ratings farther and farther in front of the two other local stations.

"What the fuck am I supposed to do then, Dave? Wear a wig and get the job myself? Huh? You can't just shut me down. This is a great idea and I'm going to do it, one way or another," Laura said, glaring back at the news director, unnerved and mad. Marty, the producer, seemed transfixed by his calculator.

"Most reporters I know who need an undercover source use a friend or a relative—someone they trust completely. As you know, we have to be extremely careful of these types of investigations, given the Food Lion ruling about false hiring charges and trespassing with undercover cameras. In the absence of such a person, you are—pardon the language—screwed," Robinson said. "Do you have any friends, Laura?"

Of course she didn't, Laura fumed to herself. Dave knew that too. All she had was Angie Brown.

It had to be Angie.

Little, troubled, confused Angie.

So Laura had made time to visit the mouse while she was recovering in the hospital. At first, Angie would mumble stuff, like she was talking to her mom or someone else Laura didn't know. She was delirious, the nurses explained. She'd pull through but would be in a lot of pain for the first week. So Laura called Dixon and arranged for a print photographer to take photos of Michael's funeral for Angie—and had a Channel 5 photog take video so Angie would feel as if she'd been there for Michael.

Angie seemed to be the only person in town who thought the psycho's demise deserved tears, Laura thought. Ellen knew he was a louse; hell, Dixon Crane knew it, too, even though he'd covered for him because it was the gentlemanly thing to do.

Anyway, as much as she hated it, Laura needed Angie. So recovering from the blast comment was crucial. Seeing the mouse brought out the worst in Laura, even when she actually tried to be nice. Laura started over.

"I'm sorry, Angie, it's just that I have a hard time showing my emotions, so I cover with bad jokes, OK?" Laura stood in the hall outside the mouse's bedroom.

"Yea, whatever," Angie said, sitting down on the bed, looking even thinner than before, with dark circles under her eyes. "You know, I really hated that hospital food. I can't wait to order a pizza. But I'm broke."

"Deal. What toppings?" Laura asked, cheerfully.

"Pepperoni, and mushrooms, oh, and extra cheese," Angie said. "And, thanks. I'm gonna go back to work at Lindey's as soon as this comes off," she said, holding up her right arm, still in a cast. The arm, the doctors had said, saved her face from the brunt of the flying glass but paid a price. The Andersons—actually Mrs. Anderson—had paid her medical bills. But because Angie lived from shift to shift and spent that way, she had no savings. Laura knew that—and was planning to get her into a personal debt she could repay in only one way.

Returning to Angie's doorway, Laura said, "Angie, it'll be here in thirty minutes. I'm prepared to pay for the last two months of your rent—I know you weren't here, but it still costs money—and for the next two months, to give you time and all, if you could just do me a little favor." She walked back into Angie's room.

What a sad little room, she thought. Balloon valances in peach, light green, and black stripes provided the only color, hanging humorously above the two small fifties-style sofa windows. Her twin bed had a thin comforter in light blue—a gift from Laura two Christmases earlier. Angie's room looked like a transient's. Angie looked like a transient. *She needs help,* Laura thought. *We need to fix her up for this.*

"What do you want me to do? I know whatever it is must be important, 'cause you wouldn't be treatin' me so nice otherwise," Angie said, knowingly. She looked at herself in the tiny mirror of a Cover Girl powder compact.

"This is going to be so fun and easy. It'll be a breeze," Laura cooed. "You want to be an actress, right? Here's your big chance. All I need you to do is apply for a job, get it, and then wear a little hidden camera."

"Are you outta your mind?"

"Angie, listen, it'll make you a star. You'll become a symbol of womanhood. A beacon of truth in the dark. Hell, your image could use a little polishing. Plus, you'll be on the station's payroll *and* your new employer's. Two paychecks and no double shifts. Think about it. You can always go back to waiting tables at Lindey's, whenever you want. I know you'll love this assignment." The doorbell rang. "I'll get the door. You just stay right there," Laura hurried out with a smile to pay for the pizza.

When she returned to the bedroom with the pizza and saw Angie's smile, Laura knew she had the mouse in her trap.

****

She considered this her real first time.

She'd blocked out the others, as much as she could. Now that she was on her own, completely alone, she could remember or forget whatever she wanted to. Anything and everything. So she kept what she thought she'd need and forgot most of the rest. She remembered her kindergarten teacher and the smell of a bad man. Sweaty. Stinky. Bad eyes. She'd recognize them from now on. Unfortunately, she hadn't figured out how to spot a dishonest man. Those, she kept meeting. They seemed so interested in you, especially once they made sure you were over sixteen but still looked it.

She'd made her way to the city, and she was living in a rat-infested apartment building with three roommates in one room with a bath down the hall for a hundred bucks a month. On the first floor below was Papa Joe's, one of the most popular bars on the campus strip.

Slowly the woman worked toward her destiny, waiting tables at night and going to school during the day. She began to believe she belonged somewhere, to believe she deserved things. While growing this way, she knew she'd never have anyone there at parents' weekend, no one to send her a care package. Nobody cared about her grades.

"I'll be here for you," she said to herself, looking in the bathroom mirror of the bathroom while someone banged on the door outside. "I will be here for you," she repeated, and then yelled, "Justa minute."

She was almost ready to find somebody. Somebody good and rich and every-thing else she'd never known. But first, practice. Sex practice. All men said they wanted a virgin, but really they wanted a virgin with experience. Downstairs, in the pulsing, beer-slimed bar, there was a smorgasbord of practice just waiting for her. So, steeling herself, she walked out of the bathroom, glared at the rude woman in the hall, and made her way downstairs.

She fixed a smile on her face and plunged into the melee of Thursday night at the campus bar.

"Hi, beautiful. What are you drinking? I'm buying," said the muscle-shirt-wearing muscle-bound jock.

"Whatever you're having would be great," she answered, exuding pheromones while staring innocently into his eyes.

"Ah, great," said the jock, flopping a huge arm around her shoulders and escorting her to the bar. Later, in his fraternity house in the top bunk of a room he shared with three other guys, they necked. It was fun. He was big but gentle. She made sure they didn't do very much, go too far.

After she said no to intercourse, he showed her how to make him feel good.

When he started to come, it scared her. He was loud—oh-oh-oh-oh—and then he shook, all over.

"What was that?" she whispered.

"That was the sound of pure pleasure, baby," he answered, lowering himself down on top of her, still breathing hard and a little sweaty. "Did you have any— ah—pleasure?" he asked.

"Yes," she answered, lying there in the dark. Was that all she had to do to make a man happy, she wondered? He seemed to like it, but he had pushed her hand away suddenly. Maybe she just needed more practice.

"I'll walk you home, if you'd like," he said. "Can we see each other again?"

"Yes, I'd like that," she said, realizing she still had so much to learn.

CHAPTER II

Tuesday, August 30

Dixon loved the corner patio table and expected it to be held for him on perfect summer days. At least until noon. The shade of the linden tree made sunglasses unnecessary, but Dixon donned them for effect as he smiled at his luncheon companion du jour and swirled the pinot grigio in his glass.

"You should've come to the funeral, Dixon. It was well done, ah, I mean elegant. Nice eulogies. All the fixings," Laura said.

"Funerals aren't for me, Sugar. I'm too close to death as it is, you know," Dixon answered, snorting and sniffing and squinting his eyes.

"Right, I'd hardly call sixty-something knocking on death's door."

"That's what Michael Anderson thought, too, Sugar, and he wasn't even forty. Hey, why did Ellen Anderson quit work right away, after the big boom? It seems like she'd need an outlet even more, you know," Dixon said.

He and Laura Mercer were enjoying what had become a monthly luncheon date outside on the patio at Lindey's. It was hot, eighty-five degrees at least, but the breeze kept the shaded terrace ten degrees cooler. Dixon was convinced Michael Anderson's death was a homicide while everyone else in the universe thought it was an unfortunate explosion.

"Dix, you're not suspicious of little Ellen Anderson, are you? You know the detectives would've found something if there was any foul flambé to be found—heck, the insurance guys would've found it," Laura said. "I know the cops grilled Angie, the Andersons' cleaning lady, and even Ellen Anderson. You said it yourself at the scene: Michael simply chose to cook out, something went wrong and boom. End of story."

"If you weren't so beautiful, you'd be easy to hate, you cold little sizzler," Dixon said, chortling. Still, he was bothered by Michael Anderson's demise. As he looked up, he saw his favorite reporter making her way over to his table. Maddie had worked at the paper almost as long as Dixon, and the two shared scoop and enjoyed the same wry, sarcastic sense of humor.

"Hi, Dixon. Dining with Columbus's newest broadcast star, I see?" Maddie said grabbing a free chair at their table and sitting down. "The newsroom certainly is quiet during the summer and now I know where everyone hangs out. I need to come here to stir up a story, I suppose. But Dixon, mixing with the broadcast folks, really? Don't worry, Sunshine, I won't be at your table too long. Or do you prefer 'Sugar'?" Maddie asked Laura, using both nicknames.

"Very funny, Maddie. I suppose if you're writing about it, nobody'll see it, so it won't much matter, will it?" Laura answered. "Remember the camera has a much broader reach than the pen."

"It makes you look broader, too, from what I hear," Maddie snapped, turning back to Dixon. "How've you been?"

"I know I am one of the only things you two have in common, but let's be civil, shall we? Am I the only soul in the city who still believes Michael Anderson was a victim?" Dixon said, sipping his glass of wine and then swirling it, for effect. He loved to be in the middle of the tension between the two women.

"You know how I hate to agree with her on anything, but I'm afraid you're out on left field on this one, Dix. It was a grill malfunction, a fluke," Maddie said. "Hey Laura, how's your Target 5 Investigation going?"

"Which one? The parking lot attendant skimming exposé is a wrap, if that's what you mean," Laura answered, sounding disinterested.

"No, I'm talking about Mr. Drummand and Squeaky Clean, actually," Maddie said with a smile.

"I don't know what you're talking about, Maddie. I've gotta run," Laura said, looking as though she were trying to cover her shock. "Dixon, thanks for lunch. So nice to see you, Mad," she called and was gone.

"Sorry, Dixon. I didn't mean to ruin your date," Maddie said.

"Ruin it? I love catfights—they're great. What've you got?"

"Oh no, you don't. You're practically one of them, now, with those television restaurant reviews. We poor, underpaid, under-lauded newspaper folks have to keep a few secrets to ourselves, you know," Maddie said, pouring herself a glass of wine from the bottle on the table. "You mind?" she asked, as she poured.

"Of course not. So what've you got on Sugar?" Dixon repeated.

"I just had to check out a hunch and it appears I'm right."

"You usually are," Dixon said, snorting. "Hey, how's your friend Janet Jones doing? Will she ever return to our fair city? I can't imagine being the queen of real estate and then just checking out."

"Janet's great. She called me a couple of nights ago, wanted me to come back and visit, sans the merry married widow, " Maddie added.

"Anyway, Janet's writing a book, believe it or not. She's calling it *The Three Types of Women*, or something like that. She's got a publisher lined up already, which is so cool. It's her theory about how each woman in today's America decides—either consciously or subconsciously—one of three different types she'll become to get what she wants in what's basically still a man's world."

"You've lost me, Madeline," Dixon said.

"Here's the theory, Dixon. You see, there are the mother women: they are stay-at-home moms, or at least home-focused moms. They are caretakers, the nurturers, the traditionalists. They hide emotions, forsake all for everyone else. But don't try to cross her on her own turf. It's her way or the highway when it comes to kids, cooking, grocery shopping, and the like. Kind of an Ellen Anderson Martin type."

"Sounds just like you, Mad," Dixon said.

"Shut up. This is interesting. The second type of woman is power women. They compete in a man's world in a man's manner. They have brains, and they're tough. They are driven, work-oriented, very determined to achieve. Very threatening to conventional men."

"And that leaves?"

"Hookers."

"Of course, now I'm interested," Dixon said.

"Not in the conventional sense, necessarily, but Janet means women who use sex—looks, makeup, sex appeal—to get their man and win in a man's world. They marry an older guy, he dies, and they're wealthy. They sleep with their professors and get As. Whatever they want from a man, they can get it with sex appeal."

"The hookers better turn into mothers by the time they turn forty," Dixon said.

"No, they can't. Even if they become mothers, their role is defined by how their husbands and other men treat them. Unfortunately, a hooker-turned-wife is an afterthought. Especially after forty. So too, sadly, are the mothers, if they don't keep up their personal interests. Once a hooker is conquered, her allure is gone. To a lot of men, it doesn't matter if you're a hooker or a mother—they allow the men to be in charge. The real threats are the power women—they try to get into the last bastion of male pride.

"But you guys do a good job trying to keep them out too, with stag bars, golf and hunting trips, steam baths—all designed to keep men ahead of the power women they're threatened by. Neosexism is very covert, but quite effective," Maddie said. "More wine, please."

"You power women take this stuff way too seriously, Mad Dog," Dixon said, pouring her a glass. "What if I want my woman to bring home the bacon, fry it up in a pan, and have wild sex—all in one woman?"

"You can't have it all. You need to hope you chose the right type for you, and each woman can have a little of the other types, but according to Janet, one type is dominant. By the way, I think you chose well. Mrs. Crane is a mother/home figure, perfect for you. You'd never last with a Madeline Wilson or a Laura Mercer. You see, most men are both repelled and attracted to power women, like Laura for example," Maddie said, smiling. "She's dangerous. Especially if she decides to pick a fight, to shake things up. Especially if she takes on a traditional male."

"She's a talking head, for heaven's sake, Maddie," Dixon chortled.

"Sometimes even talking heads pick the right story," Maddie said.

****

"That little bitch is stirring things up, Martin," Donald Drummand yelled over the speakerphone, startling the five other people in Ron's office. Ron quickly picked up the receiver as his staff made a swift exit. They had called Drummand to get his approval on Francis's latest Squeaky Clean shape, a snowflake for the holidays.

"Calm down, Mr. Drummand," Ron said. Alone in his office, listening to his belligerent client's tirade, suddenly Ron felt very old, and very tired. He wondered when he and Ellen could schedule a vacation.

"She's up to something, that pinch-nosed perky perfect-seeming reporter Mercer something. She told somebody who told me that my soap's gonna be known as filthy soap if she has her way. She must be stopped. I've paid you and your people nearly a million dollars already this year to revitalize my brand, and it seems to be working."

"It has been a phenomenal success," Ron interjected.

"Well, it's all just bubbles down the drain if she finds anything, and she seems to think she has. You better get over here and help me figure out how to fight her, because, the way I figure it, my account is worth about forty percent of your revenue. We're tied together, Ronny, and you better not forget it," Drummand added.

"I'll be right over," Ron said. Pushing the button on his handset, he called his new administrative assistant back into his office.

"Angela, cancel all my appointments today. Apologize to the guys at Kroger. We've had a client emergency, and I'll meet with them as soon as I can. Put them in my schedule tomorrow or something. Grocery guys are usually understanding," Ron said, as he rushed to gather all his things, shoving his Blackberry and a notepad into his briefcase.

"Anything else, sir?" she asked sweetly.

"Please, it's Ron, honey. Call me Ron. And no, that'll be all, for now."

*****

Once her boss was out the door, Angie—Angela, she always reminded herself—checked the tape. Plenty left. They'd be proud she taped Drummand's outburst. How lucky Francis kept including her in the Squeaky meetings. Since Ellen and Ron were married, and Ellen had quit her job, and Ron had become distracted at work, Francis had started confiding in Angela.

Even though Angie didn't get to take Ellen's place at home with Mikey, she was working on doing it at work. Since Francis had been left short a staff person, Ron told Angela to help Francis whenever she could. Francis seemed to appreciate the help on the Squeaky Clean soap account—perfect for Angela. Francis told Angela she was happy for Ellen's miracle pregnancy and she understood why she quit, but she hated the thought of training another account executive. So Angela filled in whenever she could, and so far, Francis seemed pleased.

Angela loved working at the Martin Agency. It was exciting, glamorous. She almost convinced herself the job could be real, that she could move up. With her new, double salary—twenty-five thousand from the Martin Agency, matched 100 percent by Channel 5—she was making fifty thousand a year. Her first paycheck a week ago was more money than she'd ever seen—and then the television people gave her the same amount. Direct deposit, right into her brand-new account, under her brand-new formal name, Angela. She'd had a makeover at the best salon in the city, and her long brown mane was now a professional flip. Still long, but fashionable.

The Channel 5 producer, Marty, had taken her shopping at Clothes the Loop, Macy's, and Nordstrom. She picked out a whole new wardrobe including the finest suits, and she never even had to look at a price tag. He just let her pick things out, with those fancy saleswomen helping. *They probably thought he was my sugar daddy,* Angie thought. Marty left the receipt in one of the bags, Angie discovered. They had spent $3,700 at Nordstrom alone. It was like her fairy godmother had come to life.

Her new clothes looked dreamy in her closet. Angie liked to feel the price tags and rub the different fabrics before going to bed at night. And best of all, she decided Mr. Martin might have the hots for her, but she couldn't be sure. He had really shiny shoes and drove a spiffy sports car. And he called her "honey" a lot.

Laura told her she was doing a great job. And Angie thought she probably meant it. All in all, people at the Martin Agency were impressed with Angela Brown. That was a first. The intrigue of her two jobs was a turn-on.

*****

Marty came to Laura and Angie's apartment every day to collect the video and audio tapes and give Angie new ones. They had taught her how to hide the tiny camera on her waist, concealed by a belt.

As the three of them spoke in the living room, Laura said, "Angie, we need Drummand to make a move on you or one of the other women at the agency. We really need you to get inside his offices, roam around, find macho boys'-club stuff, OK? Do you think Ron Martin or that Francis woman will include you soon?"

"Yeah, I think so. She likes me, and he's beginning to," Angie said, smiling. Laura thought Ron probably did like Angie. Ron, she remembered, had quite the sex drive. A sex drive that led to trouble. Supposedly he was changed, sober now. Laura shuddered. *Forget it, already, Laura. You'll have the last laugh.* She wasn't sure if the new

Angie Brown could entice Ron—he was married, now, of course. But Drummand was an easy prey.

"Anyway, Laura, I think Drummand's on to you," Angie said.

"Why would you think that?" Laura demanded, still mad that there had been a leak and Madeline Wilson knew about the investigation.

"Because he called up poor Mr. Martin and started yelling. It's on the tape today. Mr. Martin had to race over there, cancel all his meetings and stuff. That's why," Angie answered.

Laura and Marty locked eyes.

"We'll get him, kid, he's guilty as sin. Don't worry," Marty said to Laura. Turning, he said, "See you tomorrow, Angela."

After Marty walked out into the night, Laura pushed the apartment door closed behind him and put on the security chain.

"Is this dangerous?" Angie asked, for the first time.

"Well, yeah, I guess. Not for you, but, you know, we're going after a man's life, his livelihood. I don't see him saying, 'OK, you got me, I'm a pig who has sexually harassed any number of women blah blah blah.' It doesn't work that way, Angie, I mean Angela. Don't worry, we'll pull out if it gets too mean."

"OK. Whatever," Angie said. "I'm gonna go to sleep. I've got to be bright-eyed and bushy-tailed in the morning."

****

"We chose those girls of yours to be on the account because they're naive," Drummand said, banging his fist on the thick wood table. "We purposefully didn't tell 'em the soap isn't all natural. That it's not even close to Ivory or Dove. We're assuming the consumers, and your girls, just assume that it is, isn't that right, Ronny?

"Well, now we've got some little small-time reporter getting her panties in a wad because I don't like girls. I like girls. I just don't like bitches. Get it, Ronny?" Drummand's second chin shook when he talked, like a gloppy exclamation point on every sentence. His sad, droopy eyes still spit fire, even at seventy-two. While a little overweight, he maintained his once-a-week tennis game with the same three guys he'd played with for thirty years and played golf every afternoon, rain or shine. When he couldn't golf, he got grumpy. Laura Mercer was cutting into his golf game and he was getting grumpy.

"I don't even know what your informant thinks she's doing, Mr. Drummand. I haven't heard a thing about it," Ron said, rubbing the back of his neck.

"That's a problem, Ronny. We took a chance, you and me, Ronny boy. I invested a lump of my savings to pull my loser product out of its dying mediocrity. Remember that? That was my choice, based on your seemingly well-thought-out scenario of a new national soap brand. Well that's all hunky-dory, except my soap sucks. To really make it better costs too much. So we need some of that mind-bending advertising magic to make it seem just as good, only niftier. Cuter, as your girl would say.

"On top of that, I don't like women working. Period. Don't have woman bankers, no woman doctors fix me up. I don't play golf with women, don't talk business with women, don't do nothing with women except screw 'em. Oh, and sell 'em soap. Now this reporter has launched something called a 'Target 5 Investigation.' OOOH. Top secret. All that. Somebody sends me a memo, outlining the story. Here it is, Ronny," Drummand said, shoving a piece of paper at Ron across the thick, dark desk.

"We've already gone down our path, Ronny. We took the low road. We're stuck on the low road. Your job is to be sure we keep making money on the low road until we can figure out a way to make soap that cleans," Drummand said, pausing for effect. "Or get one of those big guys—hell, P&G is interested—to buy us."

Ron looked up from the memo resting on the desk in between them. "Excuse me if I sound out of line, Mr. Drummand, but the problem here isn't Squeaky Clean. The Target 5 Investigation isn't under way because of the quality of the product. They don't know the soap isn't quite up to par. They think the product is a hit.

"The Target 5 Investigation is based on gender discrimination, harassment. What they're saying is that you are unfair to women, really unfair. And that, given female consumers are your target audience, could be a problem if it's true. I'm afraid the recent success of the Squeaky Clean campaign may make you a high-profile target. How many women managers do you have, Mr. Drummand?"

"What d'ya mean?"

"In your plant? Your sales force? Your administrative offices?" Ron asked, staring at him.

"None. No spooks either. No spics, no homos, none of the above. Just good ol' American men," Drummand answered, smiling.

"Mr. Drummand, I'll do my best to handle your image in the market. But you need to call an attorney, as soon as possible. This sounds serious, sir," Ron said.

"Already done, Ronny. Already done. You just handle your job and everything will be fine. Keep selling that shitty soap. Got it?"

****

"I'm fine, really," she said.

"I hurt you. I went too far. I'm sorry," her muscular, fraternity-jock lover said. He finally talked her into letting him put his finger inside her, and he had hurt her.

"You've helped me more than you'll ever know," she said, and meant it. She had learned a lot from him. How to please a man. How to feel alive down there. Heck, she'd suffered much worse. Only he'd never know.

"You know I love you," he said, for the second time that night.

"I know you do," she said to the farm boy. He was from a small rural town, somewhere up North. She couldn't love him. Couldn't. He wouldn't be enough. She'd worked too hard to escape.

CHAPTER 12

Wednesday, December 7

"Welcome home, honey," Ellen called down the main stairs. "I'll be right down."

Ron hoped she'd take her time.

He felt trapped. Suffocated. By Drummand. And by Ellen and their unborn child. He didn't talk about his impending fatherhood, except to Francis. She'd been great, telling him he'd be a natural. Told him how lucky he was to have a chance to form another person's life. To share his love. Yada-yada-yada-yada. His life had become overwhelming overnight.

It would be fine. Right? Having a child. People did it every day. This would be right. His fate, almost divine retribution for lusting after a married woman. An employee, no less. He definitely had it coming, but man did he feel trapped. But he loved her, he did.

"I just had to clean my ring," Ellen said as she swooped into the room, wearing a huge shirt that looked like a khaki tent, like you'd sleep six people under during a safari. He thought she looked bigger every time he saw her. She was growing fatter by the second. "I love it, Mr. Martin." Ellen was staring at the sparkling engagement and wedding ring ensemble. On her right hand, she wore a blue topaz ring to celebrate, which he had given to her the day after she told him the secret. He'd gone, in shock, to the jeweler. Women loved jewelry. It was the right thing to do.

And this was Ron's chance to prove his character. To prove he could succeed in something besides just business. He'd built his agency from scratch. And he'd build his new life with his new family, just as well. He could do it.

Ron knew he could be faithful, although he'd never quite accomplished it in his forty-two years. There'd never been a child at stake, really, he told himself. If he started feeling Ellen trying to get too close, he'd focus on the baby and suppress his commitment-phobic side.

At the moment, the positive self-talk wasn't working. At all. All he felt was caught by an ever-growing woman whose interest in sex had departed the moment she slipped the ring on her finger. Sure, sure, she'd had morning sickness about twenty-four hours a day. Now, though, that was better. Now, though, he didn't want her. And all she seemed to want to do was cook and eat. Eat and cook.

They hugged, a lot, Ron reminded himself. And there was more and more to hug. On the plus side, she did cook. But he was putting on weight. He doubled his daily jog from five miles to ten after moving in to her home. He felt peaceful in the country back then. The problem was now he felt stuck in the boondocks.

"El, I hate to do this, but I need to work late tonight. I'll eat with you and then you can get some shut-eye, OK?"

"Sure, honey. Michael used to work late too; that meant he had a date. Do you?" she asked casually from the far side of the granite bar in the gourmet kitchen.

"Of course not. I'm just up to my ears in Squeaky Clean these days. I lost one of my most valued employees, you know. Left to stay home and birth babies," Ron teased.

"Do you need me? I'll come in with you. That'd be fun, like old times," Ellen offered.

"No. I can handle it. And I'm sorry for the long hours. I think it'll be this way for the next few weeks," Ron added, pulling up a barstool and watching as she placed fresh cilantro on each of their plates, finishing touches on a gourmet meal. "You know, pretty soon, you won't be able to reach the counter with that belly of yours. And after the baby is born, maybe we can go away, just the two of us."

"I don't know, Ron. Then we'll be parents," Ellen beamed. "Isn't it wonderful? Only four weeks to go."

Ron felt his throat tighten and he swallowed hard. Suddenly, the smell of food made him queasy.

*****

Ellen had never been happier. She loved preparing elegant meals for her sophisticated man. Taking care of their home. Preparing for the birth of their child. Being in love again.

She was Mrs. Ellen L. Martin, mother-to-be. Francis had planned a small baby shower, inviting only a few close friends. Maddie wrote about it, made the event sound so chichi. Ellen wore a stylish suit from her favorite maternity wear designer. She wanted Ron to find her irresistible, feminine, ripe and juicy all the way through her pregnancy.

"Bless you, Mrs. Martin," the saleswoman had told her, "Lord knows you've been through so much," she added, throwing in a free jeweled purse compliments of the store. Everyone knew Ellen was the tragic young widow, now pregnant with a miracle baby and married to a rich and gallant knight in shining armor who rescued her from sorrow.

Ellen felt blessed; it was her second chance to choose a good life.

Suddenly pulled from her reverie, she looked up and then stared in disbelief. Ron was looking at her with a look on his face as if he tasted something really sour. Was he sneering? Was it disgust?

"Ron? Ron, what's wrong?"

"Oh sorry, honey. Lost in thought, I guess," he answered quickly.

"Are your parents planning to visit us, you know, before or after the baby arrives?" Ellen asked.

"No, they can't. Too busy exploring the world," Ron lied, picturing his mother ironing someone else's vacation clothes somewhere in a steamy bayou back home.

"Then, it's just us this Christmas. And close friends. We'll have Francis and her kids over. And Janet is coming for a visit, she promised. I just love the holidays, especially this year. Anybody else you'd like?" Ellen asked.

"No. It sounds perfect. You know, I'm just not hungry right now and I really need to go. Sorry, honey. I'll be home late. Don't wait up."

Ellen watched as the headlights of his Jaguar lit the driveway behind the house and then disappeared. Once again, Ellen was alone. Suddenly, she pictured Ron as Michael. She tried to push the image out of her mind. Ron was just working, that's all. Work.

What am I going to do with all this food? she asked herself. *What a thankless job. I cook for him, but he just leaves. I carry a baby for him, but he doesn't care.*

Why do I want it so bad? Because all I've ever wanted is to prove I can be a good mom. Good moms were actresses, but they didn't receive Academy Awards. Good moms were the world's busiest workers—no sick days or holidays—yet they were never employee of the month.

But it was all she had ever wanted. To care for a little person. To show her unconditional love. To be there. And she would. To be in charge of a person's little soul. Motherhood was the most overwhelming, frightening, exhilarating job in the world. And the most important. No one would downplay it. No one. Even if that meant Ellen was alone.

It was OK for Ron to leave tonight, she consoled herself, but not once they were a family. Not then, that was family time. The early evening was for the daddy and the mommy and the baby to spend time together. *That's crucial, really important. Like family dinner.* They would have that. The new Martin family. Every night.

The baby kicked then, as she wrapped up Ron's dinner and placed it in the refrigerator. She'd eaten earlier but decided to eat again. She couldn't get enough. Couldn't eat enough. This baby would thrive, Ellen decided. Addy would have it all.

Suddenly, she craved Rice-A-Roni. She couldn't help it. As she frantically rummaged through the oversized pantry, she began a laugh-cry. A chuckle, gurgle, choke.

"Oh, lordy, my hormones are raging," she said aloud. Finding only a box of Minute Rice, she closed the pantry door and headed upstairs to find her good luck beans. It seemed she needed them just now.

She had made it to the top of the stairs when she felt the first stabbing pain. Like a rope pulled too tight around her stomach, and then a rolling pain. She doubled over, moaning, and crawled the rest of the way into the master bedroom. Reaching up by her bedside table, she grabbed her cell phone and called Ron. She left an urgent message on his voicemail to come home. Next, she opened the drawer and found her beads. She placed those in her socks, one in each, as another contraction forced her to scream. She remembered something about breathing. She tried, but it made her dizzy.

"Michael, help me, Momma, I can't do this, NOOOO," she cried. Her legs took on a life of their own. Suddenly she was on her back and legs were writhing, acting out her body's pain as her hands tore out whole tufts of carpet.

Finally, a break, and she crawled back over to the bedside table, able to dial 911 on her cell before the next contraction forced her to the floor.

"A baby, I'm having my baby," she screamed to the receiver lying on the carpet next to her. "Noooooo!"

Ron was halfway to the office when he noticed the missed call. As he played back the voicemail he slid the Jaguar into the left-hand lane of the highway, pulling into the median, completing a skillful yet illegal U-turn.

A Field City emergency squad and fire engine passed him on the right-hand side. Feeling a sense of impending doom, Ron followed the emergency vehicles to his street and their driveway and beat them inside his house.

Ellen was on the floor in the master bedroom. Delirious, she called out to Michael and then Ron and then her mom, whom she said was dead. Ron cradled her in his arms while one of the paramedics checked her cervix.

"She's dilated about eight centimeters. If we hurry, we might make it to the hospital. Otherwise, she'll have this baby right here," he told Ron.

"What should we do?" he asked, shaking with fear for his wife and his child.

"We should try to make it to the hospital," the paramedic answered. And suddenly, Ellen was on a gurney and down the stairs, with Ron following closely as she writhed in pain. And then she screamed again and after, the young emergency squad driver told Ron, "They always get scared, you know, with the first one, and scream and stuff. But she'll be fine, sir, just wait and see and she won't remember nothing of all this pain. That's God's blessing to 'em, after all the suffering."

Once the paramedic, Ron, and Ellen were safely inside the emergency squad, on their way to the county hospital just seven miles away, he told Ron, "Makes you glad you're not a woman, huh?"

"Yes, this and many other things—yes, I'm glad," he answered. "Hang in there, Ellen," he said, wiping her forehead as she writhed, more under control now since her arms and legs were strapped down on the gurney. It was the only way to transport her safely, they'd told him. She looked like a trapped animal; her eyes didn't focus. She had begun to speak Spanish, a second language Ron never knew she spoke. He wished he understood what she mumbled.

Ellen, sure she was dying, recited a prayer for her soul. And for the soul of her unborn child. She asked for forgiveness from all her sins. She told God she was anxious to hug her momma.

*****

Adele Martin arrived thirty minutes later, at Field City Hospital, in one of the maternity unit's two beds. Baby Adele, healthy and crying, was taken to the nursery as Ellen and Ron embraced.

"She's beautiful," Ellen said smiling.

"It's a baby girl," Ron said. Still in shock from the trauma of labor and from Ellen's relative calm immediately following delivery, he added, "You're right. Everything's going to be fine. She's beautiful. Are you sure you're all right?"

"Yes, thank you for making my dreams come true. And thank you, Lord, for letting me live," she added. "You know, I really thought I might die." And then Ellen closed her eyes. She was asleep. Ron headed off to the nursery to visit his baby girl.

By the time he had returned from a trip home to get Ellen's clothes and a bouquet of flowers for her room, baby Addy and Ellen were practicing nursing. It was a touching, moving scene that made Ron grin. Then he saw the enormous bouquet of flowers and balloons filling an entire corner of the dreary manila-yellow room.

"Aren't those beautiful, honey? They're from Mr. Drummand, with best wishes and all," Ellen told him. The mention of Drummand made Ron's stomach turn.

"Great. How are my beautiful girls doing? You two are so precious together," he said, reaching to rub the tiny, newborn head with her black head of hair, watching as she tried to put Ellen's huge nipple into her tiny mouth. "Will that really work?"

"Yes, honey, watch," Ellen answered. And sure enough, little Addy chomped down.

Once again, Ron thought, *Nipples. Amazing.*

CHAPTER 13

Monday, January 20

"Early Christmas presents aside, how were your holidays?" Francis asked Ron.

"Addy is great and Ellen is so happy. Everything's peachy, Francis. Why are you looking at me like that?" Ron asked, annoyed.

"I just worry about you, boss, that's all. It's Drummand, isn't it? I don't understand all the tension. I mean, sales are up again; last quarter we set another record. We've got a great spring line planned." Francis added, "Angela is a big help, by the way."

"Really? I didn't think you liked her," Ron said.

"No, it's just that at first, I didn't think she was on the ball. And she's not book smart—it's more just good gut instincts, I guess. And she seems to want to get ahead. She's a good kid," Francis said.

"Great. Let's go see Mr. Drummand, shall we?" Ron said, dreading the meeting. He hoped Drummand wouldn't lose his cool in front of Francis and Angela. This would be Angela's first time at Squeaky Clean's corporate offices. He hoped Drummand behaved. *This is bound to be a shitty day.* Later, that evening, he would have dinner with Laura Mercer in an attempt to quash the investigation, the investigation neither of the two women working on Squeaky Clean knew about.

Francis drove, citing an irrational fear of allowing a sleep-deprived senior citizen with a newborn to get behind the wheel. Ron happily sat in the back of Francis's Volvo station wagon. Practical. Safe. So Francis. Elegant, in a gold color. Understated elegance. Angela rode shotgun.

Ron daydreamed about little Addy. She was beautiful. Noisy. Special. Draining. He had never imagined parenthood being this tough. And he only saw a little bit of it all. With Ellen still nursing, all Ron really did was wake up and bring her the little one. Then the three of them would be awake while Ellen fed Addy in the rocking chair and Ron turned on *Headline News.*

When they'd seen the same segment twice, Addy was ready to go back to bed. Ron would carry the tiny person back to her nursery while Ellen climbed back into bed. Typically, by the time he looked at the clock, it was 3 a.m. or so. By the time he got back to sleep, it would've been 4 a.m.

So instead, he would just stay up. Working downstairs on his laptop, taking a long walk around the property in the moonlight. Worrying about the unethical client that could ruin his dreams.

Addy was worth protecting at any cost. And he would, he promised himself, he would.

Francis parked in the visitor's space in front of the nondescript manufacturing plant's offices. Big brown windows, cinderblock walls, and a large L-shaped one-story design that embodied the lack of creativity and ingenuity found inside.

Drummand's office was at the far end of the building at the top of the L, giving him the ability to see into virtually all of his corporate officers' windows at a glance. As for the only office he couldn't see into, the one next door, all he needed to do was bellow "Wiser!" and his number-two guy, Bill Wiser, came running. He'd long ago sold his soul for Drummand's money. Ron thought the price he paid emotionally and spiritually showed in his nervous twitches, chain-smoking, and his inability to meet eyes with anyone.

****

In the lobby, where they were all waiting for Mr. Drummand, Angela noticed Bill Wiser had very pretty eyes. She was shaking Bill's hand as he stared at her cleavage, and all she could think was, *What great bright blue eyes. And shiny shoes, very shiny shoes.* "Pleased to meet you, Mr. Wiser," she said.

"Where did they find you? I haven't seen a young woman as well-endowed and as attractive as you in quite some time," Mr. Drummand barked, joining them in the lobby. "What's your name, sweetie?"

"This is Angela, Don," Bill answered, still staring at Angela's cleavage.

"Should we get started, gentlemen?" Francis asked, looking uncomfortable with the banter. "Come on, Angela, help me set up the PowerPoint presentation, OK?"

"Sure, see you in a minute, gentlemen," Angela said with a smile before following Francis down the hall and into a conference room. There, she asked, "Mind if I go potty, Francis? I drank too much Diet Coke before we left. I'll be right back."

Angela wandered down the main hall of the building. She remembered they had entered in the center of the top part of the

L. To explore the rest of the building, away from Drummand's office, she took a left out of the conference room. She hoped the hidden camera was working, because the drab place gave her the creeps and she wouldn't want to come back. Everything was forest green. The carpet was, the walls were, and even the cubicles smooshed in the center of the building were green. Fluorescent lights encased in off-white ceiling tiles gave an eerie, sickly glow to the entire interior. Popping in to one of the executive offices lining the inside of the L, she saw the mounted head of a dead boar, gnarled teeth gleaming back at her. *Poor animal didn't know what it was up against*, Angie thought. On the man's desk were souvenirs of golf outings, fishing trips, and, of course, hunting trips. A poster on his door said, *Expose yourself to the bars*, with a naked man flashing folks at a bar. Angela's camera captured the entire room.

She moved on down the hall until she spotted the restroom. She kept going until she reached a group of three men who stood waiting, it seemed, for someone to make coffee.

"Look at that," one said as Angie approached.

"I hope she's in my department," another said.

"Hi, guys. What's up?" Angie asked in her best naive voice.

"Me—and uh, we're just waiting for some coffee. New here?"

"Yes, I am. Step aside and I'll make it for you," Angie offered, and did, as the sexual innuendos began to flow. After a couple of minutes of bantering, she fessed up to being an outside vendor.

"I work with your ad agency," she explained.

"I bet they don't pay you anything. We'll double it. I can do that, I'm a vice president," said the third one, sizing her up. "I'm Joe Puck. Nice to meet you."

"You're kidding, right? You're too young to be a big, important vice president, right?" she asked in her best country bumpkin manner.

"Come with me, Angela. I'll prove it to you," Joe said, putting his arm around her shoulders. "Get back to work, you two."

He propelled her back through the offices and all the way to the front of the building, into Drummand's office. Angela knew Drummand would be in there, presumably waiting for the agency presentation to be ready.

As they walked in, Drummand was drilling Ron Martin.

"Excuse us," Joe said. "I'd like to offer Miss Angela a position with Drummand Industries, sir."

"Angela works for me, Mr. Puck. I'm sure she's flattered, but no," Ron said firmly, staring at Angela, who shrugged her shoulders.

"What do you want her to do for you, Joe?" Drummand asked.

"I have that opening, you know, Julie's job," Joe said.

"Right, your administrative assistant. What do you think, Angela?"

"Oh, thank you, but I'm very happy with Mr. Martin," she said sweetly.

"We'll double your salary dear, and cut your hours. You think about it during the presentation. Is it ready?" Drummand asked.

"What?" Angela asked.

"The presentation, Angela, is it ready?" Ron asked forcefully.

"Yes, it is, come right this way," she said, hoping that was the truth, and hurried back out into the hall. She wanted to sneak away, call Marty, and find out what she should do. If the ultimate goal was to catch Drummand, she should take the position. She'd probably never get Ron anyway, now that he had a baby at home and all.

When she reached the conference room, she realized nobody had followed her. "Man, that was a long potty break, Angela," Francis said. "Are you OK?"

"You're not going to believe what happened. Drummand offered me a job."

"Doing what?"

"Being some vice president's administrative assistant. At double my salary. He doesn't even know what my salary is—hmm—and he did it in front of Mr. Martin, who looked really pissed. I need a piece of bubble gum. What do you think?"

"Do you want a career, Angela?" Francis asked evenly. "Or are you just working until Mr. Right comes along? You don't need to answer me, just yourself. Because if it's the first, I'd stay with the Martin Agency. I think you have great potential. If it's the latter, go for the money."

When the men joined them in the room a few moments later, no one was speaking, except for Bill Wiser, who hadn't been there to hear the job proposition. When Francis finished presenting the summer soap line—colors, shapes, and celebrity picks—the men all clapped politely. The room fell silent.

"I have binders for each of you outlining the campaign, should you have any questions," Francis said into the thickness. "And with that, we'll be on our way, right Ron?"

"Right. And thank you for your time, Mr. Drummand," Ron added.

"Angela, you will let us know in the next day or so, right?" Joe asked.

"Yes, I will. And thank you. I can't imagine leaving the agency when they've been so nice to me," she said, noticing Francis rolled her eyes.

****

She's gone, Francis thought, wondering who Angela would sleep with first at Drummand Industries, and wondering who she would be able to find to help her with Squeaky Clean.

****

Laura Mercer was fifteen minutes late by the time she joined Ron Martin at his table, in a corner of a dark Italian restaurant called Tony's. The spot was near the television station, but Laura had taken her time getting there. It was a power play.

Tony's, like its owner Tony Morelli, was authentic, dark, and small. Perfect for peace talks and secret negotiations. Politicians loved the joint because of the privacy and the manly feel. Only recently the sanctity of the atmosphere began to slip as female power brokers had begun to lunch there too. Much to Tony's discomfort, she suspected.

Nighttime was still man time, however.

"I'm glad you showed up. I was afraid I'd be enjoying the Roman bread alone," Ron said, standing to pull out the chair for Laura. She murmured thanks as she sat, and a waiter came to take their drink order.

Laura was dressed in black, with discreet jewelry and a well-hidden microphone. She wouldn't take any chances with Ron Martin. He was slick and driven, she knew. In fact, she knew far too much about Ron.

"I haven't had Tony's fettuccine in forever. You can always lure me here with that," Laura said, keeping up the idle banter. "But I'm sure you have more in mind than dinner. What's up?"

"I know about your investigation of Drummand Industries, and I'm wondering what you're up to. The Squeaky Clean brand is my agency's biggest account, and what hurts it hurts us. I know you don't want that—after all, we buy a lot of time on WCOL. A Target 5 slam job could affect our media spending."

"Is that a threat, Ron?" Laura asked, looking up from the menu.

"No, Laura, that's reality. Mr. Drummand is seventy-something. He resurrected a brand everyone thought was washed up. He's provided jobs to the community, created a national novelty item. He should be applauded, not investigated," Ron said, shaking his head sadly.

Ron looked like the cowardly lion, Laura thought, and then she wondered, *How much does Ron know?*

"Ron, it's my job as a reporter to investigate wrongdoing. The fact that Squeaky Clean is fun and popular with the college crowd doesn't change the fact that Drummand is a pig. Your agency has done a fabulous job making more money for an unscrupulous man," Laura said, as the waiter walked up with Roman bread, a glass of Chianti for Laura, and sparkling water for Ron. *Why doesn't he remember?* she wondered. She stared into his eyes then, willing Ron to make a connection.

Nothing. Maybe he really doesn't remember...Impossible, Laura thought. She shivered.

After they had placed their orders, Ron decided to try another approach. "Look, as a friend, I'm asking you to stop your investigation. I'll help you find another story. There are plenty of sexist pigs out there—heck, there are even some in their forties and fifties you can really ruin. Please, leave Drummand alone."

"I can't. He stinks," she answered simply.

"Laura, it could be dangerous for you and your career. He knows people. You're being watched. I care about you, I do," Ron said, reaching for her hand.

She allowed him to hold it, and then she asked: "How's your baby, Ron?"

He didn't flinch. Still holding her hand, and then brushing his thigh against hers, he answered, "She's beautiful. Like you. She cries more. How would you like to finish here and go someplace more private. My office? Your place? How about it? I think we could work things out better that way," Ron said. He was a desperate man.

Slowly, she extracted her hand from under his and slid her leg away from him. Staring straight into his eyes, she said, "You had your chance, Ron, a long time ago. I'm not interested now. You can threaten me and you can try to seduce me, but it won't work. Either way, I'm working on a story and you're trying to obstruct it. I won't be threatened off, bought off, or fucked off. Got it?"

"Fuck you, Laura. You're playing with the big boys, and you're gonna get burned. Just remember, I tried to help you," Ron sneered.

And, as she stood to leave, Laura added, "Big help, thanks. Oh, and thanks for the wine and bread, it reminds me of communion. Maybe you should encourage your client to come clean. Confess. It could help—maybe your business would even last through the scandal. Get away from Drummand, Ron. Fast. I shouldn't even help you, but I do feel sorry for you."

And then, pausing to turn off the microphone, she looked straight into his eyes and said, "You just don't remember, do you? I can't believe it."

****

"Remember what?" Ron said to Laura's back. Watching her walk away, through the dark restaurant, turning heads, he knew she knew more about Drummand and his dirty ways than Ron did. But that wasn't all she was talking about. Remember what? Something with her, about her? There was nothing.

He should resign the Squeaky Clean account, Laura was right. Extract himself from Drummand's control before he pulled him into an ethical pit. But he couldn't. Without another big account to fill in the void, he'd be forced to lay off half his staff. Of course, one was down with Angela, who had abruptly resigned to work for the pigs. But Francis, and the others. No. He couldn't be rid of Drummand.

"Tough night, Ronny?" Tony asked, sitting down in the chair formerly occupied by Laura.

"Not the best," Ron answered.

"You weren't trying to get that one, were you? You'd be crazy, man. That chick is bad news with a capital B," Tony said, shaking his head with manly disgust. "She's messed with a lot of guys' heads, man."

"Maybe that's because she can," Ron said, staring into his glass of sparkling water, before finishing it with one gulp. "I've gotta get home, see the baby."

"Right, the baby. Just what the world needs, another girl, huh, buddy?" Tony said, slapping Ron on the back and disappearing into the restaurant. Ron hurried to finish the meal he'd ordered.

He was having dinner at Tony's the following evening, too, he realized. Ellen wouldn't be pleased, but he hoped she'd understand. Business was pulling him away too much, she'd complained. Coming between him and his family, she'd said. It would only be for now, until he could get through this Drummand mess, he'd told her. She told him that's what Michael used to tell her.

He'd call her during the drive home; hopefully she'd be in a good mood. They could talk about Addy. That's really all he wanted from her: understanding and a little love. And a happy baby girl, of course. Ron shoveled his pasta into his mouth.

*****

Outside, it was cool and Laura shivered as she waited for her car. The valet parking attendant drove it around quickly, as if sensing her need to flee the restaurant. He looked surprised by the generous tip.

Laura drove home slowly, wondering how a man could block out a rape. That's what it had been. She had been a young reporter, just starting out at the Dayton CBS affiliate, WDAY-TV, when she answered the phone and it was the Dream Call. The general manager at the CBS affiliate in Columbus was interested; he'd seen her tape and wanted her to interview for a lifestyle reporter position. The Dream was coming true, faster than she'd ever imagined. Unfortunately, she had no one to share the good news with at the station, no friends, just enemies she'd made in her drive to excel, stand out, be the best. Her family wasn't going to jump for joy, either, but they were all she had then.

Her born-again parents were still shocked by her career decision, thinking journalists, especially broadcast journalists, were dirty sinners, carrying out the work of the devil on earth. Growing up, as her family traveled the Midwestern countryside every summer, hosting revivals in tents throughout Kentucky, Ohio, and Indiana, Laura would read. It was her escape. She wasn't reading the Bible, although that's what her parents thought. She'd ripped out the center of her King James, making a nice false cover for any number of best-selling paperbacks.

She'd sit in the back seat of her parents' Rambler station wagon, the one with fake wood sides on the outside and the spirit of God boiling over on the inside. Her father practiced his hellfire and brimstone sermons at the top of his lungs in the car, making her false Bible book escape even more important. Pulling into whatever town, they'd toss their suitcases—one for the front seat and one for the back seat—into their two dive hotel rooms—one for the kids, one for the parents, courtesy of the revival organizers—and head out to the site. Once there, Laura and her brother helped set up the baptismal tub, if there wasn't a shallow stream, and helped set up row upon row of folding chairs.

That night, they'd eat supper at the local coordinator's home—usually a pretty good meal—and then head back to the hotel for prayer and bed. That's when Laura was free. From the night before the revival until it was teardown time, she and her brother could roam the town, read, be kids. Her parents' attention was focused on saving souls while Laura focused on expanding her horizons.

By the age of fifteen, she'd traveled the back roads enough to know her future was in the city, with the sinners. Drawn to beauty parlors and record stores and any type of pop culture outlet in the towns they visited, Laura had blossomed into a tall brunette symbol of everything her parents preached against during the revival, although they didn't notice. As soon as the revival began, she was free to make her transformation: she'd wear makeup, curl her hair, dress in short, tight skirts, and walk along the main street, looking for pop culture fun. She loved Barbies, playing Monopoly and winning all the money, and reading *Glamour* magazine. She was, in essence, somehow normal.

Her brother called her a sinner. She told him to get lost.

Her senior year in high school, she was crowned homecoming queen and that night celebrated with her quarterback boyfriend by sleeping with him. She liked it; he did too. Unfortunately, in what Laura considered a twist of fate and what her parents considered divine intervention, her boyfriend had parked the car illegally in a city park, and naked, the kids were discovered by a Dayton cop.

The cop drove her home after allowing her to dress. Took her to her front door, rang the doorbell, and told all. The rest of senior year was spent repenting. She taught Sunday school at their church and led the prayer warriors' group on Wednesday evenings. All the while, she kept her "Bible" close by her side, stealing glimpses of the world beyond her parents' home. She won a full scholarship to Ohio State University's journalism school, and when August came, she never looked back.

Until she had to, of course, when her first big break brought her back to Dayton. This time, though, she was back as a minor celebrity in town. A local girl on the fast track—at least that's what the *Dayton Daily News* said about her. When Laura called her parents to tell them to watch the paper for the story about her, they called her a sinner. She never called them again.

Her cell phone rang, jarring her into the present. *Who would call at midnight?* she wondered. It was Angie. Desperate to talk. Laura told her roommate she'd be right there. Angie had surprised her, doing an awesome undercover job. They almost had enough tape to put together the Target 5 piece, to show sexual harassment as it really happens, enough to convince even the biggest cynics. Almost.

It was dark as she pulled into the apartment complex. Blackout. Ron's friends had claimed Ron had a blackout, that he hadn't touched alcohol since, that it hurt him more than she'd ever know, that he would remember someday and apologize. Yes, he would remember someday. She'd make sure.

"Hey, Angie, I'm home," Laura said, walking into their place, smelling the mildewy smell so familiar after four years in the rat hole.

"OK, here's the thing. I was thinking we've seen enough with Drummand to take the Martin Agency people totally out, OK?" Angie said. "I don't wanna hurt them 'cause they've been so nice to me, really."

How ironic, Laura thought, and said, "Who've you been talking to? Anybody threatening you?"

"No, of course not. I mean at Drummand, the same ol' thing: yesterday, he closed his office door and dropped his pants, Laura. He started rubbing his thing, right there, in the office. I couldn't get out, so I just rolled tape and screamed."

"Are you ready to quit? I don't want you getting hurt, Angie," Laura said, meaning it. But this was great stuff.

"I'm fine. I'll finish up this week; there's a company picnic on Friday—promises to be interesting. But back to Ron and Francis and the others at the Martin Agency. I really don't think they knew," Angie said.

"They know, at least Ron does. You have the conversation, or the part of it he couldn't hide when Drummand came on the speakerphone. What do you think that was about? Get real. Vendors who work with a company like this are just as unethical as the company. They make money off the company either by looking the other way or by participating. Ron Martin participates," Laura said.

"What do you have against him? You hate him, don't you?" Angie said.

"It was a long time ago when Ron and I had a run-in," Laura said, suddenly so exhausted she couldn't even rally her typical disdain for any deep conversation with the mouse. *What the hell,* she thought, and plopped down on the orange velour sectional's end piece. "Ron's a rapist. Or he was. When he still drank. He doesn't anymore. I was working in Dayton, mostly weekend stuff, trying to get ahead, when I got a call from a station here. Not Channel 5, a different one. They wanted to interview me. I was pumped, so I got the day off and then my car died. Died. My parents were driving through Columbus on the way to a revival, so they offered me a ride."

"What's a revival?" Angie asked.

"It's not important; I'm sure you've been saved," Laura said, sarcastically. "Sorry, anyway, they dropped me off at the station and waited in the parking lot for me to come out."

"That was sweet," Angie offered.

"Sweet? Paranoid. They thought I'd get into trouble in the big city. I guess they were right, because after my interview, I rode with them to the motel where they'd spend the night before driving on the next day. They turned in early and I was bored, so I went for a walk. Next thing you know, this big ol' car is following me. It slows down and this guy says something like, 'Hi, babe, wanna ride?' or something stupid. I said no, but he wouldn't go away. We were in a bad part of town, I guess, I don't know, but I started getting worried.

"He had a big green BMW," Laura said, picturing the car clearly, still, almost seven years later. "When we came to an intersection, I kept walking and he turned right in front of me and parked on the side of the road, right in the crosswalk.

"Nobody else was around. Just a traffic light and a baby crying somewhere. And suddenly, we were face to face, and he grabbed me around the waist and put his other hand on my mouth and pulled me into the back seat," Laura said, staring at the ceiling.

"My God, who did this to you?" Angie asked softly.

"Ron. Ron Martin. He kept mumbling how he'd pay double, and he wondered why he'd never seen me around before, and then he told me I was a perfect weight, one hundred fourteen pounds. I started begging him to let me go, and I wondered what kind of kook he was, and I thought I was going to die, right there on the tan leather seats of his green BMW," Laura said, catching her breath. "And then he just pinned me to the seat. He was so strong and so drunk, and when he was finished with me, he said thank you. He had ripped my underwear in his frenzy and one of the buttons of my shirt was torn off, but otherwise, physically, my wrists were sore, but you couldn't tell anything."

"Did he, you know, rape you?"

"He put it in but didn't come. It deflated or something. I'm not sure," Laura answered. "He handed me five hundred-dollar bills and his business card and said he'd be interested anytime, and then—I guess I was in shock—'cause I stayed in the back seat and he drove me to the hotel where I was staying and walked me up to the door. My mom opened it and saw me and started screaming and Daddy dialed 911, and my mom was yelling, 'Sinner. The devil took her! Sinner!' Ron freaked and tried to grab his business card and said it was all a mistake, and then he pushed me forward into my mom and turned outside the door and threw up, and then he ran to his car and drove away. When the police showed up, Daddy told them he didn't want to press charges yet. He needed to talk to me, make sure it wasn't my fault.

"Daddy saw money that night. Cha ching. Ron says he doesn't remember any of it, but through his attorney, he paid and paid. My parents, through their attorney, got a new car. I got a BMW—black—and Ron, I guess, got away with it. I got a call from one of his friends. He said Ron had hit rock bottom that night, had been drinking all day, and was looking for a hooker. He thought I was a hooker. After that night, he went into rehab. Supposedly, he's never had a drink since. Supposedly, he doesn't remember that night and he never found out my name."

"Wow, and I thought I'd been through a lot," Angie said, "I guess you never really know what somebody else has been through, even if they look like they've had a cushy life. That's how you look, you know. Kinda snobby. Like, cold and mean and above everybody. Guess you're a survivor, you know?"

"But, I somehow can't get past it, with Ron's agency across the street and all," Laura said. "And then, when I did finally get a break with Channel 5 and I move here and and I saw Ron at one of those advertiser-ad agency schmooze cocktail parties, what did he do? Ask me out! Now, my name was never in the paper, and he was only cited for DWI and went to rehab and stuff, but still, I thought people would know. I thought he'd know me, remember me."

"Nothing."

"Nothing. Except, of course, I turned him down," Laura said. "But I make sure I flirt just enough to rile him up. I keep thinking maybe that'll—"

"Maybe he just blocked it or blacked it all out or whatever," Angie said. "Maybe you should just tell him? He probably would like the chance to apologize."

"Nope. He's chosen to forget. I want to try to force him to remember. Actually, I think linking him to Drummand can help, make him repent a bit. Maybe even force him to remember. After all, before he went on the wagon, Ron was a sexual predator." Laura's arms were covered with goose bumps. "I need to get some sleep, Angie. You can't change my mind. Really. And you can't change people. Ron might not drink anymore, but he's still the same. He tried to hit on me again recently, over dinner."

"Recently? But he's married and has a baby—there has to be another way. Please, think about it. I hate what happened to you, but do you really want such public revenge? What about just talking to him?" Angie suggested.

"I tried that. Good night," Laura said, walking away down the hall.

****

Angie couldn't stop thinking how sad Ron's life had been, thinking how cute he was. Turned out he was just another one of Laura's cast-offs. *Ron needs to know,* she thought. If she could tell Ron, he could apologize to Laura, and then Angie could convince Laura to keep the Martin Agency out of the Target 5 Investigation. *Yeah. Right.* Not so simple, but at least she had a plan.

Why did she care about Ron so much, she wondered? Was it just his shiny shoes? Or was it that he was nice to her? Or maybe because he was another pawn of Laura's. *Ron treated me like, well, like a professional,* Angie thought. That was different, for sure. And even though Marty had made her take the job at Drummand, Angie secretly dreamed of working at the Martin Agency again. Someday. She'd fix everything.

****

Maddie had told Lyle she hated to ask, but she thought it was time for him to get involved in the Drummand mess. She asked him to help out, offer whatever he could to help fix the Drummand account and the morale at the agency. Lyle loathed office politics and sucking up to hateful clients. It was much easier to just be creative, detached, aloof, and artsy. He didn't want to expend emotional energy on a job.

Besides, he told her, he didn't want to work there anyway. He wanted to write screenplays or a novel or something. Do something important someday. Not just commercial. Lasting.

He knew Maddie was talking to Francis too much. That just needed to stop; that was the real problem, he knew. But it was too late. Maddie was expecting him to follow through. Francis was in a panic; she needed help and so did Ron, Maddie said.

"Hey Ron," Lyle said, while jogging down the hall to catch his boss before he reached the conference room for a staff meeting. "Say, hey, was just wondering if you had time for a quick lunch?" Lyle felt as awkward as his invitation sounded.

"Ah, well, thanks for the offer, but I'm busy," Ron answered, smiling but breaking eye contact fast.

"OK, cool, maybe some other time," Lyle said, slowing down to let Ron get ahead of him into the conference room. It wasn't like they were friends or anything. He didn't even know if Ron had friends, just the agency people. He knew Ron was "in recovery"— meaning no booze. Maybe it was hard to find a guy to hang with without drinking.

Lyle sat down in the chair next to Ron and tried again. "Well, ah, Ron, maybe we could go grab dinner tonight?" Lyle asked feebly. If only he was a more manly man, he could take Ron golfing. Once there, swinging their sticks, they could talk about life, pee behind trees, get back to nature, and bet on their game. Too bad. *I wonder if he digs cooking shows...Probably not*, Lyle thought.

"I've got dinner plans tonight, Lyle, but is something bothering you?" Ron asked, looking up from the stack of papers in front of him, and for the first time really seeming to see Lyle. "If you're just the latest in a stream of big-hearted well-wishers, I appreciate the sentiment, but I'm fine. Now, if you have an idea about any new business, that's what I'd like to hear about."

"I do. But I'd like to get out of here to pitch you on it," Lyle answered, thinking he'd come up with something by the time they went to a meal together, about the time hell froze over.

"Great. That's what I like to hear. I have tomorrow night free. How about it?"

Shit. "Sure, that sounds great," Lyle said.

"Let's meet at Tony's, seven o'clock. That'll give me time for a workout. I think I need it," Ron added, patting his stomach.

The conference room continued to fill with the rest of the agency's staff members as Lyle murmured, "See you there" as enthusiastically as he could. He looked calm to anybody walking into the conference room, but inside he was panicked. He needed to call Maddie. She had to help him find a new client and a campaign by the next evening.

After the meeting, he hurried back to his office, reaching his desk, panting. Man, it wasn't like he hadn't hustled before. But it'd been a long time. He was pumped. Inspired, even. And out of breath. Although he hadn't a single idea about a potential new client, he had the opportunity to dream. But he had to hurry.

In this business, you could say whatever you wanted and if you said it often, or bought enough rating points, it'd be something everybody said soon enough. "Just do it" and "You're in good hands" were among his personal favorites.

A quiet, shy boy, Lyle Boardman grew up in what would later be described as the all-American family: one mom, one dad, one boy, and one girl, in a split-level, white stucco ranch with a wrought-iron

B hanging proudly next to a picture window. Mom cooked, cleaned, and basically managed the home. Dad worked at Union Fork & Hoe, making rakes and gardening equipment, starting in the shop and ending up as manager, hoe division. Sally, Lyle's sister, was two years older and stereotypically popular at their elementary school, middle school, and finally, her crowning glory, high school. Lyle, the little brother and only son, was tragically gangly, introverted. A bookworm.

Lyle's dad didn't dig what Lyle did; Lyle liked to learn. To study leaves in the fall to figure out what the growths on them were; to diagram the exact shape of snow crystals in winter; to catch bugs and frogs in the spring and summer, some to feed and keep as pets and others to kill and dissect. Sam Boardman liked to play softball, drink beer, lift weights, and tinker with his car. Father and son, much to Olivia Boardman's despair, couldn't hang out together like Olivia and her daughter did, at the beauty parlor, shopping, and being together. And while the female Boardmans bonded, the male Boardmans grew apart, internalizing their dreams and goals. For the thin, thirteen-year-old Lyle, his first day visiting his father's factory was one of the most terrifying experiences of his life.

The furnaces used to weld the tools spit ferocious flames out of their belching mouths. The workers, covered in soot, smiled and waved at him while he was near them, and immediately began snickering about the beanpole once he'd walked past them. Lyle saw them, heard them. He vowed never to work among men like these. And Sam never asked him back.

Meanwhile, in school, while his sister became a cheerleader and talked on the phone every night, all night, Lyle wrote poetry. He never showed it to anyone, not even his mother. She would've liked it. But it wasn't worth the possibility of his father or sister discovering his writing. So he hid out in the library at school, tried to ignore his father's disgust, and later, when he told Maddie about his life, he included only his favorite family vacations, his scholarship to Northwestern, and his dog, Kaiser. That was a wrap on life from zero to eighteen.

At Northwestern, Lyle became a stud, but he didn't realize it at the time. His thin physique slowly filled out and his reddish blond hair gave him a striking presence, while his freckles made him "approachable." His shy demeanor became mysterious. All in all, Lyle was a hunk. Working during the summers as a waiter forced Lyle out of his shell. Without a job, he would've been forced to return back home, to Columbus and the rest of his family. To stay in Chicago, in Evanston, he had to make enough money to live. That left waiting tables.

Lyle Boardman, waiter at the Golden Peacock, was a draw, with a regular customer base who requested his section. Especially female customers, who left uncharacteristically big tips. Once he'd stashed away enough cash, he purchased his first car, a used Jeep Wrangler. With the ragtop off, summer in the city was great. Windy City winters, seeming so far off in the middle of summer, didn't seem to worry him. Later, he seemed the stud for not caring.

As a first true girlfriend, Shelby Lawrence was perfect. She should've intimidated Lyle Boardman from Columbus, Ohio. She of the North Shore, the wealthy Chicago suburb of Winnetka. But Lyle wasn't looking for love, and so he didn't know it when Shelby, his coworker at the time, set her sights on him. He still thought about her with a smile. She was, he realized now, the opposite of Madeline Wilson.

Shelby was tall and thin, blonde and translucent. She laughed a lot, and when she did, heads turned. Her laughter, like a child's giggle, was contagious. It was easy to become hooked on Shelby. Outside the restaurant, she dressed in designer clothing, although Lyle couldn't care less about that. All he saw was the vision of Midwestern purity standing in front of him, eye to eye in the matching uniform of white T-shirt embellished with a ridiculous peacock and khaki shorts.

"Oh, excuse me Shelby, am I in your way?" he asked the beautiful waitress blocking his path. Lyle didn't know Shelby had begged her parents for a chance to experience the real world, to work, to have a menial job.

"No, Lyle, actually, I was wondering if you'd like to go see a movie or something tonight?" And that, as Lyle remembered it, was the beginning of bliss, of love. And until the end of summer, when Shelby Lawrence bravely invited him home to her mansion on Lake Michigan and stunned her parents with the nobody English major on scholarship from Ohio, Lyle's life was full of love.

Shelby's parents made sure it was simply summer love, and Shelby suddenly no longer waited tables at the Peacock. When Lyle dreamed of summer in the winter, smelled sunshine in the air, he pictured Shelby. He always would.

Moody, creative, brilliant Maddie was winter. Dark, brooding, beautiful, and difficult. And hopefully, an especially quick and prolific marketing campaign creator. Lyle realized it was time to start. He needed Maddie and a brainstorming session.

He was lucky to have Maddie, Lyle knew. *Summer is fun*, Lyle thought, knowing he'd always wonder what had become of Shelby. *But life is really more like spring and fall and winter. Changing. Unpredictable. More Maddie.*

"Call Maddie, Boardman," he scolded himself. *Now*, he told himself, punching in the phone number.

"Lyle, are you serious?" was the first thing Maddie said. "An entire campaign, a new business pitch, by tomorrow evening?"

"Yep."

"I guess we better get started right away. Meet me at home in an hour."

"Maddie, I do love you," Lyle said.

"I know. Thanks. And Lyle, no matter what, be home on time. We have a lot of work to do before tomorrow night. Oh, and bring your laptop home, you're going to be doing some graphic design work too," Maddie said.

"I'm a writer," Lyle whined.

"So am I, Lyle, but we're trying to save your butt, so you'll be the designer on this project, got it?"

"Yes, Maddie. See you at three," Lyle said, hanging up.

*****

Maddie had the big idea. Ideas were her forte. She had come through again.

By the time Dixon Crane rang the doorbell, they'd been working on the campaign for five hours and it was coming together. Maddie couldn't believe it was already eight at night.

"Thanks so much for coming, Dixon," Maddie said, escorting him into the living room. "All we need you to do is give us a witty quote and let us take your photo. Then we'll use that video camera to tape a little piece. No big deal for a broadcast star," Maddie said, and Dixon chuckled.

"I won't ask you much, but what the heck are you up to?" Dixon said.

"We think—Lyle and me—the *Daily Journal* needs an advertising campaign, promoting its writers as celebrities just like the broadcast folks do. We'll use a mixed-media campaign—web, print, television, billboards, and even radio—to tell people that print reporters bring depth to life. Right, Lyle?" Maddie asked, hoping he'd jump in, and he did.

"The idea, Dixon, is to sum up your essence, your experience, as one of the most renowned newspaper reporters in the city. It'll be one short segment about ten seconds long for broadcast, and then a print ad. I'll adapt the rest. If you look at most broadcast people, they're kids. Young pups. No wrinkles. Print reporters are proud of their wrinkles," Lyle said. Maddie shot him a look and Dixon laughed.

"We're proud of our experience and our years in the community, and we don't hop around like those talking heads do, gentlemen. We have roots," Maddie said. "Anyway, Lyle needs to present this campaign tomorrow night, so we need you, me, and maybe one other reporter or columnist to dummy up a campaign."

"I fit the dummy qualifications, for sure. Let's get started, Mad," Dixon said. "I suppose you'll want my help convincing the board at the *Journal* an ad campaign is worth it, right? Even though the thought probably hasn't crossed any of their collective minds, what with the great fear of print going the way of dinosaurs."

"Would you? That would be awesome," Lyle said, as he snapped photos of the character seated before him.

"Did you capture enough wrinkles to impress 'em, Lyle?" Dixon asked when they were finished.

"Oh yeah, this'll be great. But do you really think the *Journal* guys'll go for it? Maddie and I really think you need it," Lyle added.

"I agree. Let me see what I can do. I'll let Maddie know tomorrow," Dixon said. "And now, if you'll excuse me, I have a dinner date."

"Thanks, Dixon. You're a sport and a gentleman," Maddie said, shutting the door behind him.

"And you, Ms. Wilson, are a genius," Lyle said, walking over and kissing her on the lips.

"And you, Mr. Boardman, have too much work to do to mess around. And I've got to write my column. We'll celebrate tomorrow night, OK? Once you land the Martin Agency its biggest account since Squeaky Clean. I can see your big office now. But just don't get a big head, OK?" This was going to be great. Hopefully.

"Yes, my love," Lyle said, kissing her hand.

****

Ellen stood in the kitchen, looking out the window, waiting for Ron. Again.

Perched on her toes, she leaned forward. Her beans were in her pocket. Her jet-black hair was in a low ponytail, tied with a hot pink ribbon.

Ron had told her he'd be late, that it was business, but she didn't believe him. She would've followed him herself, but she didn't have a babysitter she could trust. Ron complained on the nights he made it home at a decent hour that Ellen was becoming a shut-in. She didn't care. She would rather stay home with little Addy than go out. And if Ellen and Ron had to go out, for an agency function or some sort of society event, Addy went with them.

"She's only five months old," Ellen said. "She needs her mommy."

"How come children all over the country are thriving at day care centers, huh, El? How come normal people get babysitters and have adult time all the time and their kids don't die or anything? What is wrong with you? I think you need help, OK? Go talk to your doctor, please," Ron said, fed up.

One night, a few weeks earlier, he had actually planned a romantic evening. Francis had offered to watch Addy, said she'd even bring Sophie and they'd come out to Field City, to Ellen and Ron's house, so Addy wouldn't be in strange surroundings. With dinner and the movie, they'd be gone four hours. Tops, he'd explained.

Ellen, tears streaming down her face, said no. Not even Francis could watch Addy. She couldn't leave her, not with anyone. But he didn't understand. Ron had left then, stomped out of the house and didn't come back until the eleven o'clock news.

Ellen was sure he was having an affair then. It cinched it for her.

Ellen walked away from the window and into the powder room by the front door. She looked at herself in the mirror and saw what Ron saw. She had yet to lose thirty of the forty pounds she gained with Addy. With her normal weight being ninety-six pounds, Ellen knew she was fat. Plus, she hadn't been wearing much makeup. She was happy just fussing with the baby, dressing her in three different outfits each day, ordering special toys and clothes from the catalogs arriving in her mailbox daily. Addy had a bright pink bow taped in her hair today to match Ellen's.

And Ron didn't give her any credit, but they did get out, now and then, she and Addy. Why, they went to the mailbox at the bottom of their winding driveway, Ellen thought proudly. Addy loved to sit in her stroller as Ellen pushed her past the pond and down to collect the mail and packages. Ellen kept the gates closed, so the UPS driver just left the brown boxes next to the mailbox. She had a delivery almost daily. When the UPS strike hit, Ellen's lifeline to the outside world suffered. But before that, daily, there were packages waiting. After the strike's resolution, it looked like a brown Christmas at the gate.

On a typical day, by the time she loaded the mail and the boxes onto the stroller and walked back up the winding drive to the house, she'd be sneezing, the fresh country air already causing her sinuses to swell and her eyes to itch and burn. Quickly, she'd roll the stroller holding Addy and a stack of brown boxes into the garage and push the button for it to close. Grabbing Addy, she'd climb the stairs and be safe inside for the rest of the day.

Walking backward out of the powder room, away from the mirror, Ellen hurried back to the family room to watch the baby. Addy was in her ExerSaucer, gurgling at herself in the mirror and screeching. Her little legs worked hard together, propelling her backward. Ellen picked up the camcorder again. She didn't want to miss a moment. Watching the tapes was fun for Ellen, but her own incessant babbling eclipsed her child's gurgles.

"You are perfect, you precious little dumpling, come to Momma, oh, good, that's it, get those legs moving, good girl... your daddy will be so proud of you."

During Addy's naps, she'd open the boxes and order things. Ellen was happy. Except for Ron's cheating. She was sure of that, and she told Addy all about it. Late every night. Not eating at home anymore. No sex. Just like Michael.

Ron was making Ellen mad. But besides that, life was perfect.

CHAPTER 14

Tuesday, March 13

Maddie wished she hadn't picked up the phone, or at least checked caller ID. She was on deadline, her desk covered with notes, and now, she was stuck on the phone with a distraught, irrational Ellen. Her patience was waning. She took a deep breath and tried again.

"You're crazy. No way, Ellen. He's just working too hard," Maddie said, exasperated. She'd been trying to convince Ellen that Ron wasn't cheating on her. Maddie told Ellen she would know. She was a society columnist, code word for gossip columnist for heaven's sake. After all, Maddie was the person who had finally convinced Ellen to see the truth about Michael. Ron was a different story.

"I hear nothing but great things about Ron. The only negative is that he works too hard. Period," Maddie said, and sighed audibly. Ellen didn't seem to hear the hint.

"He's gone all the time, and poor little Addy isn't even going to know her father," Ellen sobbed.

"You know, that's pretty common with entrepreneurial men, and women, I'm afraid. Work absorbs them sometimes. Plus, he's dealing with all the Drummand fallout. That's gotta be tough," Maddie said, exhaling a big puff of smoke. Why was Ellen so whiny? She had all she wanted. A baby. A faithful husband. A family. Maddie was tired, tired of this lame conversation.

"Maybe I should call Janet; she'd understand," Ellen said finally.

"Great idea. Do you have the number at the pink palace?" Maddie asked. She hated to have Ellen bug Janet, but she couldn't take it anymore.

"Got it. Thanks. Could you still try to check it out for me, Maddie? Just try, you know, so I can be sure," Ellen said.

"Yeah, I'll keep my ears open, but I think you're wrong this time. You've got a great guy who loves you, a beautiful baby, and the life of your dreams. Sometimes that means he's going to have to work hard to pay for it all," Maddie said. "I've gotta run. Take care. Be happy."

*****

Francis was surprised when Ellen called. She hadn't heard from her one-time protégé since the baby was born, and try as she might, Francis seemed to have been cut out of her life. As Ellen talked, Francis felt like the younger woman was accusing her of sleeping with Ron. She needed to end the call.

"I just need to know, Francis, that's all. It's OK to tell me if it was in the past," Ellen said.

Francis had had it.

"Go see your doctor, 'cause you're going crazy," she told Ellen. "Ron loves you so much. You should see how he stares at that picture of Addy. He's just stressed at work, that's all, honey. That's all. I think maybe you're suffering from postpartum depression or something." Francis didn't add that the Drummand deal was enough of a problem to push anyone over the edge. Why couldn't Ellen be supportive, instead of doubting Ron? "He needs you, Ellen. Your love and support."

Without Ron sharing everything, Francis had pieced together the Drummand saga. The image she had of Squeaky Clean was one she had created. The reality of Drummand Industries, and even the product she'd promoted with all her heart, was much dirtier. Disheartening and eye-opening. She couldn't burden Ron with her own feelings of disappointment and betrayal, so she turned to her daughter. Francis called Sophie and told her everything. She rambled on for at least twenty minutes, with Sophie giving her the "Uh, uh, uh," treatment.

Self-centered Sophie, Francis thought. Her college-aged daughter still couldn't listen to anything that didn't directly influence her life. Ellen was beginning to sound just like her. After twenty minutes of listening to her mother's troubles, Sophie said simply, "Sorry mom, I *have* to go." She *had* to go, Francis thought. Had to, you know, Mom.

Francis had no one else to confide in for comfort. Her own mother had never understood her or her need for a career. Friends weren't a great option either. Ellen was becoming a wacko shut-in, suffering from some type of self-centered baby blues. Maddie was a journalist; Francis couldn't share all of this with a journalist, even Maddie. And Janet—she had moved to a deserted island.

The women who were Francis's friends before the divorce, when she played tennis at the club and lunched, were long gone. They belonged to a different world, admission requiring a wealthy spouse, a great body, and lots of money. That world was a lifetime ago now, Francis thought.

She'd dabbled in the part-time job life while she was still married, becoming manager of a local Hallmark store. She needed fulfillment, she had explained to her then husband, and for a while, the luxury of part-time employment, the chance to be part of the time in the real world, satisfied her. That luxury ended up being a trap. She was halfway in the working world—and halfway out. The other store employees were teenagers, far too young to "hang" with, and she was stuck. No new friends, just fewer old ones.

Francis had zippo experience in the real working world. And she was bored. Her country club friends were all get-to-stay-at-home moms whom she decided could no longer carry on any substantive conversation about anything other than parenthood and worthless husbands. Francis's other acquaintances were full-time working-outside-the-home moms. Most weren't part-timers; they were committed one way or the other, and if they were part-time, they were so stressed out they had no time for a social life between kids, day care, school, and the job that barely paid for child care.

So, after two months, Francis quit the Hallmark job and turned to exercise. Francis jogged. First three miles, then six miles, and then ten—and then, a blowout. It was her knee. Arthroscopic surgery and three months on crutches later, and Francis knew she needed a life.

Her first day off crutches was when she had found the note from her husband. That night was the evening she met Ron Martin at the grocery store. He was in the soap aisle next to her when Francis joked about how boring buying soap was, and Ron immediately agreed. He asked her: "What would you do?"

"I'd make my soap a different shape—I mean, I'm sure ergonomics have something to do with this, with this rectangle shape. Boring. And I'd make it fun colors. Different packaging, different smells. Maybe it would change," Francis said, and then stopped. "I really do have a life, or a so-called life, promise."

"No, don't be embarrassed, you're right. In fact, very right. I'm Ron Martin, owner of the Martin Agency—advertising—and my client is Squeaky Clean," Ron explained.

"I've never heard of it. Oh, and I'm Francis Hall," she said.

"That's the problem, Ms. Hall. You should've heard of it and you haven't. This might sound personal, but do you work outside the home?" Ron asked, suddenly getting a great idea. "Because if you're interested in a job, I could sure use some help positioning this brand. I love your ideas for shape and size and color, and the client will too. How about it?"

"Well, I'm flattered, really. I'll have to ask my daughter. I'll need her to cooperate, pitch in until school starts again. Are you for real?" Francis asked.

"A little crazy but definitely for real. Here's my card. I'll look forward to seeing you, day after tomorrow. Eight thirty a.m., if that's OK." She nodded. "Have a nice evening; it's been a pleasure," Ron said, smiling. "You're right, you know. None of the soap looks fun. Mr. Drummand, my client, will be intrigued, seriously, when I—we—tell him we recommended soap with a shape, a texture, a color. Squeaky Clean will be fun. Cool. He'll love it. See you Wednesday, and call me with any questions," he added, handing her his card.

"Ron?"

"Yes, Ms. Hall?"

"This is a paid position?"

"Of course. You'll become an account executive from the start."

"And the pay?"

"Very good, Francis. Very good."

"You know, is Mr. Whipple going to come around the corner and squeeze the Charmin? I feel like I'm in a dream. Or a commercial or something."

"No, it's real and I'm serious," Ron had answered.

And the rest, well, had been great. Until now. Ron was crumbling under the stress of an investigation yet to be revealed. It was smoke, mirrors, and scandal waiting to erupt. Ron told Francis about the dinner with Laura Mercer. She was even more committed to the story now, Francis assumed. But she couldn't figure out what was wrong with the soap. Ron told her about the sexual harassment and gender discrimination—but even he didn't know what they'd uncovered about Squeaky Clean. Did it harm people? Could it? Francis supposed the best-case scenario was that they'd green washed—called the product all natural, environmentally friendly when it wasn't. Was that it?

And then there was Angela. So young, so vulnerable. And she'd left for money and an undefined position. Francis tried to picture herself as a twenty-eight-year-old, tried to imagine herself free, unencumbered by a spouse and children. Would she have chosen money or a career? She knew if she hadn't already been a mom, she would've loved a career. But not Angela.

Francis sensed there was something sinister in Angela's job offer. A deep evil lurking at the core of Drummand Industries. She'd asked Ron and he'd agreed. "Angela surprised me," was all he said, but she knew he agreed. She also knew Ron had moved on—he was fixated on replacing the Squeaky Clean business. He poured over the names in his Outlook contacts of the top companies in town. He thumbed through his iPhone, calling men for golf, women for lunch. He was a man possessed, working fifteen and sixteen hours a day.

So Francis worried, stewed, and tried to keep working on the Squeaky Clean account. It was hard to imbue a bar of soap with spunk when your agency's morale was going down the drain. But she tried, because she cared, and she could, and she loved Ron for giving her a chance.

And she called Janet for support, and tried to hug Sophie after they had lunch together. Francis had even allowed her to drop psychology. Sophie was right—everyone knew too much about dysfunctional families through experience. Why should she have to study it?

****

Ron smiled into the Channel 5 camera.

Mr. Drummand and his attorneys had insisted on Ron as the designated spokesperson for Drummand Industries. This was some sort of test of his character, Ron thought, hoping he'd pass.

"Have you personally witnessed any sexual harassment while visiting Mr. Drummand, your client?" Laura Mercer asked. "Anything out of line, Ron, ah, Mr. Martin?"

"He's not going to answer that, Ms. Mercer," the attorney in the shadows said, for the seventeenth time in the past eighteen minutes.

"He's bugging me, Marty," Laura said to her producer, who was, like the attorney, simply a presence outside the dome of light. "We should just get out of here. We have enough anyway."

Ron felt sick. He had looked sick, too, in the greenroom beforehand. He'd glanced at his reflection in the mirror and been aghast. Huge circles dragged down his blue-green eyes, and they had lost their sparkle. His skin was sallow, pasty. Even his hair seemed limp, lifeless.

His life was drained of all joy. Work was a mess. At home, Ellen was withdrawn, sure he was having an affair despite his repeated assurance otherwise. Addy, she was perfect. Cooing, smiling. The only light in his life.

Drummand had stopped paying his monthly retainer to the Martin Agency: fifty thousand a month, gone, even though they were all working double time to ward off media inquiries and plan for future positioning.

****

Angie called Ron, but Francis intercepted the call. She told her to leave Mr. Martin alone, that he'd been hurt enough. Angie tried to explain she wanted to help, that she missed everyone at the agency and had information that could really be important to them. Francis told her she'd helped enough, and hung up on her.

Angie decided she'd try again, later. She missed him; she just wanted to meet for lunch or dinner. She'd make it worth his while, in the business sense, of course.

Of course. Unless he was interested in something more.

CHAPTER 15

Thursday, April 11

Angie was tired of being a spy.

So she quit. She walked into Joe Puck's office, told him she was leaving and to mail her check.

"What's wrong, honey? Mr. Drummand really likes you. He wants me to keep you happy. Why aren't you happy?" Joe asked, walking toward her.

"Because you're a creep, he's a creep, and I hate it here. Leave me alone or I'll scream," Angie said, backing up. "Just send me my check and we'll be even. OK?"

"Fine, whatever. Mr. Drummand isn't going to be pleased. I believe you'll need to tell him about your decision personally," Joe said.

"Mr. Drummand doesn't own me. I'm an employee, not a slave. Get out of my way," Angie said, disgusted. "You hired me and you're supposedly my boss, although I still have no idea what you do every day except golf and hunt things. I'm outta here."

Once she was safely on the road, with her shoe box full of personal things from her desk at Drummand Industries, she called Ron Martin. He took her call.

"Angela, what's up?" he asked.

"I'd like to come back to work for you. I hate it at Drummand—in fact, I just quit, but I really need to share some stuff with you, to help you. I miss you," she gushed.

"Um, Angela, I appreciate the sentiment, but I'm going to be out of the office today."

"But I need to tell you some things, very important things, to help you with Drummand and Channel 5, OK?" she pleaded into the phone.

"You're not going to believe this, but I'm a celebrity judge for the Yacht Club's annual sailing regatta today. I guess you could join me up there? We can talk in between heats, or whatever they're called."

"Sure, thanks, Mr. Martin, and sorry I left the agency so suddenly. I'll fill you in. I can be at your office in ten minutes, OK?" Angie said.

"I'll be waiting by the curb in my car. You can follow me up," Ron answered, sounding intrigued.

✳✳✳✳

Ron took a deep breath as he stood on the sidewalk in front of his office building, waiting for Angela. He was happy to be getting out of the office—and now maybe he'd learn something important from Angela. Something he could use to get out from under Drummand's control.

What an interesting few days. First, Lyle Boardman had surprised him with a great campaign idea for the city's daily paper, a new client opportunity Ron had never imagined possible. And now, the paper's board was considering it. Unbelievable. While not quite as big as Squeaky Clean, the prestige of the account would draw other new business opportunities, Ron knew. And then, he'd talked Ellen into going to a doctor. Everybody kept assuring him the only thing wrong was the baby blues, and that it would pass. Ron decided her mood, rather than passing, was getting darker. Not toward the baby, but definitely toward him. Suspicious. Teary. Fat.

Is she a good mother? they'd ask. *Yes,* he'd answer, *the best. The baby is great, it's just we have no relationship anymore. She has nothing in her life except the baby,* he'd explain. *Stop being so selfish,* they'd say. *You can handle no sex for a while, big guy,* they'd say. *That wasn't what it was about,* he'd tell them. They didn't believe him.

Angie honked her horn and Ron, standing beside his own car, jumped, cracking them both up.

"Nice car for an administrative assistant, Angela," Ron said, leaning into the open window of her white Mercedes.

"It's used, but thanks," Angie answered, smiling. "Do you want to ride together? I'll drive. Just tell me where to?"

"Sure, sounds great," Ron said, climbing into the passenger seat. "It's a long drive up the river road. Just take Broad Street to Long, and we'll stay on Riverside Drive for half an hour at least. It'll be pretty since spring has sprung." As Angie pulled out into traffic, Ron said, "So tell me about Drummand Industries."

She told him about the gross things that had happened to her in her short time there—the groping, dropping, ogling, and other "ings" encouraged among the guys at Drummand. "I had no choice but to put up with it," Angie told him, explaining that even if she had wanted to turn anybody in, there was nobody to turn them in to.

"So even though it was great money, I quit," she said, as Ron shook his head in disgust. He couldn't believe he'd introduced her to the likes of the Drummand gang. He was such an idiot. Angela was a wonderful young woman, and of course, they'd taken advantage of her.

"I'm sorry I even introduced you to them. And believe me when I say I knew nothing about this behavior before all of this Channel 5 stuff brought it to the surface. I golf with Drummand. He tells dirty jokes, but a lot of guys do. We don't go out together. I had no idea he hated women, didn't hire them except to exploit them, until he so much as admitted it to me. I wish I hadn't taken you over there. Francis and I both realized our mistake too late. It wasn't your fault. You needed the money. I'm sorry you had to go through all that."

"Thank you, but I really don't blame you or Francis. I loved working for both of you. And now, I need to tell you something I'm sorry about, because the next thing I tell you has to do with you," Angie said, inhaling deeply. "I've been wearing a camera since you met me. My name is Angie, not Angela, and I'm Laura Mercer's roommate." Angie looked over then in time to catch his wince.

"Oh my God, this has been some setup," Ron said, staring at the young woman.

"I know this will take a little time to sink in, but ever since I met you, saw how nice you were, I've been trying to help you. I'm still really trying to help you by telling you all this when I'm not supposed to. You see, I told them I'd get them the real stuff, you know at Drummand. To leave the Martin Agency out of it. That's why I quit, once I got to know you, to work at Drummand so I could spy on them and leave you out of it. Out of the Target 5 thing, you know." Angie waited for him to speak. He was staring out of the front windshield of the car. She plunged ahead.

"Well, Laura wouldn't let me get you out of it. Even when I told her how good you are, how honest you are. I begged. I stayed at Drummand extra long, just to get more video to use about them, instead of you," Angie said, hoping he'd believe her. "The thing is, Mr. Martin, Laura hates that you don't remember raping her, that's what it is. So if you could just call her up and apologize, and say you suddenly remembered and you need to make it right and all that, then I think I can get you outta all this. Are you following me? Mr. Martin?"

Ron was in shock.

Inside the deepest part of his mind, the subconscious part inaccessible without a prodding poker of truth, memories of a young Laura Mercer came out. She had shorter hair but otherwise looked much the same as today. That was it, he knew as completely as he had blocked it out before, that was why she intrigued him, why he tried to stay close to her. Why, even when she kept saying no, he pursued her. He didn't do that with anyone else. Didn't need to with anyone else.

He had raped her, in the back seat of his old car, a car he'd sold as soon as he completed his in-patient treatment program. Of all the blackouts he'd suffered during his drinking days, this was the one that mattered. He'd never forced himself on anyone, attacked a woman. It was the worst moment of his life, and the searing guilt flooded his conscious now. It hadn't been mutual, the way it was with the Lemon Shake girls. No, this had been predator and prey. The hunter and the hunted. He'd grabbed her with sheer force. She was a hooker, at least she'd looked like a hooker, he'd willed her to be a hooker. She was young and thin and—Ron turned then, and saw Angie Brown again.

"Now I know why she hates me," he said stupidly to Angie and she nodded.

"Yes, and now you know you can apologize and fix things," Angie said.

It wouldn't be that simple, Ron knew. Laura Mercer wanted him to feel pain, pain as deep as he caused her. She'd ruin his life, his business, whatever it took to make him feel. To destroy him the way he'd destroyed her that night. There could be no equalizing. What could compare, equate to rape?

"In rehab they told us all we had to apologize, to make amends with people we hurt while drinking and ask for their forgiveness. I did that, apologized to everyone I could remember. I suffered blackouts while drinking, so I knew I didn't get to everyone."

"But how could you not remember her? She said you bought her parents a new car, you bought her a BMW?" Angie asked, looking amazed.

"No, my attorney took care of all that. He told me he took care of the girl and her family. I never knew their names. We settled with them, gave the parents a lot of money. Maybe Laura doesn't know that part. I always wondered if the girl knew her parents stole the money—because I knew they would. The money was supposed to be for her. A car wasn't my idea. Her parents were some sort of preachers or something, but my attorney said they were con artists. I was lucky to get out of it without losing everything," Ron said. "And now, she wants me to pay again."

"I don't think she knows you paid before. She thinks a car was your payoff, you know, for raping her."

"You know how messed up I was, Angie? I thought Laura was a hooker. Isn't that sad and pathetic? I was pathetic, back then, and she sees me that way still," Ron said. " Ron put his head on his right hand, right elbow perched on the ledge of the window. "Now what, now what?"

"What? Did you say something?"

"Well, since you've figured everything else out, what now?" Ron asked the young woman driving. "And are you still wired?"

"To answer your first question, I don't know, because she won't see you again. She let you have a chance—and you hit on her at a restaurant or something?" Angie said, shaking her head.

" I thought that was what she wanted," Ron said. "God, I'm an idiot. What a mess."

"No, I'm not wired. And just so you know, the ice maiden only wants sex when she wants it. And only from married rich men who haven't raped her," Angie said. "I'm not as picky." She didn't look at him.

"Are you two friends?"

"Nope, just roommates. She's paying me to spy, first on you and then on Drummand. We both needed a roommate to help pay rent. We got stuck with each other, but not for much longer. She told me she's moving out soon. Really, we kinda hate each other," Angie said, frankly.

"Not as much as she hates me," Ron said.

"No, probably not that much," Angie agreed. "Hey, there's the sign for the race. Ooh, a regatta. How formal. Do I get to help you?

"You already have," Ron said.

"No, judge the sailing I mean."

"Sure. You didn't think you were just my driver, did you? No, I need you, Angela, um, Angie. And, thank you. Very much."

*****

Another late night, he had told her. Why didn't he just bring his woman over so Ellen could meet her?

"No honey, it's a sailboat race. Do you want to come?" he had asked.

Yeah, right, she thought.

"Watch it on TV. I think Channel 5 is the media sponsor. You'll see me. I'm a celebrity judge," he said.

"Why?" Ellen had asked. "Are you famous? I didn't know."

"Not famous, famous. But you know, I do those guest spots about advertising on TV and then that column in the weekly papers. I don't know, honey, I guess some people just like me," Ron had answered.

"Well, lucky you," Ellen had said.

"Come with me. Bring the baby. It'll be fun," Ron offered again.

"Maybe we'll surprise you," she had answered.

****

Laura Mercer was broadcasting live from the sailboat race.

Even though temperatures were in the low sixties and the wind was more of a breeze, it was chilly. It was her first live remote of what hopefully would be her last springtime in Columbus. Lately, her agent John told her, there had been renewed interest in her at the network. At least in Chicago or LA, if not straight to the Big Apple, he said.

So she was, for Laura, happy. Her long brown hair was pulled back in a low ponytail and tied with a bright orange and pink scarf. Her simple black dress complemented her eyes. They'd get calls, she knew, from viewers wanting to be sure she hadn't cut her hair. Kooks. Maybe she'd turn and show them all so the phones wouldn't ring. No, they'd find something else to critique. Her clothes. Her lipstick. Even, unbelievably, they'd call about fingernail polish. Get a life.

"Ah, excuse me, Ms. Mercer, they're ready for you," some media relations type was saying to her.

"I'm coming," she answered. "I still haven't seen a list of the judges. I need to make sure I know how to pronounce all these *celebrities'* names, got it?"

"Yes, Ms. Mercer, it's coming right up."

Around the edge of the reservoir, both on the Yacht Club side of the water and on the other shore, brightly colored sails reached to the sky, adding color and a vibrant feel to the day.

Laura and the camera crew were set up on the bridge spanning the water. Below them, the judges were being helped onto the replica of the Santa Maria positioned under the bridge. Their services weren't needed beyond appearing. Once they were on the vessel, they enjoyed a floating cocktail party. Occasionally they were asked to pause for commentary or smile for the photographers.

*****

The local celebrities included sports figures, politicians, successful businesspeople, and others who simply had risen to the top of Columbus society. Angie was thrilled when Ron grabbed her by the elbow and escorted her on deck.

"Anchors away," she cried, wishing she had remembered her gum but enjoying the VIP treatment. She spotted one of her former crushes, an old shiny shoes, on the other side of the floating party but ignored his attempts at eye contact. No, she was with Mr. Ron Martin. The advertising agency mogul. A really good guy.

"Angela, Laura is up there," Ron whispered into her ear.

Angie froze. "She can't see us together, Mr. Martin," she said.

"Please, call me Ron."

"Ron, she'll know I told you everything. We gotta go," she said.

"No. It's a beautiful day. We won't let her chase us away. Let's go over to the Yacht Club and grab a seat on the grass, and maybe one of those sailors will take us out. You do swim, right?"

"Uh, yes, but not in freezing cold water," she answered. "I think I'd like to stay on this nifty ship or on shore, OK?"

"Sounds good. Let's go hide by the Yacht Club, shall we? If we drive over the bridge fast enough, she may not notice us," Ron said.

"Yeah right. The ice maiden knows all."

*****

Why are they always so sneaky? Why, why, why?

Her jock could've just broken up with her, but no. He had to find someone else first. Then, then he could leave her. High and dry.

Not that she needed him, or anything. He was poor, farm dirt poor. It was just nice, having someone to depend on, someone to come home to and stuff.

Well, he left her no choice. She had to move on. And she was ready.

But first, she made sure he would remember her. He would, because she was good, he said. To be sure, she told his house mom at the fraternity she needed to collect her things, that jocko had found another.

The older woman looked at the young woman, smiled, and said, "You'll be fine, honey. Better off without him. They're a dime a dozen. Trust me. Now go on up before I get in trouble for letting you in."

Why couldn't you be my mommy—instead of mommy to a house? *she wondered climbing the stairs. Jocko and his three roommates were all at classes.*

She took out the lipstick—All Day Cinema Red, guaranteed to last, kiss after kiss after...—and started writing. She wrote on the walls, she wrote on his pillowcase, his sheets, the bunk beds, the mirror. She wrote on the linoleum floor. She had gone through all three lipsticks she'd brought when she felt better.

Love hurts. Remember me when you do her. Sorry you cheated, aren't you? Be a man. Too bad it's small...*and more, all over the room. She had to teach him. Reach him.*

And she would. When jocko and his buddies came home, they would think the room was covered in blood. Shocked, they would back away until one of them realized it was lipstick. Bloodred lipstick.

And on the pillow, the pillow she'd kissed over and over, was a note that said, "Good-bye, sweet dreams. Love and kisses, me."

*****

"Francis was right about you," Ron said to Angie as they sat on a borrowed blanket by the edge of the cold, brown water. It was a perfect day and he was enjoying their chat more than he could imagine. They hadn't discussed his predicament with Laura, and they hadn't talked about Ellen and the baby. His mention of Francis was the first about the office. Mostly they'd shared relaxing small talk.

"I like Francis. Or should I not? What did she say?" Angie asked.

"She said something about the fact you have street smarts, not book smarts, and that's more important," Ron said. "And she's right. You're very bright. What will you do if we can't hire you back at the agency?"

"Waitress. It's my fall-back position. Everyone needs one. I make good money, the hours are kinda long, but I meet interesting people. I gotta pay for my new car now," she added. Angie studied Ron's face then, saw the signs of stress tighten his jaw, squint his eyes. "Sorry, I didn't mean to remind you of the car thing."

"No, that's fine. I'm anxious to face it. Get it behind us, if she'll allow it," Ron said.

"Would you like to go out sometime with me?" Angie said, looking directly at Ron. "I mean, I know you're married and all, but you don't seem real happy, and I think I could make you smile. I know I could make you feel good."

"Angie, I'm flattered, but I have enough problems without complicating things further. You're a beautiful young woman—how old, twenty-eight? Right—and you have your life ahead of you. I'm forty-three and married and I have a baby at home. My business is teetering on the brink of ruin if your roommate extracts her revenge, and I'm being implicated in a sexual harassment investigation. All in all, not a good time to start a relationship," he answered.

"Maybe it is," she said, leaning over and kissing Ron on the cheek. "I think you're the most handsome man I've ever kissed."

"Angie. Wow. Thank you. For everything. I need to sort out my life, OK? Can you understand? I'll find a job for you, a place at the agency. I'll never really be able to repay you for telling me everything, but I'll try."

"I can't believe you're turning me down," Angie said, hurt and mad at the same time. Standing, she placed both of her hands on her hips. She looked like Francis. "I tell you things to save your business. I tell you things I'll get killed for sharing. You say maybe you can give me a job—is that what you're saying?"

"Calm down, Angela," Ron said, jumping to his feet, trying to calm her down. "I'll hire you back. Call me in the morning, and we'll work it out," Ron said.

"Fuck you, Mr. Martin. Fuck you," Angie said, running up the riverbank with tears in her eyes.

CHAPTER 16

Monday, April 15

Ellen waited until three o'clock Friday afternoon, and then she called the police. She explained Ron hadn't showed up at the office this morning, that he hadn't come home Thursday night after the sailboat regatta. She was worried, really worried, she said. It wasn't like him.

When she gave her name, the detective who had been asking perfunctory questions in a bored, nasal tone, perked up. He asked her to hold. Ellen decided his voice sounded like a combination of pity and awe that a "celebrity" might be in trouble.

Addy was crying for her feeding when a Detective Moore came on the line and said he'd be right over. *Is Janet coming today, or tomorrow?* Ellen thought as she hung up the phone. *Maybe Wednesday? And I thought Janet's life was tragic,* she thought ironically, placing Addy under her right arm, in the football hold position, to nurse.

All I asked for was a normally dysfunctional family. Quiet, happy, and problem-ridden. Normal. I have Addy, Ellen thought looking down at the little miracle she'd been handed. *I have Addy,* she thought again.

The doorbell rang.

"More later, baby. Maybe they've found your daddy," Ellen said, settling Addy into her playpen and then walking slowly to the front door.

****

Angie sat transfixed, legs pulled up, knees under her chin.

The orange velour sectional took on a brown fuzzy tone when the only light in the room came from the television. She reached for her vodka and 7UP. Finding it wedged between the cushion she was sitting on and the next one over, she took a deep, cold sip.

I really shouldn't be watching this alone, she thought. *They should've invited me down or something. Oh well,* she thought. *Typical ice maiden move.*

And then her segment began. Angie watched as all of her undercover spy work paid off in the most gripping exposé of sexual harassment ever broadcast. She also watched as Laura Mercer ruined Ron Martin and Don Drummand and his male employees, and put the fear of God and the hidden camera into male employers everywhere.

It was good, Angie thought. Definitely as good as Dateline NBC, maybe almost 60 Minutes level. She wondered if she'd be watching the ice maiden on the nightly news from New York some day. Laura told her she'd be in the big time, might even be moving up sooner than they thought. Angie did hate her, but even the ice maiden was better than nobody. *And if she becomes a famous ice maiden,* Angie thought, *maybe she'll remember me. I'll make her remember me.*

She'd need to start picking up more shifts at Lindey's. They always took her back. Even Ed the bartender seemed happy to see her, she thought. He must've been bored without her life to watch, she thought.

Laura looks like the big time, Angie thought, watching her introduce the segments of tape from inside Drummand Industries, as Ron Martin, acting as a spokesperson for the company, officially denied any woman was ever treated poorly there. Then, the viewers watched it happen.

Laura's voice told the viewers that fortunately, Ohio still allowed reporters to use a hidden camera to uncover wrongdoing. This story, she explained, wouldn't have been possible without the hidden camera and the brave woman who agreed to wear it undercover.

"That's me. Angie—Angela—Brown. Say my name!" Angie screamed. Laura didn't say her name, but instead, the undercover footage began on-screen.

"Wow," Angie said, watching as Mr. Drummand dropped his pants—they put one of those black circles over his privates although they really didn't need to, Angie thought. "I bet Drummand will know who the mole was now."

She saw the meeting with Francis and Ron and the creatives, talking about Squeaky Clean when Mr. Drummand's voice boomed over the speakerphone, his cussing beeped out of the broadcast. Laura Mercer's face filled the screen, explaining Mr. Drummand had been tipped off about the Target 5 Investigation, and that's when she and her staff began receiving anonymous phone threats.

"This type of behavior is consistent with Mr. Drummand's contempt for women, and really, people in general, and his continued and blatant disrespect for the law. Target 5 has learned a class action lawsuit filed on behalf of all current and former female employees and applicants for employment, naming Drummand and his senior management team as defendants, will be filed in Common Pleas Court in the morning," Laura added grimly.

"An amazing piece and pioneering work of journalism, Laura. Thank you very much for that report," John Taylor gushed, smiling into the camera. "In fact, in addition to filing that wonderful piece, Laura has some other news of a more personal nature to announce."

"Yes, I do,," Laura said. "I've been offered the evening anchor spot at the NBC affiliate in Chicago. It's a great opportunity for me, and while I'll sincerely miss all of you I've gotten to know in Central Ohio, I just can't pass up a great opportunity like this one, John."

"No, you certainly can't, Laura, but we will miss you around here for sure," John said in his inimitable flat baritone, Malibu Ken hair shining under the lights. "I know I for one will be very sad, indeed. And now, on to the day's news..."

Angie clicked off the television. *The ice maiden must've had a special moment with Mr. John,* she thought laughing about the way the male anchor drooled over Laura. But then Angie grew serious again. Reaching for her drink, she chugged it and then began crunching on an ice cube.

I tried to help Mr. Martin, she thought, still angry over his rejection. *I guess he got what was coming to him. He looked so stupid, denying everything when they showed it all on the screen a second later. He never should've done that. He was making some really bad decisions. Rejecting me was his worst. We could've had a great time, a family, a really big house...*

Maybe I'll follow Laura to Chicago. Be her roommate, work at a nice restaurant in the blowing city or blustery city, or whatever they called it. No, not blustery. That was from Winnie the Pooh, Angie thought, laughing. *Chicago's the windy city.*

Her phone was ringing.

"Angela Brown?" a woman asked.

"Yes, but if you're selling, I'm not buying," Angie said.

"No, that's not it. It's Madeline Wilson, with the *Daily Journal.* Are you aware Ron Martin is missing?"

"What?"

"Yes, his wife says she hasn't seen him since Thursday morning. He didn't come home Thursday night either. Sources say you gave him a ride to the celebrity regatta. That's the last time he was seen. He didn't show up at work today; no call either," Maddie said. "Do you have any idea where Mr. Martin could be? Is he there with you, Angie?"

"No, of course not," Angie stammered. "I left him on a blanket by the Yacht Club, on the grass. I drove home without him. He stayed there."

"Interesting how you keep ending up with Ellen's men, isn't it Angie? Where is Mr. Martin, Angie?" Maddie asked again.

"Oh my God, I have no idea," Angie answered, and slammed down the phone.

*****

She thought, There is no pain if you don't think about it. *That's what her momma said. The mind could do powerful things, especially in a woman. Men, they were weak, but women, once they set their minds to something, they could do it. Anything.*

Fortunately, the boy didn't press charges or anything. A guy at the bar one night told her the boy jock still felt bad about dumping her, missed her and all. But she'd moved on by then, way on down the road of life. Down the road to freedom. To her dreams.

She'd met him the next night, the night after her lipstick frenzy. This one, he was Mr. Right. Older. Successful. Handsome. Considerate. Prince Charming with money and a spine and big plans and dreams.

He wanted her, she could tell. But she needed to be careful. Needed to hold back the sex. Make him want her. Make him take her virginity—or make him believe he had.

Yes, Momma, if only you had believed your own words, you would've lived. Lived well, like I will, *she thought.* You had the choice, Momma.

And now, so do I.

****

It was midnight and Laura Mercer sat in shocked silence behind her desk in the now-quiet newsroom.

After the eleven o'clock newscast ended, the kudos—even from Dave Robinson—were nonstop. A huge bouquet of red roses from her new station in Chicago was delivered to her desk.

And then, the real news, from one of the assignment editors. Ron Martin had disappeared, presumably before the broadcast of her Target 5 Investigation. In fact, the segment hadn't even been promoted prior to airing, since final legal clearance wasn't given until just before broadcast time. The station promos would run hot and heavy now—but it was after the fact, and a day and a half since Ron Martin had been seen.

Laura thought back to that day at the sailboat event and chills raced through her body. As emcee, Laura had a bird's-eye view from the center of the bridge. Standing there, the media relations lackey had pointed to each and every so-called celebrity, pronouncing the hard names slowly, so she could practice. And that's when she spotted Angie, wearing her purple suit.

"Hold on a minute, I need to make a private call," she told the media relations kid, and dashed around the far side of the remote van for privacy. When Marty came on, she screamed, "We have to air that piece tonight, Marty!"

"It's not through the legal guys yet, Laura," Marty answered calmly.

"Angie is down below me right this minute, and she's probably on a date with Ron Martin. I'm not, repeat, not kidding."

"Shit."

"No shit; get our piece on the air, Marty."

"I'll try, kid, I'll try. Stay calm. Don't let her see you watching them. Don't spook her. Maybe she hasn't said a thing. She's a sneaky one, that one," Marty said, hanging up.

"Not as sneaky as me," Laura had said to nobody, but the media relations kid, having followed her behind the van, overheard.

"Excuse me?"

"Nothing," Laura answered. She'd taken Marty's advice and done her job at the race, and didn't look for Ron and Angie again. They could have been among the crowd of "celebrities" on the Santa Maria just below her, but she didn't know. When the race and club officials asked her to join them on the ship, she declined, saying it was a busy news day and she needed to get back to the station.

And now, Ron Martin was gone. And a police detective was asking her if he acted strange or suicidal when she interviewed him for the Drummand exposé. "Did he feel personally threatened? Did he seem at the end of his rope? Ready to end his life? Go on the run? Do you think your story went too far, Ms. Mercer?"

"Ms. Mercer has no comment, Detective Moore. Excuse us. You can take your fishing trip to somebody else's pond, got it?" The station's lawyer was crusty and competent and fighting off a yawn. He'd been summoned to the station by the general manager. Although he'd clearly been asleep, he was there by midnight, bathrobe and all. It was hard to look dignified in your slippers, but he still sounded commanding. And it seemed to work. At his answer, Laura felt a little better and smiled faintly, and the detective stood to leave.

"Ms. Mercer, that's all for now. We'll be in touch," the detective said, walking out of the conference room.

✻✻✻✻

Pretty cool roaming around a TV station, Detective Pete Moore thought. He went into a door marked "makeup" and was blinded by huge lightbulbs surrounding a large mirror. It was hot in the small room. A teenage girl's makeup dream was spread out all over the counter. A guy was at the far end of the room, in front of the mirror. It was that TV anchor dude.

Pete thought it was gross that he put all that stuff on his face. He didn't know if he'd be able to watch the news from now on, knowing the guy wore makeup.

"Excuse me," Pete murmured, turning to leave the guy scraping makeup off his cheeks. *Sickos everywhere,* he thought.

It was time to call Maddie Wilson. She might have something by now. Maybe the guy was in Bermuda or Grand Cayman—someplace exotic, hiding out until after the Target 5 thing blew over. But it wasn't really that awful for Ron Martin. Drummand's the one who should have disappeared, Pete thought. Heading back out to his car, he called Maddie on his cell phone.

"What is it, Pete?" Maddie asked.

"Have you got anything?" Pete asked.

"You know, you should apologize for calling at one fifteen in the morning first. Then, you should tell me what you know, and then, if I feel like it, I'll tell you what I know."

"Sorry. No Ron Martin. No leads. Laura Mercer was cute, but no help—wouldn't even talk without her station's lawyer, and he wouldn't let her open her mouth."

"They're worried about being sued over that story, Pete, that's all. You don't think she had anything to do with him disappearing other than chasing him out of town with her story, right?" Maddie asked. "I'm surprised you even went to see her."

"Well, we know they were both at the regatta. And, of course, there's the interview they did when he talked for that Drummand guy a few days ago," Pete said, shaking his head to ward off sleep as he slouched in the driver's seat of his white Taurus. "His right-hand gal at the agency, Francis, didn't know anything, but of all the folks I've talked to, she's the most shook up. Says Ron wouldn't just leave town, that there has to be foul play. She's a mess."

"I know. I talked to her too. She's a friend. She and Ron, well, they should've been married or something. They're very close," Maddie said. "I think little Angie Brown knows something, and she was the last person seen with Ron Martin, smooching along the banks of the Scioto River in fact. Everybody in town saw them there, together."

"No way, isn't she the one who—"

"Yep. She almost blew up at Ellen's house with Michael Anderson. Before that, she was caught with Janet Jones's husband, and now Ron. Creepy, if you ask me, and more than just coincidence."

"What is it with that girl and trouble? Has a thing for married men. Can't she find a man of her own?" Pete asked.

"It's 'woman,' Pete, not 'girl.' She's definitely a woman. And I don't know what her deal is—it's almost like she picked Ellen's husbands. When I talked to her, she acted like she didn't know Ron was married to Michael's wife. Yeah, right. After all the stories in the paper, on television. Everyone in town knows who Ellen is. This place is so small," Maddie said. "You'd have to be a complete idiot not to know."

"Well, Mad, believe it or not, not everyone's as brilliant as you, and not everybody makes it her business to know everything about everybody in town like you do. It is possible."

"Thanks, Pete. I think you should question Angie Brown though. Arrest her or something."

"For what, Maddie? There's no crime. Ron Martin disappeared, but maybe he's gone up to Lake Erie or down to Cincinnati or to Grand Cayman to chill out," Pete said.

"Yeah, right. I gotta go. Keep me posted, Pete."

"I will, Maddie. Sweet dreams."

CHAPTER 17

Thursday, April 18

While Janet Jones's airplane landed on the runway in Columbus, a fisherman in the Scioto River hooked what he thought was the largest carp in the history of the river.

While Ellen and Janet embraced inside the airport, at baggage claim, the fisherman reeled in his catch.

As Ellen drove Janet to her home, Janet sitting in the back seat next to baby Addy, the fisherman was trying to find a motorist with a cell phone. Finally, somebody stopped and the man yelled, "Dial 911, there's a dead guy floating in the river."

As Janet oohed and ahhed over Ellen's gorgeous home and rolling estate, the emergency squad driver zipped up the bag and waited for the coroner's car to transport the body to the morgue.

And after the doorbell rang, indicating somebody wanted in down at the gate, and Ellen pushed the buzzer to ask who it was, the sheriff bowed his head and said into the speaker, "I'm afraid I have some bad news, Mrs. Martin."

"Now, that's one unlucky lady," the fisherman said to his wife, at home after his terrible find.

"We are so sorry," the sheriff said, just before Ellen fainted.

****

"I think it was Angie; something's not right about that young girl," Janet said to Maddie as they shared a bottle of wine at Lindey's. Janet needed a break from Ellen and Addy; she'd called Maddie at work. Maddie, anxious to see Janet but conscious of Ellen's need for privacy, had kept away from the Martin house and thus the Martin mess. Directly, at least. Indirectly, she'd been working it. She would find out the real story on Ron's death.

A guy in his situation didn't just drown. Poor Ellen. How would she live through being widowed twice?

"I agree, Janet. Angie Brown either has really rotten timing, or Chuckie's lucky to be alive. Either way, what are the odds of all that? She has to be involved," Maddie said, staring into her glass of Chardonnay. "Pete and the rest of them are convinced Ron went on some sort of binge drinking episode, fell off the wagon so to speak, tried to pee off the side of a boat, fell in, and drowned. That's how most drownings occur, I guess. And his fly was down. But that doesn't fit Ron, no way. And Francis Hall—do you remember her?"

"Sure, how's she doing?" Janet asked, sitting back in her chair and relaxing for the first time since she'd arrived in Columbus.

"Great until now. She was Ron's number two at the Martin Agency and probably his best friend. Francis said there was no way Ron would've had anything to drink. He'd been sober since she met him and there wasn't anything wrong that he couldn't overcome. He just had a bad client. Francis had already drafted the letter stating the Martin Agency and Drummand Industries were through. Taking a sip, Maddie added, "She was waiting for his signature."

"So who controls the agency now? Ellen?" Janet asked.

"I suppose it depends on his will. Wonder if he had one," Maddie mused.

"Who knows? Life's much more simple in the pink palace," Janet said. "Cheers."

"Cheers," Maddie answered, wishing she had a pink palace where she could hide.

*****

"I won't be any trouble, I promise," Angie begged Laura for the seventieth time. Laura was a little afraid Angie would chain herself to one of Laura's suitcases or her car or something. Laura would just run over her, or leave the suitcase behind. Anything to escape the hellhole and her roommate. "Please, please?"

"No, Angie. It's been fun, you know, being roommates and all. But I'm moving on. You can't go to Chicago just because I am. The station's taking care of me. I have an apartment and a roommate and everything. There's no room for you," Laura said.

What she said was mostly true, all except the roommate part. She never would have a roommate again until it was the man of her dreams. That was it. Certainly not the mouse turned mole. She'd given her money, made her life a little more exciting for a while, and now she wanted more. No way.

"But you'll need somebody, you know, to do errands. Maybe you'll wanna do another undercover thing and I could help," Angie offered.

"If the need arises, I know where to find you," Laura said coldly. "Now, please, I need room to pack and you're plunked down right in my way. Don't you have to work today?"

"Not until four. That police detective is still out front, you know," Angie said.

"I know, the jerk."

"Is he watching you or me?" Angie asked.

"Hell if I know. Like we pushed Ron into the water, the lush. He'll leave us alone soon. Well, he'll have to leave me alone, since I'll be outta here," Laura said, smiling and tossing a pile of clothes into one of the cardboard boxes. The movers had dropped them off for her. Taped them up, three sides with the tops ready for all her stuff, and would be back to pick them all up. Didn't want her to move a muscle. Would've packed her clothes but she decided to do it herself. She wanted to make sure they were all there.

"By the way, Angie, did you return my purple suit?" she asked, obviously startling the mouse.

"Yes. How did you know?"

"I just knew. Did Ron? Did you tell him?" Laura asked, intentionally using Ron's name.

"No, I didn't tell him a thing. Of course not. You can trust me, Laura. I did a great job, didn't I?"

"You did. And you made a lot of money and you had a lot of fun. And, as an extra bonus, I'm leaving you all of the furniture. My half of everything, plus my bed and the bedding. Everything except my clothes, so if you could check your closet for the rest of my things you secretly borrowed, I'd be thankful," Laura said, still smiling as she turned to unload a couple dressers.

"I don't have nothin' else, promise," Angie said.

"It's 'nothing.' 'Anything,' actually. But just in case, you should check," Laura added and Angie got up and left the room. *She'll never be part of my new life, never,* Laura thought. *I'm moving up, out of here. The big time.*

Laura was so happy about her future, she even forgave Ron Martin. Forgave him for raping her, for forgetting, for being a drunk coward. Forgave him for hitting on her, for lying on behalf of Drummand, for being a coward before he'd even seen the broadcast. In what to Laura seemed strange and ironic, she was sorry Ron was dead.

But now, with her life on fast-forward and her dreams coming true, big time, she was unable to sustain an unhappy thought. That, in itself, was amazing.

She was off to Chicago in the morning and this mid-level mid-market Midwest city would be nothing but a distant memory. Or rather, a distant stopping point in a forgotten past. That, too, was her choice.

****

Janet was sure there was nothing more she could do for Ellen. Mostly because Ellen was so in control.

"I've done all this before, Janet. I need to stay strong for Addy, and so I will. Day after tomorrow, Ron will be resting with his family and I'll be moving on, too, for her," Ellen said.

"What about the agency?" Janet asked, curious after her dinner with Maddie.

"I'll sell my interest to Francis. She wants it, I'm sure. He left half to me and half to Francis. She can have it. It means a lot to her," Ellen added cheerfully.

"El, I'm glad you understand why I need to head back to the beach. I'm sorry I'll miss the funeral, but I'm glad I got to meet Addy. She's beautiful. And I'm glad she has such an adoring momma," Janet said. "Please do call if you need anything, I'm always there to talk."

"Janet, I'm still surprised you need to leave early. Are you sure?" Ellen asked. Janet had originally said she would stay with them until the weekend.

"My publisher asked for a meeting—and yes, I need to go," Janet said, not adding that Ellen's denial was too hard to handle. Tears would've been preferable to the happy, controlled smiles.

"It's OK. Shall I wake Addy up from her nappy to say good-bye?"

"Never wake a sleeping baby," Janet said with a smile. "Oh, that's my cab," she said, hearing the horn blow. "I hope you will be all right." Janet stopped then and gave Ellen a hug, looked into her eyes, and then pulled away.

Nestled safely in the back seat of the yellow cab, Janet thought about Ellen some more. *Maybe Ellen needs to use denial right now. She's lost two husbands. A little denial is nothing, really. But still—*

Ellen had lost something that used to shine in her eyes, she thought.

CHAPTER 18

Monday, April 22

Dixon Crane, still convinced Michael Anderson was murdered, and now convinced Ron Martin was too, had pleaded with Maddie for support, leaving her three e-mails to convince her there was foul play even before the body was discovered. Now, two days after the fisherman found Ron, he was even more convinced.

Maddie bounced the theory off Lyle. He actually knew waitress-turned-spy Angela Brown from her days at the advertising agency. He told Maddie she was crazy.

"That little thing couldn't murder two men, Mad. She's tiny—maybe this big around," he said, holding up his little finger. "And shy. She only smiled at me and never spoke during meetings. She called Ron 'Mr. Martin.' And I know she wore a camera, but she had to be tricked into it by that brunette tease on Channel 5, because

Angela wouldn't think up something like that. You're wrong, Mad."
He added, "You should spend your time helping me figure out how
to become creative director under Francis's new regime. She's your
friend and all."

Maddie hadn't known until that minute that Lyle had any
desire to be anything but a copywriter. She was stunned, happy to
be witnessing a glimmer of drive. "Creative director? You? Lyle, you
hate the agency business," Maddie stammered. "You want to be a
novelist or screenwriter, right?"

"You know, Madeline, you underestimate me as always. I just
might've found my calling. Francis needs me. I know all the clients. And if I made it big, here in the good ol' heartland, I could
stay here with you, instead of moving to Hollywood," he said,
winking.

"Right," Maddie said, thinking she'd suddenly fallen into some
bizzaro world. "I'll approach Francis about you when I talk to her
about Angie. And then you can all come visit me on my long, well-
deserved vacation, someplace like the beach with Janet."

"What does Janet think?" Lyle asked, further surprising
Maddie by sustaining interest in a subject other than himself or sex
for more than five minutes.

"Janet thinks the little slut did it. But what's she going to think?
Angie is the same woman who she caught with Chuckie, remember?" *Duh.*

"No, I forgot. You're all wrong. Both of you, and Dixon too.
I think it was that television news anchor, that Laura Mercer.
Anyway, Maddie—"

"I know, I'll talk to Francis about your newfound type-A career
desires," Maddie said, hustling out the door.

Work wasn't a haven either, of course, since Dixon was there,
waiting to pounce. "Don't you have a column to write or something? Go eat, would you," she said seeing him looming over her

desk. "Really, Dix, this is turning into some sort of obsession with you. You just seem haunted by the affairs of Ms. Brown."

Dixon was adamant. "Madeline, Ms. Brown just happens to be there when Anderson is toasted; then she's the last person to see Martin before his final swim. Hell, we have a witness who saw them kissing. No, no, she's not guilty," Dixon said, and then sniffed and pulled his beard. "Come on."

Maddie knew Michael Anderson was the hapless victim of an accident. An adulterer, yes. Deserving death by Weber grill? No. But accidents did happen. Ron Martin was another story. New baby, bad press, but nothing insurmountable. And what was the mole doing cavorting with her prey? The enemy? All a seedy, questionable mess. *But murder? Nah.*

Dixon said, "All I'm asking is that you go with me. Is that too much to ask, after all these years?"

"OK, Dix, I'm in. Let's go talk to Mincy," Maddie said, grabbing her reporter's notebook. "You realize this has nothing to do with my gossip column or your food section. Mincy'll think we've both gone off the deep end."

"That's why he should listen to us," Dixon said. "Slow down, Mad woman. I've got this cane to drag around with me, but I'm right behind you. Right behind you."

"You know, you're gonna owe me big after this, Dixon," Maddie called over her shoulder, slowing down to accommodate the relentless restaurant reviewer pursuing her through the newsroom.

"Name it. Anything."

"Lyle needs a promotion at the Martin Agency and I don't want to ask Francis directly. We're friends and I don't want to jeopardize that. But Lyle would be awesome, I know it. So, can you think of a way to let her know he's a good choice for creative director?" Maddie asked.

"You serious?" Dixon asked, huffing.

"Yep."

"Consider the request made; just no guarantee on outcome, all right? The big dogs did really like the new campaign you and Mr. Boring came up with," Dixon said, climbing into the elevator next to her.

"Boardman, Dix," Maddie said, smiling.

"Right. Maybe you've found a man with drive after all, Maddie. Stranger things have happened," Dixon snorted, as they walked outside into the sunshine.

"I'm driving." Maddie steered Dixon toward her Jetta. She'd let him drive her once, in his broken-down frog-green Honda. Never again.

"That's your choice, my dear. I do find it interesting your main man's found a spine, ah, a calling, so to speak. Maybe these recent deaths have triggered some sort of career crisis in his mind, you think?" Dixon asked, shoving his cane in the back seat and settling into the front seat.

"Well, it does make you realize that life, even at it's longest, is still very short," Maddie said, punching in her lighter. "I mean, I smoke these, and they say every pack is something like ten minutes off your life. When you're twenty, ten minutes is nothing. At thirty-five, it's starting to worry me. But then, we could get hit by a car pulling out of here and poof, it's all over anyway."

"But the one action—smoking—is your choice. The other—a car wreck—is fate. By choosing to smoke—" Maddie rolled her eyes. "—now, now, listen, would you? They are starting to learn that you change your genes. So while you may escape lung cancer, and you haven't, I see, escaped the early aging smoker's wrinkles, you are passing along genetic mutations to your children and their children. We know fifty percent of your genetic makeup comes from your parents, your aunts and uncles, and something like thirty-five percent from your grandparents and great-aunts, and like twelve percent from great-grandparents and cousins. All those genes coming together, mutated by choices, and kaboom. You give your kid a predisposition to cancer before it's even born. Interesting, huh?"

"It's a wonderful life, Dix. In fact, I just heard a bell. You must've helped somebody up there earn her wings," Maddie said, blowing smoke out the window and tossing the cigarette butt. "No lectures about litter, please. I can't take it today."

"Hey, what if there's another suspect?" Dixon said. "Maybe Francis Hall wanted the business so she bumped him off."

"The police have questioned her, Dix. She's devastated. Yeah, she wanted to inherit a struggling, publicity-slammed advertising agency that just lost its biggest account," Maddie said.

"Yeah, lost its biggest account due to the stupidity of Ron Martin's comments and Don Drummand's actions."

"Right. So Francis was honked off with Ron's interviewing skills, and before she'd even seen the story on Channel 5, she decided to bump him off. Or maybe Ellen did it. Hell, she's even more frail than Angie. Yeah, she'd want to murder her husband, the father of her baby girl. Right," Maddie said, shaking her head. "Are you sure you're not senile?"

"No, I'm not."

Soon Maddie Wilson found herself in the coroner's office with Dixon Crane, pleading with the coroner to reexamine the body of the deceased, before it was too late. The publisher of the *Journal*, they told Mincy the coroner, would seriously consider future political favors if he could respond to this small request.

And they did it. Persuaded the coroner to reevaluate his findings. To consider foul play, for them and the publisher. Fortunately for Maddie and Dixon, Mincy didn't check with the publisher, who knew nothing about the case or the promise.

The results were due two days later, four days after the body of Ron Martin was fished out of the Scioto River.

And so once again, Maddie and Dixon were in her Jetta, headed to the medical examiner's office. Maddie knew Dixon was hoping to discover he was right about murder; she was hoping Ron was a victim of his own desire to pee.

****

"It's not like he really felt anything at all," the coroner said to Pete Moore. "I mean that stun gun kinda numbs you out, you know, so by the time his lungs realized he was breathing in water, he would've been about dead. Are you following me, Detective?"

"Yes, and don't try to gross me out, OK? Just stick to the stuff I need to know, Mincy," Pete said back into the receiver. He didn't go to see the coroner in person anymore. After throwing up five times, he decided he could read and listen to the autopsy reports from the comfort of his own desk chair. "But why was his fly unzipped? I mean, that was one of the strongest clues to indicate a drowning, right?"

"Well, yes, detective, that's why. Most drownings occur just like that. Guy takes a leak, falls in, and he's never goin' fishin' again, if you get my drift. We didn't suspect any foul play, you know, until hotshot Mayor Mac talked to the widow, who insisted the deceased was a great swimmer even in freezing water and that something musta happened. That's one part of the story," Mincy said.

"Mac's up for re-election again," Pete said thoughtfully, cleaning his glasses on his left pant leg. "That's why he's suddenly interested in twice-widowed women and their fatherless children. But what was Mr. Martin doing out in the water on a sailboat, after all the festivities were over? That's the question. Was he waiting for someone? Was someone with him?" *Someone he was comfortable enough with to pee over the side of the boat with them nearby*, Pete mused. "What's the other part of the story, Mincy?"

"Madeline Wilson and Dixon Crane," Mincy said chuckling. "They've never bothered me about anything together. And they've got the publisher's support. So, I figured, what's it hurt, you know, going over him one more time. And voilà. Really, it was a perfect crime. I almost signed off on an accidental death. A murderer would've gone free, forever."

"Did the murderer unzip Martin's pants, you know, to make it appear to be a normal drowning?" Pete asked.

"Unlikely, detective. The force of the electricity from the stun gun would've knocked Mr. Martin into the water immediately. As soon as the electrodes hit his body. More likely, he was taking a leak, someone blasted him, and bam—he's toast. Soggy toast," Mincy said.

"It just doesn't make sense. I mean, he's helping the bad guy Drummand, who's also got an airtight alibi. He's a great boss, according to all. A great husband and a devoted new father. His business is going through tough times, but nothing insurmountable, according to his number two. And he knew it. Who'd want to kill Ron Martin?" Pete asked.

"You'll figure it out, Pete. And you know, you should stop by sometime, detective. We miss seeing you around here," Mincy said, chuckling.

"I wouldn't be caught anything but dead in your office, sir," Pete said. "No offense. By the way, have you told the dynamic duo yet? 'Cause as soon as you do, it'll be all over town, you know."

"I've just made my first statement to you, detective. I'll give you a couple hours' lead time. That's all I can do," Mincy said.

"I understand, and thanks," Pete answered, hanging up. "Now what? Now I need to find a murderer and a murder weapon is what," he said to no one. *Stun guns.* You could buy them in Soldier of Fortune, pawnshops, upscale security mail-order catalogs, and on the Internet. There was no way to track purchases.

Dredging the river in the area where Martin was last seen alive resulted in no gun. The undercurrent would, they said, carry any weapon downstream eventually. If the weapon had existed, if the murderer had tossed it into the water.

Angela Brown agreed to come down to the station for questioning. She said she had nothing to hide. Pete was grasping at straws. He would have to get her to confess because he had no evidence. No weapon. No real motive. No nothing.

"So, Ms. Brown, do you own a stun gun?' he imagined himself asking her. *Oh, that's real clever, Detective Moore,* he said to himself. *You'll have to do better, Peter, to solve this one.*

"Pete, you're barking up the wrong tree," Officer Sandy Meyer said, walking down the hallway, nodding toward the closed interrogation room door. "I'll be back with Ms. Brown's Diet Coke."

It has to be Angela Brown, Pete thought. *Who else could it be?*

He'd exhausted every lead, followed every tip. Dixon Crane and Madeline Wilson had a story in the paper, complete with a tip line and reward. A good story, written by Dixon Crane, asking anybody with any information to come forward. Mrs. Ellen Martin and the baby had posed in silhouette—Pete didn't want their faces shown. They'd been through enough. So beautiful, so tragic.

The door to the interrogation room was green, metal, thick. He pushed it open and saw the frightened woman standing in the corner. She shrunk, it seemed, as he entered the room. She backed into the corner.

"Please, Ms. Brown, take a seat," he said, sitting heavily with his own words. *What a strange, strange case.* And then, as she sat, he asked Angie Brown all the usual questions, all the basic *where were you* and *what have you done* questions. All the *Why were you with Ron Martin at the sailboat race when you were wearing a hidden camera to expose his client's wrongdoing?* questions.

Nothing. She liked Mr. Martin. Wanted to warn him about the story. Left him by the edge of the water. Watched the broadcast of all her work. Was mad she didn't get invited down to the station by her selfish roommate.

"Have you considered checking into the ice maiden's alibi?" she asked. "Laura Mercer was raped by Ron Martin almost seven years ago. She told me she'd get even with him someday. That since he'd blacked out the whole episode, she'd want him to remember it slowly, painfully. And then she'd get her revenge."

"But Laura did the evening news that night—I mean, that was your big story, Ms. Brown. You think she had time to murder Mr. Martin and then host the news?"

"All I can tell you is she did the news that night, came home and packed, and now she's gone to Chicago. Kind of sneaky, huh?" Angie asked. "And what about his wife, Mr. Detective? Don't you think it's odd she'd be widowed twice, under really weird conditions? I mean, maybe she needs more insurance money or something," Angie said. "I know he wasn't happy with her. She'd gotten fat; I mean, he was kissing me and he liked it." Angie sat back and took a big sip of Diet Coke, looking smug.

"That's enough, Ms. Brown," Pete said, bristling at the attack on Ellen. Angie stopped smiling, apparently aware she'd struck a nerve. "That's enough. Thank you for your opinions. You're entitled to your theories, I guess. But you should know everyone else says they were a truly blessed couple. She became pregnant, which was a miracle. They were in love. Had a beautiful baby girl, a huge house—oh, you know about the house I guess," Pete said forcefully. "Maybe you were jealous, jealous of their love, when you had nothing. And no one."

"You know, I might not be rich, but I'm pretty happy. I'm having fun. I'm young. I don't owe you anything, and I really don't owe the widow anything. I wish I could help you. I can't. I have to get to work. I'm late already. I'm pulling a double today," Angie said, sounding exasperated. "Can I go?"

"Yes, yeah, you can go," Pete said, and slumped down onto the green metal chair again as Angie Brown walked out of the room. He sat, staring at the ceiling for a long moment. Then he shifted in the seat, and the chair squeaked and groaned under his weight. "Shut up, already," he said to the chair and then self-consciously grabbed his gut. Yeah, it was time to work out again, he thought. That could help him solve the case. More stamina.

Pete picked himself up and hustled out the door.

"Got something from her?" Officer Meyer called out.

"Yeah. I'll be back tomorrow, I've got to follow up on some things," Pete said, lying. Actually, he had the urge to punch something, and decided it better be a bag at Silver's Gym. *That'll do it.*

On the way to the gym he called his boss for authorization to fly to Chicago to interview Laura Mercer again. The ice maiden anchor had motive, opportunity, if she met him after the broadcast, and had fled town immediately after the murder. She could be a really hot lead, now that he knew about the rape.

Would a woman kill her rapist? Especially if he didn't remember his crime, was now rich, successful, and happily married?

Why wouldn't she?

****

"To your health, Dix," Maddie said, raising her glass of wine but looking past and over it to follow Angie, who was waiting on a table of four businessmen. Watching her smile and flirt, Maddie shook her head. "You were right. It was murder."

"And to yours, my dear. But she just doesn't look or act guilty, you know?" Dixon said, also staring at the young woman. "What about Sugar? I hate to say it, but she did leave town in a flurry, right after the body was found."

"You know why, Dix. Her dream finally came true. No, Laura used men, but she didn't murder them, just played with their hearts. Why are you such a softy when it comes to Angie?" Maddie asked.

"Sometimes, using men and playing with men is just one step away from killing them, you know. It's almost the same thing, Mad," Dixon said, adding, "And, as Mincy told us, if it was a stun gun, which he thinks it was, it had to be somebody Mr. Martin knew. Laura was no stranger. She knew a lot of men in town. I hear Michael Anderson was one of them."

"I'm not surprised, Dix. But you're way off on this. She made it to the big time. She didn't need to kill anyone to get there. Heck, she got a great story out of knowing Ron Martin. He was more useful to her alive."

"So you really want me to believe it was her," Dixon said, pointing to Angie. "Look at her. She's a stick figure with a perky haircut. What exactly are we doing here? Will she suddenly turn around and confess over a plate of angel hair pasta with shrimp? I mean, what do we expect? We're not private investigators or anything."

"I just keep thinking if she sees me and she knows I'm friends with Ellen, that, well, all of a sudden she'll come clean or something. I'll look into those baby brown eyes of hers and unnerve her. Lyle thinks we're crazy. How about Mrs. Crane?"

"'Stark raving mad,' I believe she said," Dixon answered. "Dessert?"

"Yeah. Oh, and have you spoken with Francis yet? You know, about Lyle?"

"Called her. Told her how pleased the board of the *Journal* is with the campaign. Hell, even the reporters like it, which isn't easy, as you know. I told her what a great job Mr. Bored-man did. She was glad to hear about Lyle's accomplishments, but she sounded very sad, Madeline. You should call her. She needs friends right now. She seems overwhelmed," Dixon added. "But I did recommend your man for the position."

"Great. I'll call her tomorrow, Columbo. After we're finished with our stakeout. I've been spending too much time on this wild-goose chase with a crazed restaurant reviewer. I'm sure Francis'll understand when I tell her what we've been up to, stalking waitresses in trendy restaurants," Maddie teased, trying to lighten the mood. "We'll have to leave the rest of the investigation to Pete and the city desk."

"Have you talked to the widow squared?"

"Yes. Actually Francis asked me to go to lunch with them yesterday—so see, I haven't blown off my friend duties all together. This investigation stuff is forcing me to eat at all the finest restaurants in town—and it's business," Maddie said.

"Isn't it always, my dear?"

"No, not for me. Anyway, Francis says Ellen is giving her the creeps for some reason, so I went along with Francis for moral support."

"So you have been being a good friend. Good girl," Dixon said.

"Thanks," Maddie said, smiling. "Ellen showed up for lunch about twenty minutes late with the baby. All that baby stuff would be enough to make me late a whole day. She had the diaper bag, the car seat, the bibs, the toys, the stroller. A big production. And she was happy. So happy. I guess it's not right to say she was too happy—I mean, is that fair? If she chooses to be happy, to move on, for the sake of little Addy, who's to say that's wrong? It's not me who lost a husband, for heaven's sake."

"No, my dear, you would have to find one first," Dixon said.

"Very funny. But her happiness did bug Francis. In fact, when Ellen went to change the baby, Francis begged me to help start the takeover talks. She wants Ellen out of the agency before Ellen decides to get interested in advertising again."

"I always thought Francis would've been a good choice for Mr. Martin," Dixon sniffed, and then asked, "So what does that mean? That Francis hates Ellen? It's natural. Did you help initiate the sale?"

"Of course. You saw the column. Writing about it should help make it de facto sold."

"Yes, that's what I thought when I read it. And seeing is believing, of course," Dixon said. He reached out a hand to stop Angie. "Ah, Miss, I know you're not our waitress, but could I bother you for some water?"

"It's Angie, Mr. Crane. Of course, I'd be happy to bring you water if you promise to stop watching me. Is water all you want?" Angie demanded.

"It'll do for now," Dixon answered, still smiling, as Angie turned and walked away. "You know, Maddie, I'm beginning to think Ron's murder was an act of random

violence. A friendly mugger he let get too close. He picked the right place at the wrong time. Or vice versa. Along the edge of the river, in a boat, without the oars, and without a coat. I mean the water's almost ice in April. What was he thinking?"

Maddie didn't respond. Shaking her head, she said, "I don't know. Francis seems to think Ellen had something to do with it. Janet and Ellen and I suspect our friendly water fetcher, and you suspect Laura Mercer. Anyway, I've gotta run. Pete will get to the bottom of things, Dixon. He's good. Thanks for the cheesecake and dinner. I think this will look better on your expense report than mine."

"Sure, Mad. Are we tossing in our hats? Giving up the tail, as they say?"

234 | KAIRA ROUDA

"Unless something else shakes out. I'll be in touch. You too," Maddie said pecking him on the cheek and waving good-bye to Angie across the crowded restaurant. Angie waved back. "What was that?" Maddie said aloud, surprised at the young woman's carefree manner when she knew they were watching her. Maybe she had nothing to hide, Maddie thought, pushing her way through the crowded bar toward the front door of the restaurant.

"Bye, Ms. Wilson," Ed called from behind the bar. He was one of her best tipsters, alerting her to divorces in progress and the like. He thought Angie Brown killed Ron Martin.

"See ya, Ed. Keep your eyes open," she yelled back to him.

"I always do," he yelled, winking as she disappeared into the night.

✳✳✳✳✳

Pete Moore, ace detective, plunked down at the crowded bar exactly five minutes later. Every muscle in his body ached. He ached in places he didn't even know he had muscle. This was bad. He had worked out from three to four thirty and then checked in on Ellen and Addy.

Ellen had invited Pete to stay for dinner and he eagerly accepted. After dessert, Pete headed straight downtown to Lindey's. It was 11 p.m. He was stiff as a board and the last place on earth he wanted to be was a bar, on a wood stool with no back. He'd never last.

"Hey Ed, I need a painkiller."

"You mean the island kind, Detective?"

"What's that?"

"A painkiller: rum, orange juice, coconut juice, and nutmeg. Created on Jost Van Dyke in the British Virgin Islands, and I don't mind telling you, I like to go back there as often as possible to freshen up my drink skills," Ed said in a reverie.

"Fine. I'll take a double. How's our favorite waitress?"

"Cool as a cucumber," Ed answered. "I'm beginning to think she might be innocent."

"You and everybody else. But she can't be, 'cause she's got to be guilty. The widow thinks so, the public thinks so, I thought so—and I've got nobody else. I mean I'm going to check out Laura Mercer's alibi again, but would she kill Ron Martin? I'm lost. Not one sure suspect, Eddie," Pete said. *Man, why did I do so many crunches?* he thought. "Hey, this is good. Thanks," He told Ed, taking a big sip of his painkiller.

"Yeah, but take it slow, 'cause it'll sneak up on you—and whammy, you're buzzed and a cop and you're in trouble. I've got customers. Be back," Ed said, waltzing away.

Pete swiveled his barstool so he could watch the restaurant. The late-night drinking crowd pressed into the small cocktail area as the restaurant tables cleared out. Angie walked calmly and sweetly— yeah, tough but sweet—through the restaurant, clearly in control. Her head was high. She flirted with the man whose wife went to the restroom and, Pete was sure, earned a big tip.

The four businessmen practically ran into each other trying to touch her arm, to thank her, Pete saw. *Cha ching.* Nobody else saw Angie as the pathological killer Pete saw. He leaned forward, and as his feet touched the floor, his thighs screamed. *Damn. This so-called painkiller isn't.*

"Ed, I've gotta go," he yelled down the bar. Ed seemed immersed in a joke fest.

"Catch me next time, Pete," Ed yelled back with a dismissive wave.

Once Pete was outside the restaurant, on the sidewalk, the valet parking attendant appeared: "Sir, your claim ticket?"

"Right, thanks. Here you go," Pete said to the kid who looked a lifetime younger than Pete's body felt. Toned, in shape.

He'd look like that again, Pete assured himself. Ellen and Addy were worth it.

CHAPTER 19

Two Weeks Later: Friday, May 18

"How's my baby doing?" Detective Moore asked, peeking in the playpen at Addy, who smiled up at him. She had been cooing at herself in the mirror suspended from one of the playpen's rungs. "You just get cuter every day, Addy."

"She has you wrapped around her little baby finger, Peter," Ellen said. "Here, you must try one of my cinnamon rolls. I insist." She placed a pot of coffee and fresh-baked rolls on the coffee table and then sat by Pete's side on the family room couch.

"You shouldn't have," Pete said, his face feeling a little hot as he took a roll and summoned his courage. "I was wondering if you and Addy ever get out. I mean, would you two have dinner with me sometime? Or, you know, lunch or something. It's important for the little one to get out."

Ellen looked at the detective for a moment, and then smiled. "You know, Addy has only been to a restaurant a couple times. And you're right, we haven't been out, not since the funeral and all. That would be nice. But it's definitely my treat," Ellen said, adding, "I owe you so much. You found out my Ron was killed. If it wasn't for you, I never would've known. Coffee?"

"Yes, thanks. I'm afraid nothing has shaken loose with the investigation. Angela Brown's got no record, and has, as far as we know, never visited a pawnshop or gun shop in the city and, while we still have a tail on her and we're hoping for a break, we're really frustrated. We don't have a weapon. In fact, aside from the coroner's report, we have no reason to suspect Ms. Brown or anybody else of wanting Mr. Martin dead, except of course, Laura Mercer, but that was understandable at the time she said it. And that was a long, long time ago. I do think she's sorry Mr. Martin is dead; she wanted to do a follow-up piece to the Drummand scandal. Would've won some big award. But with Mr. Martin dead and Drummand retiring to Florida, well, there's just nothing there.

"Hell, all in all it seems your husband was a nice guy who was in the wrong place at the wrong time," Pete said, then, realizing his mistake, said, "Excuse me for swearing; I hope the baby didn't hear that."

"What about that Mr. Drummand guy? He seemed like such a bad guy when I watched that television report about him," Ellen said.

"Actually, your husband was just about his only friend in town. Drummand himself was drunk the night of the broadcast, and stayed that way for a long time after. Said Mr. Martin was like a son to him. He cried when I interviewed him," Pete said, sucking in his stomach so flab wouldn't fold over his belt.

He'd been working out every day. He wondered if Ellen noticed. "We're pretty sure it was an amateur. With these types of unsophisticated criminals, they slip up. It's just a matter of time. I'm just sorry I don't have better news," Pete added, stirring two cubes of sugar into his coffee.

"So you don't really know who killed my husband. It seemed everyone was so sure Angela Brown killed him. This is so, so frustrating, not having a resolution," Ellen said, bowing her head.

Pete saw her pain. "We checked out Laura Mercer's alibi, of course. Solid. You know how she was when I flew to Chicago. Cold. Matter-of-fact. She didn't deny hating Martin, didn't deny the rape or the revenge wish. But she did deny killing or wanting him dead," Pete said, thinking back to his second interview with Chicago's hottest new television star.

By the time he and Laura had sat down to talk a week earlier, in a conference room at the television station she now called home, she seemed to have found her place, her calling, ensconced in a room overlooking the spectacular coast of Lake Michigan. The only thing to mar the setting was Pete, a Columbus homicide detective, and the station's attorney.

As they sat down, Laura looked indignant. Pete couldn't think of any other word to describe her. Throughout the interview, she gave abrupt answers to his questions and seemed disgusted that anyone in her past would dare to cloud her future. She showed complete disdain at the mention of Angela Brown. Called her a mouse, then a mole. As far as Ron Martin was concerned, she said she felt sorry for him.

He was a tragic figure. A victim of his own addiction to alcohol. Protected by well-meaning friends, and favored by a system where he knew all the right strings to pull. She believed he had blacked out the rape. He wouldn't have hit on her for all those years if he'd remembered her. No way.

"Detective Moore, all I wanted out of my time in Columbus was to pass through it, to learn and grow as a broadcast journalist.

I found my breakthrough story with the Drummand Industries piece. That it happened to involve Ron Martin was circumstance. Do I wish I could've forced him to remember the rape before his demise? Yes. Did I kill him? How absurd. I'm so far past Columbus, Ohio. It was simply a five-year stepping stone to here," Laura said, spreading her arms to encompass the city and the waterfront below, and then smiling at the station's attorney.

"If I were you, Detective Moore, I'd return to Midway, climb on whatever cheap airline brought you here, and follow around Angie Brown. She desperately wants whatever I have. Always has. Once I told her about Ron raping me, I think she wanted it too. You know, in her sick little mind, she wanted him to rape her. She went after Michael Anderson because of me, and really, it was a pattern," Laura added, pausing for emphasis. "That's who had motive and opportunity. I mean, she didn't even show up to watch all her hard work the night of the Drummand Industries Target 5 report. I invited her to sit on set and everything. No show. I guess she was busy."

"Will that be all, Detective Moore?" the station's attorney asked, his first utterance of the meeting. He smiled at Laura then. *Why do all of these television stations use such fancy law firms?* Pete wondered. *Do they always have a lot to hide?* "Yes, that's all for now," Pete said. "I'll be in touch, Ms. Mercer."

"Oh goody, Detective," Laura said as she stood, nodded to the two men, and walked out of the room.

One cool cucumber. No one could really pull off being that cool, Pete decided, unless she was innocent. And the venom for Angie Brown seemed based more on her personal feelings about the woman than on some sort of inkling regarding Ms. Brown's murderous rampage. All in all, the meeting then, as it did now, gave him a rotten headache and another reason to hate the fact the department did require him to fly on one of those cheap, cattle-car airlines. Laura Mercer had been right about that at least.

Flying home, his system stuffed with Extra Strength Tylenol and an airplane "snack pack" that was supposed to be dinner, Pete decided the murder, if it truly was murder, was an accident. A robbery gone wrong. Nothing else fit.

As Pete had told Ellen, Don Drummand had been very vocal at the Outer Inn Bar from three o'clock that afternoon until the bar closed. He had tons of witnesses; the bartender even ended up driving him home to his house, the old guy was so wasted.

Francis Hall continued to be crushed, trying to hold the business together at the advertising agency, all the while suspecting Ms. Brown. The rest of the employees of the Martin Agency were uniformly distraught at Mr. Martin's premature demise, wondered about the security of their jobs, and spoke highly of Francis and Ellen. Many made reference to Angela Brown, who was quite famous now, thanks to Maddie's column.

Angie Brown had been an infamous source of barbs for Maddie, almost like O. J. Simpson always would be for late-night comedians, ever since the Chuck Jones saga.

"Basically, Ellen," Pete said, finishing his coffee, finishing his thoughts, "Everybody in town still suspects Ms. Brown. And don't worry: if she did it, we'll catch her. I'm not one to let a crime go unsolved, you know." He sat up straight and smiled over at Addy, who was whining for some attention. "Hello, pretty baby. Is it OK if I hold her?"

"Of course, Peter, you're so great with her," Ellen said, smiling. "But if Angie didn't do it, who did?"

"Sometimes these things are just random acts of violence, Ellen. I know that's not a good answer, and you've suffered so, but I'm just not sure what's going to come of it all. I think it's best for you to get on with your life and leave the worrying to me. I am the detective, after all," Pete said, holding Addy on his lap and starting to tickle her. "You're busy enough caring for the little one. Nothing's more important than that."

Ellen smiled happily as Pete continued to tickle Abby. "Let's go out tonight, for dinner. At the Refectory. We'll celebrate something—we'll celebrate celebrating, OK?"

"That's the nicest place in town. I've never been," Pete said self-consciously.

"Well, it's time you went, then," Ellen said, standing up and snatching baby Addy from Peter's lap. "Please pick Addy and me up at five p.m. sharp. A bit early, but she needs to go to bed by eight. That'll give us time. And Peter, wear a suit, OK? I've never even seen you dressed up. And I'm looking forward to it."

Oh, my gosh, she likes me; she's taking me out on a date, he thought. "Yes, ma'am. A suit. I'll be here. Do you want me to make a reservation?"

"No, I'll handle everything, Detective," Ellen said, taking Addy back over to her playpen, and then, walking up close to him, Ellen slipped her arm into his, by the crook of his elbow, and kissed him lightly on the cheek.

"See you tonight, Detective," she said and closed the door behind him. He heard her call, "Coming Addy!"

****

Red-hot heat. Searing hot heat. That's what her kiss, her touch, felt like. Even though she barely touched him, barely kissed him, his body felt as if her arm was a hot fireplace poker and her lips, a lightening bolt.

Even now, driving home, Pete still felt the tingle of her touch on his arm and the feel of her lips on his cheek. The light turned red and his glasses suddenly got foggy. He took off his glasses, held them in his left hand, and wiped the lenses across his thigh. Then, he huffed a hot breath onto the lenses and repeated the wipe. By the time the light turned green, his glasses were back on his nose.

He hoped he could get everything done in the next two hours. Two hours to go buy a suit, shower, shave, and be back at her door. No problem.

Suddenly, there seemed to be traffic everywhere. He was stuck, anxious. The cars weren't moving at all. *What's the deal?* he thought.

Hell, he thought, *I feel like a high school kid on his first date. On his way to a first date. No, naked, trying to get to his clothes, stuck on a highway on his first date.*

This was the first time he'd ever dated somebody he met through work. Pete knew he was pushing the code a bit. But it wasn't like she was a suspect; the case was simply unsolved for now.

Was he taking advantage of a widow? He didn't think so, since she'd asked him out. *That baby's so precious, and that home, so big, so many acres.* She really needed a man out there, protecting her and the little one.

Could it be me? He fantasized then. Pictured himself coming home, unbuckling his gun belt, slipping it into a special hiding place as Addy ran around the corner screaming, "Daddy!" And then he'd pick her up and walk into the huge kitchen—it was the biggest kitchen he'd ever seen—and there'd be Ellen, apron on, cooking up a huge feast. All healthy and low-cal. In his fantasy, Pete was twenty pounds thinner and two inches taller and his hair was thick, but it was his dream, after all.

And then the baby would cry in the bassinet and he'd bend over and pick up little Pete Moore Jr., or P. J. He looked just like his daddy always dreamed, and then Ellen came over and kissed him—a big juicy kiss right on the mouth—and then they sat down and had dinner and it was great…

Oh, for heaven's sakes, he thought. *I'm never going to make it at this pace.* He hated to do it, and he really didn't do it often. But this, this was an emergency. So Pete reached under the seat, grabbed his police light, and placed it on the top of his car.

Nodding at the other trapped car dwellers, he maneuvered his way to the shoulder, where, with full lights and siren and completely illegally, he sped down the right-hand side of the highway, exiting at the Gentry Shop exit and flipping off his siren.

A man's gotta do what a man's gotta do, he thought, parking in front of the store, pulling the light in, and returning to life as a private citizen.

As he walked into the discount suit store, Pete started to wonder if he needed a new cologne. New boxers? *Shit, I should probably have liposuction on my love handles*, he thought. His *Men's Health* subscription had helped him stay current—he knew what was in, what was out. He'd read about what women wanted in bed, in a mate, in a husband. And he'd had his share of girlfriends. Nobody quite as mature as Ellen, what with her other two marriages and all. No, at thirty-four, Ellen was a year older than Pete but seemed much more. But he'd gotten past that in his mind. In fact, way past that. He was thinking so far ahead that he dreamed of their wedding day, with Addy as the ring bearer, even though she wasn't walking yet. Pete was surprised he'd daydreamed all the way to the clothing store and found himself wandering around inside, following a kid with a nose ring who was holding up suits.

"Man, you've fallen hard. I hope she's worth it, dude," said the kid with the piercing, holding a suit in each hand. "Just try to focus, OK? Stay with me here, bud, and we'll get you what you need, alrighty? If you keep up that spacing out or whatever, man, I'm gonna have to go help some other dude in love, got it? Do you have a preference?"

"Yeah, sure, no problem, OK. This one's good. I'll take it," Pete said. *I think I'm losing my mind*, he thought. *But it's not bad.*

"Charge," he said, tossing his Discover Card on the counter and rubbing his neck. "I'm in a big hurry, big hurry," he mumbled to the cashier kid, not that it mattered. *Why do young people today have no sense of urgency?*

****

They were seated at a long conference table in The Hyatt's most formal meeting room.

"If you added a little more lemon, you could create a more acidic aftertaste I think—don't you agree Dixon?" Walter, the annoying food critic from the city magazine asked.

Dixon could barely tolerate Walter, who dressed in impeccable three-piece suits, no matter the occasion, and affected a highbrow demeanor even at chili cook-offs. Walter sported a pinky ring, a perfect manicure, and silver-gray hair parted to the right. He exuded elegance and status. He made Dixon's lips curl.

"Yes, perfect," Dixon drawled, bored out of his gourd. Dixon became grumpier the longer he was in Walter's presence. Unfortunately, as the two food experts in town, their paths crossed with regularity. Dixon, the crusty sailor type, and Walter, the elitist, would never be friends.

"Now when you submit recipes to *Bon Appétit*, do they just jump at the chance to print them?" Walter asked Lillibet Season, formerly of Columbus, now of the *East Coast* and a successful cookbook author. The Cookbook Queen, as she called herself, came back to town before each new release, confident an appearance would lead to sales. She was seated at the head of the long table, the seat of honor, looking much like an advertisement for Lilly Pulitzer in pink and green.

"Yes, of course they do, Walter," Lillibet answered. "Remember all those years I tried and tried. Now it's almost a given."

Dixon snorted. He was there only because someone from the *Journal* had to be, per his publisher. So here he sat, tasting the Queen's cooking.

"The sweet potato soup with orange crème fraîche and lobster has just a hint too much citrus, don't you agree Walter? Dixon?" Lillibet asked in her gracious, *don't you agree with me of course you do because I'm the big time now* voice. She paused, then said conspiratorially, "When I last flew between the coasts, I had the most horrible experience."

"What? Do tell us," said Walter.

Why can't he just shut up? Dixon thought, *glaring at him.*

"Lunch in a bag. I mean, honestly. They tossed a sack at us and it had this awful hard roll, pretend deli meat and fake cheese, barbecue potato chips, and a cookie. Four hours, and that was all," she said, "And that was in first class."

"That's terrible," said Walter.

"You want to know what's terrible?" Dixon asked, and all of the guests sitting around the long dining table stopped eating. Dixon paused for maximum effect. "It's terrible that Ron Martin was murdered by a local waitress and no one can prove it," he said, looking around the room. "Were you aware of that?" he asked the queen, seated at the head of the table.

"Why, Dixon, I believe I did read something about it; we do still get the city magazine on the coast," she said smiling, as everyone nodded. "It's a shame, really. What do you all think of the wild rice and pecan salad? Isn't the asparagus just beautiful, so green? And the rice, parboiled perfectly. The plum chicken could use some more sauce; you'll want to tell the chef to follow my recipe more closely," she added to a young woman taking copious notes while standing to her left.

"Dixon, I really don't understand your fascination with the case. There've been other murders in town. I'm thinking it was a suicide," Walter said. "Isn't that what they've finally decided?"

"I don't know what 'they've' decided, Walter, but I'm not satisfied. I guess, since the rest of the city feels the way you do, I should just move on. Forget about it," Dixon said.

It wasn't like Dixon was friends with either of the victims. No, he realized, it was starting to get weird, weird for him to care. His wife was beginning to resent his fascination with stun guns. In fact, since he'd ordered a catalog from a website advertising unique ways to protect yourself, they'd been added to a lot of strange and sadistic mailing lists. She was getting the creeps. Somewhere, he was convinced, someone else in Columbus was on the same mailing list, because he or she had a stun gun. But the lists were private. There was no way he'd ever know.

"Don't you agree, Dixon?" the Cookbook Queen was asking.

"Whatever you say, dear. When's your book signing? I need to bring the wife—she wants a signed copy," Dixon said, ignoring whatever question she'd tossed his way.

"You don't need to bother, Dixon. I'll give you one for Mrs. Crane, right now. To…what's her name?

"Mrs. Crane."

"Right, 'To Mrs. Crane: Good luck with the recipes and with Mr. Crane. Fondly, Lillibet, the Cookbook Queen.'" After drawing a little crown over her name, she handed the cookbook to Dixon.

"Thanks, Lillibet. I'll tell the readers to go out and get their own copy of *Creative Convenience*, by the queen of 'Speed Scratch Cooking.' You've practically created a whole genre for these dual-income, upper-middle-class folks."

Dixon decided Lillibet's success was dumb-luck, and of course, he was a little jealous of the Cookbook Queen but he'd never admit it. Maybe he should spend some time making a cookbook instead of trying to solve murders, he realized.

***

"Fins to the left, fins to the right, and you're the only bait in town!" Lyle and Maddie sang in unison, arms above their heads, pointing the different directions along with the other ten thousand or so Jimmy Buffett fans—or Parrot Heads, as they called themselves. When Buffet took a break, Lyle and Maddie sat down and talked for the first time since the concert began. They'd been too busy singing. Drinking margaritas. And smiling.

"You know, listening to his music brings back so many great memories," Maddie said. "And a lot of those memories are foggy ones from too much time in Margaritaville, if you know what I mean."

"Yeah, after the year we've had, I'd just like to stay right here, listen to Buffet songs, and pretend we aren't grown-ups. You were right to be shocked about me wanting the director job. Maybe I'm tired of watching guys like, well, like that guy—" Lyle pointed to a forty-something man wearing a Styrofoam parrot on his head "—moving up while I chase stupid dreams. But then I realized, it doesn't have to be overkill. I can have success without giving up everything for it like my dad. And Maddie, I'm so happy. I mean, I'm stressed, I have more responsibility, but I'm happy," Lyle said, smiling broadly while reaching out for her hand. Dressed in his Parrot Head attire—including boldly patterned Hawaiian shirt—Lyle knew he looked anything but successful or stressed.

"I know, Lyle, it's great. I mean, it's only been two weeks since your promotion, but so far, so good," Maddie said, cautiously optimistic the current burst of energy and motivation Lyle was experiencing would turn into something permanent. "I'm proud of you, honey."

He grinned. "Thanks," Lyle said, squeezing Maddie around the waist with his left arm. Maddie reached up to be sure her Parrot Hat didn't fall off. She wore a fake flower lei on top of her signature black T-shirt and black shorts.

"Janet says congrats, too, by the way," Maddie said.

"How is the conch dweller doing? And don't kid me; you think her house looks like the inside of a conch shell in bright sunlight. I know you do," Lyle teased.

"It's great, and so is Janet. Her self-help book is selling well, and her publisher's sending her on a promotional tour. Network television and everything. Just the sort of limelight she was escaping, ironically," Maddie said, laughing.

"She can retreat whenever she wants to now, though. That's the difference: she has choices and the freedom to make them," Lyle said.

"I hope he plays 'Mother Ocean,'" Maddie said, smiling over at the man Lyle was becoming.

"Well, if he doesn't play it tonight, maybe he will on New Year's Eve," Lyle said, smugly.

"New Year's Eve? Does he have a special or something?"

"No, you and I will be in Key West then, and he's giving a concert, in the heart of Key West," Lyle said. "I've been planning this for a month."

"Oh, Lyle. I'm shocked. That sounds so awesome."

"Maddie, will you marry me?" Lyle asked, and then kneeling, he took her hand and said, "This is without a doubt the biggest choice a man and a woman can make. But I really believe we can make it together, Madeline Wilson. Marry me?"

Maddie's lips moved, but nothing came out. She'd never been speechless before. She'd never been proposed to before. The crowd started to scream as Jimmy Buffett walked back on stage. Still, Lyle knelt, and Maddie stared.

"Lyle, how's it going?" Jimmy Buffett called out as soon as he'd grabbed his microphone.

Oh my God, Maddie thought.

"Yes, a Parrot Head out there is proposing. Can we have the lights up? Thanks; Lyle wave your hands, son," Jimmy said, and Lyle stood and waved his arms.

"Did she say yes yet?"

"Maddie?" Lyle asked, staring at her, back on his knees.

Maddie nodded, tears rolling down her cheeks.

Lyle jumped up, kissed Maddie and gave the thumbs-up sign to the stage. The Coral Reefer Band began "Mother Ocean" as Maddie leaned into Lyle and they swayed together to the music.

****

It was 10 p.m. in Chicago.

Tonight would be Laura's first anchor assignment, filling in for the popular weekend anchor who was scheduled to move up to weekday night anchor, bumping the talented yet aging current female anchor.

Laura's arrival at the station had sealed the older woman's fate. The chain reaction of younger women would reach all the way to the top this time. Laura was aware of the chain reaction her arrival at the station would cause, but she couldn't care less. She'd worked too hard to get there to be intimidated by the reigning anchor. So she ignored the evil stares, smiled at the hostile makeup woman who was the soon-to-be retiring anchor's friend. She befriended Debbie, the woman who was moving to the weekday anchor spot. Someday, of course, Laura would bump Debbie out of the way too. Unless, of course, she leaped over her to New York. That could happen, her agent promised. But first, she had to become a star in Chicago. Laura was ready.

In the meantime, she needed another friend, a friend who knew who was important in town and who wasn't. Debbie would help, although she'd only been in the market for three years. She needed a Dixon Crane, and so she had called Dixon, leaving a message on his voice mail, apologizing for not saying good-bye, asking if he had any friends in the Windy City who would know people she should know.

Dixon called her back and left a message. "Sugar, in this business, it's important not to burn bridges. To repay kindness with kindness. Common courtesy with the same. It was always your dream to make it to the big time, and I'm happy for you. But Sugar, you'll never make it all the way if you keep burning bridges along the way. You'll need me someday, remember? Just like you need some of the folks you met back here in Comfortable Columbus.

"You'll see, Sugar. Choices are a chain reaction. Everybody you know is affected by what you do, when you do it, and how you do it. You left town with quite a mess brewing, and you didn't even care, did you? You were rooming with the number-one suspect in a murder investigation and all you had for the detectives was 'no comment.' That's not nice, Sugar.

"You didn't call the ladies over at ProMusica, the chamber orchestra to let them know they'd need another celebrity emcee. Heck, the AIDS Task Force wants me to do your duties next month. That's not right, Sugar. You committed to these people.

"What I'm saying is, if you want to try to live a life without connections, fine. But it has to work both ways. So no, I won't let my many friends in the Windy City know a friend of mine moved up there, because none have that I know of, do you?

"Have a wonderful life. Oh, and Dave Robinson, the general manager down here in little old Columbus, says, and I quote: 'Columbus says good-bye, Sunshine.'

"We'll be watching you on TV," Dixon added before hanging up.

Jerk. Laura deleted the message. *Yes, you will be watching me, Dixon Crane. I'm just sorry we couldn't stay friends. I really don't need some old guy in Columbus, Ohio, to help me out, that's for sure. Pretty soon, I'll know everybody who's anybody here anyway.*

"Laura, how's it going?" asked Justin Ambler, the station manager, her boss, who she noticed was wearing a black Italian-cut suit.

It was Armani. "Do you need anything, anything at all?" His voice was soothing. He reached out his hand and held hers, like a father holding a young child's. His palms were completely soft. And a little moist, Laura noticed. Not a lot of physical activity going on with those hands. He did have a nice manicure, though, and a very kind touch.

"Everything's fine, Justin. Just fine," Laura answered and then looked away.

"What is it, my dear?"

"Oh, I guess I'm just a bit lonely. I don't know anybody here, and it's such a big city. But it'll be all right, and I'll be fine. Thank you again for the chance," Laura said, water seeping into her eyes. "It's my dream come true."

"Well, then, the rest will follow," Justin murmured. "Please, join me for dinner tonight, after the show."

"Yes, that would be lovely," Laura said smiling. *Gotcha*, she thought. "Now, if you'll excuse me, I need to go into makeup. Shall I meet you somewhere?"

"My limousine will come for you, say midnight," Justin answered. "I know the address, my dear, since I am paying the rent."

"Of course. See you tonight."

"Make me proud tonight. I'll be watching."

****

Justin watched the beautiful young woman walk down the hall. She was going to work out fine, he thought, just fine.

"You don't waste any time, do you, Just Man?" Debbie, the stunning, five-eight blonde anchorwoman said, coming up behind him. "I feel like I'm watching a play, some sort of déjà vu play. Three years ago, that was me." She pointed down the hall toward Laura.

"Yes, it was. And now, you're my big star, honey," Justin said, kissing her on the cheek, careful not to mess up her makeup. Debbie's bright blue eyes flashed at him.

"Yes, we've come a long way—or I guess I should say I have."

"Don't forget, you made me come too, for a while. Go get your beauty sleep, sweetie. If Laura works out, you'll take over in prime time next week," Justin said.

"Are you serious. Finally? Oh wow," Debbie said.

"See you on prime time," Justin said, kissing her hand. And then, he turned and walked away, leaving Debbie as happy as Laura.

"I love TV land," he said, passing by a news editor whose name he could never remember and walking out the newsroom door. He pushed the elevator button. He'd head up to the executive suite and watch his new girl from above. She wouldn't see him again at the station.

From now on, their personal exchanges would be behind closed doors. It had worked with Debbie, and Marcy before her.

****

She knew he was the one, because she decided he'd be the one. Then it was easy.

Men are so, well, predictable, once you take control. A girl at work told her, whined really, about wanting to get married, but her man wouldn't. She told the girl, you—the woman—are in charge of when the marrying thing happens. There aren't but a few guys who fall for a girl and then say, Man I gotta get married.

No. They want sex. Companionship. Dinner. Somebody to pick up after them.

Marriage. Yeah, right. So you have to plot. You gotta plan. You need to decide you want him. That's your choice and then you exercise your power. Give him a deadline. Withhold sex. Whatever it takes.

With my Mister Right, she told the girl, she just used nonverbal communication. She batted her eyes. Touched his skin gently when they came in contact. And smiled. And served him drinks. And she made him feel important. And he was.

That's silly, said the other girl.
Maybe. But I'm married and you're still dreaming. Your choice.

****

Leaving the long, nasty voice-mail message for Sugar earlier in the day had made him feel great.

Sweet revenge, Dixon thought, as he poured a half glass of port and sat down to write. Rather childish, he knew, but sometimes, life just dragged you down into the gutter. *Enough*, he chastised himself. *It's time to focus on food. Not murder.*

Dixon decided to end his obsession with the Anderson–Martin cases, at least until new information surfaced, if it ever did.

"I still know I'm right," he typed slowly, a closing left behind in case he died before the killer was discovered. He still used a typewriter, although he surfed the net with the greatest of ease. Just one of his many quirks.

"Someday, someone will figure it all out and prove that I, Dixon Crane, being of sound mind and body, knew there was a killer getting away with murders." After adding the rest of the details, Dixon folded the piece of typing paper and placed it in his strong box with his other treasures. He labeled it in black pen: "The answer."

"Mrs. Crane can play Clue with her friends someday and open the secret box," Dixon snorted aloud, laughing. "I believe it was Ms. Brown, in the park, with the stun gun."

"Dinnertime, Dix!" Mrs. Crane yelled up the attic stairs. "Come on down from there, you old fool. You've worked enough this week. It's Friday."

"I'm coming. I'm coming."

"I fixed a special meal right out of Lillibet's new cookbook, honey!"

"Great, great. Just what I wanted," Dixon said, wondering why he hadn't waited until Mrs. Crane's birthday to give her the damned cookbook.

****

What's she gonna do? Angie wondered. *She's used to me, she needs me. I'll just go there, go to Chicago, go to the TV station, wait for her to get off the air, and then follow her home. Then, the next day, while she's at work, I'll pretend I'm her kid sister, visiting from—well, Ohio—and they'll let me in as a surprise, and then, voilà. I'll cook for her, or at least, order food for her. Go undercover for her and work at a restaurant nearby where lots of great-looking, successful guys hang out.*

Angie had made up her mind to move to Chicago. She wasn't going to change it, she told herself. No matter what. She was leaving in the morning. She printed out the MapQuest route and thought the clunker car could make it to Chicago. Her white shiny Mercedes had been repossessed once she'd lost her real jobs. She'd make it in the clunker. It was only a six-hour drive.

And once she was there, she'd get another map at the TV station. She'd just walk in and ask for Laura. That's it. And Laura would be so happy to see her, 'cause she'd be lonely already, and she'd give her a key and the taxi money and say *I'll see you later, Angela. You're like a sister to me.*

No, that's not how it would be. Not with the ice maiden. And why would Angie want to follow her anywhere? *Because I have nowhere else to go.*

"Damn," she said to the empty walls of her apartment. *Everybody in this stupid town thinks I killed somebody, killed Mr. Martin. This is crazy. And now nobody'll date me. I might as well have a big X on my back, with "kick me" on it. Of course, it all started with that stupid Chuck Jones thing, with his stupid wife walking in on us.*

None of that was her fault, despite what that guy sitting in the car outside the apartment thought. She was getting used to being followed.

"Follow this!" Angie yelled out the window, sticking out her tongue. She knew he probably wouldn't get the full effect, but she felt better. Hadn't she been through enough? Why couldn't they leave her alone? Ed the bartender always teased her, mocked her. And that creepy restaurant reviewer and that lady smoker with the gossip column. *Staring at me and following me. Trying to get me to confess or something.*

She hadn't had a date, hadn't kissed a man since she kissed Ron Martin. She looked great. Still had all her fancy clothes, and even some of Laura's she hadn't given back. Her hair still looked great. Even that push-up bra that made her look like she had boobs. But nothing. Just a dead man's lingering kiss, an empty apartment, and a closet full of clothes.

Angie wandered into the kitchen and poured herself a seven and seven. The phone rang as she cracked ice cubes out of the tray. She almost ignored it, but picked up at the last minute.

"Just tell 'em you did it, Angie. Confess," the voice said.

"Leave me alone!" she screamed into the phone. It was the third call today. The prank caller had been bugging her for at least a week. She had nobody to tell, so she hadn't. She just stopped answering the phone. She had tried pushing *69. The recording said that callback service couldn't be used for the number the prank caller was calling from.

She had to get out of town.

Everybody was closing in on her. Making her nervous. Angie started rummaging through the kitchen cupboards, looking for trash bags. She'd put all her stuff into big green trash bags, as many as she could fit into the back seat of her car. The trunk would be for her clothes. She'd spread them all out flat, so they wouldn't get too wrinkled, and then she'd be gone. She'd leave a note for the stupid landlord with a bunch of cash for the month's rent.

She'd need to write a letter to Mr. and Mrs. Lindey. Even though they didn't come into the restaurant anymore, they had been so kind to her. Hiring her in the first place. Sticking by her through all of this mess. Giving her a break. She really liked them, the more she thought about them. She'd write them a letter. But right now, she had to get out of this stupid town.

It only took half an hour and one drink to pack the kitchen. She was leaving all the stupid orange velour furniture and the stupid TV. The only other furniture was the two twin beds. She'd leave those—ice maiden's cast-offs, really.

The real question was whether to drive north or south, to ice maiden country or to the beach. Angie scooped up a huge armful of hanging clothes and carried them down the narrow hall to the orange couch. She needed to pull her car up closer to the apartment door. She had loved her white Mercedes. It had meant she was going to be somebody, that she was somebody. She needed to start over. She just needed to be somebody else somewhere else. She'd get another fancy car, someday.

She'd park in the fire lane for loading purposes, just like Laura's moving men had. Maybe the guy watching her would move in closer, so she could really do something to him.

One of the ice maiden's moving guys, named Frank or something, said he was an escape artist in real life. Said he'd be famous someday. Showed Angie his handcuffs and all. Said he always needed a lovely and talented assistant if she was interested. The creep. But he did give her an idea. She could go to Las Vegas. Lots of waitress jobs and showgirl jobs and warm weather and it was close to California and lots of guys with shiny shoes.

And then she knew. She decided. She was leaving for Las Vegas in the morning. She had no idea how she'd find it—just head west, she thought. She had money and clothes and a car. She'd make it.

She sat down then, to write a note to the Lindeys. She wrote:

Dear Mr. and Mrs. Lindey,

I would like to thank you for all you did for me during my time here in Columbus. It has become necessary for me to leave town because people think I killed Mr. Martin, which is stupid, but I wanted you to know I like you two very much. Thank you for all the pasta.

Your friend,

Angie Brown, waitress

P.S. I will be traveling so I will send you postcards.

P.P.S. Ed is mean and you should watch him.

P.P.S.S. The plant in the corner of the restaurant by the wait station needs water every Tuesday. I did that. Please ask Bob or somebody to take care of it.

****

"It's a good thing we went to dinner early, Peter," Ellen said, as they pulled up to the gate at the bottom of her driveway.

She got out and punched in the code and then hopped back into the car. Pete was driving her black Infiniti, at her insistence, and Addy was asleep in her car seat in the back. "The storm seems to be imminent. The air is so still, and thick with rain. Something's coming, that's for sure. The storms always seem so bad way out here in the country and all. From the house, I can see them rolling in, across the McNallys' farm, past all those pine trees. It's eerie."

Pete flexed his arm muscles. She probably couldn't see them move under his new dark blue suit jacket. "Don't worry, Ellen. I'll stay until the storm passes tonight, if you'd like."

"That would be nice, Peter. I'll get little Addy changed into her pajamas and tucked into bed if you'll make us a nightcap. Just push that button and pull on into the garage," she added as Pete navigated the car into its spot next to Ron's Jaguar. The car didn't send a chill down Pete's spine anymore, as it had the first couple of times he'd taken Addy for a stroller ride and walked through the garage. There was something odd about your car surviving, living longer than you. Pete didn't know why that had bugged him. He didn't know why Ellen kept it, either. Sentimental, he guessed.

The evening, so far, had been perfect. He had made it home from the suit place, with alterations and everything, in an hour. That left him enough time for a shower and a stop by the florist on the way back out to Field City.

At least he wouldn't have a clothes crisis. His old girlfriend had teased him because he used to try on five different shirts before he'd settle on one to wear out to the movies. She said it was a clothes crisis, and only girls should have them. He had thought, *Well, tonight, I'll wear this new suit.* He was set.

He wiped the steam from the mirror and carefully shaved. The phone rang. It would be Ellen, he was sure, canceling their date. Crestfallen, he dashed to the phone. It was Doug, his sometimes partner, telling him Angie Brown seemed to be packing her things, tossing them into her car. Pete told Doug to keep up the surveillance. And to stay in touch. Maybe she'd leave some clues behind, Pete said. Maybe she'd take the evidence with her and they'd never solve the case, Doug said. All they could do was watch her, Pete said. Doug teased him about his date with the widow, then, of course. Why would he want to go out with a lady whose last two husbands met tragic ends!? Pete told him to shut up and hung up.

Because she's the most perfect woman I've ever seen, Pete thought. *Inside and out. And she needs protection and she needs a man. And I need to protect someone. And the little girl needs a dad.* And, shit, he only had ten minutes if he was going to stay on schedule.

He'd arrived at the gate at five on the dot, and the gate swung open for him before he even had a chance to press the buzzer. *Neat,* he thought.

Pulling up to the house, Pete decided to go to the front door. It was their first formal date and all. She opened the door wearing a black, skintight dress. The dress's fine straps supported a plunging neckline in the front and a deep V in the back. Pete was speechless as he handed Ellen the bouquet of red roses.

"Peter, you look so handsome. And thank you, these are beautiful. Come on in. Addy's dying to show you her dress. Or, I guess I am, since she can't talk yet," Ellen said, apparently noticing Pete's eyes frozen on her cleavage. "Would you like me to spin again? Speak, Detective, speak."

"I've never seen a more gorgeous woman, ever."

"Come on in," she said, taking him by the elbow and leading him into the family room. Addy did look cute, of course, in a frilly black dress with a white petticoat and white lace tights. But Ellen. *Wow.*

"Just let me put these beautiful flowers in water and we can go," Ellen said, going to the kitchen and selecting a large, cut crystal vase. "You clean up well, Detective," she added. "I never pictured myself with a, you know, blue-collar fellow. In fact, Detective, you don't seem like a blue-collar type. You're smart. Articulate. Handsome. Brave."

"For some reason, I always wanted to be a policeman," Pete answered. "From there, you know, since I had a college degree and all and a lot of guys didn't, it wasn't too hard to move up to detective. End of story. Probably it's this new suit. I wanted to look my best," Pete said, blushing a little as he put Addy back into her bouncer seat. He got busy cleaning his glasses.

Ellen's hair was swept up in a topknot, making her neck look longer and her shoulders look broader. Since Ron's death, she'd been dieting and had lost at least fifteen pounds. Her figure, while not back all the way, was perfect to Pete. Her bust, with the extra weight, was very large, and the black gown enhanced that feature.

"Just to get stuff out of the way," Ellen said, "Any word on the case?"

"Angie Brown appears to be leaving town. I'll know more in the morning."

"What if she does leave? Where does that leave the investigation?"

"Unless new evidence surfaces, Ellen, I'm afraid—"

"It's as dead as Ron," Ellen said. "You know, Peter, I know you've done your best. And I don't want to dwell on this anymore tonight. Deal?"

"Deal."

"One last question before we go. Do you have a girlfriend, Detective?"

"No, ah, no, I don't," Pete answered.

"Good," Ellen said. "Voilà. Aren't they beautiful in this vase? Come on, little princess," she said, "We have a date."

And what a date.

Pete had never been to the Refectory. He'd never seen so much silverware. Ellen helped him, telling him what fork to use and where to leave his soup spoon, and even helping him order. The quiet wealth of the restaurant would've been intimidating—was intimidating—Pete thought, if Ellen hadn't made him feel so comfortable. So needed. Fortunately, the maître d' had pulled out the chair for her. Pete would've forgotten. And when Addy got fussy, he held her and she calmed right down. Actually went to sleep right on his shoulder during dessert, drawing admiring looks from patrons being seated.

"You're a natural, Peter," Ellen had said. "She loves you already. Do you prefer 'Pete' or 'Peter'? I'm afraid I've been calling you Peter all along."

"It's what my mom calls me, actually," Pete answered, trying to spoon a bite of ice cream and apple crisp—at least that's what it tasted like even though it was called something fancy—into his mouth without bugging Addy.

"It suits you. Mothers always know best, you know," Ellen said. "By the way, did you know Uptown is my favorite florist?"

"You never know all the things I might already know about you. I am a detective," Pete said, smiling. "The guy in there knew exactly what you'd like. Oh, he said to tell you hi."

"Oh, that's Brian. Did you know he's Stuart Mitchum's lover?"

"What? He's married, president of a division of Chase Bank, right?"

"Yep. Anyway, how'd you know where I buy flowers? Have I been followed? Am I under suspicion?" Ellen asked. Her smile had faded.

"I told the department to knock it off. Of course, right after Mr. Martin's demise, some people found it a bit odd that a woman would lose two husbands in such a short span of time, under such tragic circumstances. I told you that, Ellen, back when we first met. I called off the dogs, though. Got myself assigned to you. End of story. They turned over all of their surveillance files—only about a day and a half's worth, really—and that's where I came up with the florist. You used him for the funeral, I believe. Can we change the subject?"

"Sure. And I'm sorry, it's just…well, I hope she does leave town, actually. We can put all of this behind us," Ellen said, her smile brightening again as she looked into his eyes.

Pete kept thinking he was in a dream. A classy, beautiful, rich woman with a beautiful child who happened to be drooling on his new suit was asking for the bill and paying for what had to be a four-hundred-dollar dinner. And then she'd asked him to make the after-dinner drinks while she and the baby changed.

On his salary, he could afford, he calculated, to pay for the kitchen in Ellen's home. The rest of the house, no way. She must have some serious cash—and more to come with the Martin Agency's sale. Her husbands took good care of her. That was good.

He started the coffeemaker, found some Baileys, and poured two drinks in sparkling crystal glasses. Too excited to sit, he decided to explore the gourmet kitchen. As he rummaged around, he discovered her home computer, cleverly concealed inside a pop-up cupboard. He pressed the button and a motor raised the machine up to counter level. *Now this is high-tech*, he thought. He turned it on.

"Peter?" Ellen demanded. "What are you doing?"

"Just checking out your computer. Ah, you don't mind, do you? You startled me, El," he answered. "I'll shut it down. It's so cool how it just zooms right up here and all."

"How'd you find it? I mean, it's fairly hidden."

"Yeah. I just noticed a split in the countertop, saw a button. I am a detective, you know. Is it hooked into that TV up there?"

"It sure is. One day, I think I'd like to teach cooking classes here at my house. I thought the computer would be helpful. Cooks share a lot over the Internet these days," Ellen said. She gestured to the family room. "Let's go sit down in there."

"You can learn about just about anything on there, nowadays," Pete said, pushing the button to lower the machine back into its hiding place. "I didn't mean to snoop or anything; I was just poking around."

"I guess I'm still a little jumpy with the storm coming," Ellen said. Bringing the Baileys, they sat together then, on the couch. Hearing the machine beep, Pete told her the coffee was ready. They decided to drink Baileys straight up without it.

When she leaned over to kiss him, he could see down her white V-neck T-shirt and he saw that she wasn't wearing a bra, as he had suspected. "Kiss me, Detective Moore. I've wanted you from the first moment I saw you," she whispered into his ear.

Pete's reaction was instant. A lurch, something between a lunge and a reach, and he managed to grab hold of her, bend her back into the cushions of the sofa, and kiss her deeply. As his tongue explored the inside of her mouth, she groaned.

He rolled onto his side, took off his glasses and yanked off his tie. He paused then, to look down at her full, shapely body. She was completely naked under the long T-shirt.

"Oh, Ellen, you're beautiful," he gasped, rubbing his hands down her bare legs and up again, to her thighs.

"I want you, Peter," she murmured, still breathing heavily, and wriggling with the heat of the moment.

He fumbled with his new belt, but finally managed to yank it and his pants off. Still standing, looking at her figure, which was hazy without his glasses, he dropped his underwear to the ground, revealing his full erection. He sat back down next to her, and she grabbed for his penis and told him it was so big.

After, they held each other on the couch. He was still in shock. She seemed sleepy but not asleep. "That was wonderful, Peter. I feel so safe with you," she murmured.

"Let's drink to that; I'm parched," Pete said. "Where are my glasses? I can't see a thing."

"You don't need them right now, Peter. Here—" Ellen said, handing him a glass of Baileys. "Let's have a toast."

"Yes, to us and to the future," Pete said.

"Yes, and to choosing wisely. That makes all the difference," Ellen said, taking a sip of the sweet thick liquid and then helping a blinded Peter by taking his glass, placing it in his hand, and then steering it into a collision with her own.

CHAPTER 20

Five Years Later

She'd had to do it of course, and she knew how to do it. She'd taken lessons. Lessons called life. From Momma first. Then Momma's men. They had taught her well.

When Momma decided to go back to her man, and leave her alone in Dayton, to go on, she just couldn't allow it. She knew she'd be dead, as good as dead. So she made sure it would happen sooner, rather than later. She didn't want her momma to promise anymore. She would tell her she loved her and cared about her, and that she'd be there, and then, she'd pick them. Every time.

So she called him. Disguised her voice. Told him Momma was on her way back to him after sleeping with two other guys, told him one of them was her husband, told him Momma better not come back. Said that if he couldn't control his woman, what kind a man was he? She kept it up until he hung up on her. She was sure her momma would die. She didn't know how, but he'd get her good this time. And this time, she had her momma's lucky beads.

"Sorry, Momma. It was your choice, wasn't it? You chose wrong,

When it rains out here, it sometimes reminds me of that trailer home. The big field that held me captive, the smell of the grasses. The sound of the thunder when I was standing outside, being punished. The fence between me and freedom. Yes. I'm real sorry, Momma.

You, too, Michael. All it took was an electrical ignitor. I just whipped up some plastic explosive—they teach you how on the Internet—and cooked it up. It felt like Silly Putty, smooth and cool. Did you know common household cleaning supplies, if mixed together in the right way, can create some really dangerous compounds? Now you do. Well, I made my own goo and I placed it on the propane tanks. Good thing we had a deluxe grill, with two tanks to explode and all. Industrial-strength power. Did you know your gas grill just needs an extra kick start to make it into a dangerous bomb?

You discovered, of course, all that wonderful food I'd made, perfect for a little picnic for two. And perfect for a little grilling out for two. Two lovebirds. Why did you let her sleep in my bed? When you pushed the button to ignite the gas, you got a big surprise, didn't you, love? All those years of marriage, up in smoke and fire. And I didn't even know, before I killed you, about your really big lie.

Sometimes, like now, I wonder if you pushed me over the edge, Michael, or was I already there after Momma?

And then there was you, Ron. So powerful. So important. Everybody in town liked you. A decent, creative man. Gave me a break when I thought all I had left was me. It was, until I found you and the life grew inside me. A gift. From Ronald Langly Martin.

But then Ron cheated on her. It took a while, but it was inevitable. He kept telling her it was business, just business, just like Michael had said. But it wasn't business at all. When she found him on the bank of the river, he had just finished kissing the slut. The same slut Michael had had over to their house. Of course, Ron acted like he didn't like it, her kiss.

After the slut left, she walked to Ron's side. He seemed happy to see her. They climbed into the tiny boat. She had brought her backpack, of course. And her gloves. And some wine. Ron wouldn't have any, of course. But she did. And they floated, drifted really, in a little tiny rowboat, and the sun set, and he thought they should go back, and she agreed. He had to go to the bathroom, so he unzipped his pants. She called his name and he turned, and the two electrodes stuck, and he made a strange noise, sort of like, "Why?" and then he fell into the water. And it was so quiet. And she rowed the rest of the way to shore. Drowning is really such a silent death.

And now you, Peter. You kept saying you would solve the mystery of Ron's death, but you won't. You won't because I can't allow it. I don't know if you're suspicious or just tired, but I don't think you like me anymore. We don't make love like we did.

She got pregnant with Pete Jr. that first night, after their dinner out with Addy. By then, he was so in love with her. When she told him she was having his baby, he was all rushed and said they had to be married, properlike, and she reminded him he'd be her third husband, and it should be pretty quiet, and they had his family over to her house, and Addy, and a couple of his cop friends, and they were married.

And his mom cried big alligator tears and kept repeating, "I wish Peter's daddy could see this," and his grandma kept patting her hand and telling her, "Take care of our boy—treat him kindly," over and over again. They were talking about the Moore family's curse. The heart problems. That's why he never married before; he worried about a wife, kids. Didn't want to leave them. I told him it would be fine. Just fine.

She thought the yellings were finished. But they arrived in the middle of the night sometimes, and Peter held her, worried, and she told him, always, of course, that it was nothing. She wondered if she told him more, when she didn't know it, when she was asleep. She looked at him sometimes those nights, to see if he saw her differently, but he could barely see at all.

The bad yellings were with Addy. Addy was so whiny, and she never listened. She sent Addy outside sometimes, or locked her in the basement where it was dark, but then Addy told Peter, who said not to do that, to put her in time out in a chair in a corner. Then he bought her a parent magazine to teach her about discipline.

I know about discipline.

I know a lot of things you don't know. Too bad for little Petie; he probably would've liked to have had a daddy growing up. Too bad. A lot of us want that and just don't get it. Dad's at work. Dad's at play. Dad's golfing. Dad's screwing his secretary. Dad's on a business trip. Dad's on drugs.

Peter never had a problem with allergies before moving out there with them, so she started him on her Seldane. She had saved a big supply of it even though it had been taken off the market. And it helped; he felt better.

The only downside is that some medicines actually cause a lethal reaction with other things, sometimes things as simple as a glass of grapefruit juice you might drink every morning with your Seldane.

Too bad for you with your weak heart. When you swallow Seldane with a big glass of grapefruit juice, just like you've been doing since we got married, well there's a risk of dangerous—even deadly—heart-rhythm abnormalities. And there's also a problem when people combine certain antibiotics—you know, like for sinus infections or the flu—with certain antihistamines. The antibiotics affect their livers somehow, and that slows the metabolism of the Seldane, and all of a sudden, a person's blood is just coursing with antihistamines, and his heart is racing, and sometimes it can just... stop...

*****

"Ellen? Ellen? Something's wrong. Help!" Peter yelled from the bottom of the stairs. "Call the squad, I think it's a heart—"

"Attack, Peter?" Ellen said, gliding slowly down the stairs, looking down at her third husband as he stared up at her. She was smiling. Wearing a yellow chenille bathrobe, her long dark hair spilling over her shoulders, and her wedding ring sparkling in the setting sunlight. Her eyes glistened, and she held her beads in her left hand. With a sigh, she sat on the middle step and began to cry—another choice made.

****

I do not see why I should e'er turn back,
Or those should not set forth upon my track
To overtake me, who should miss me here
And long to know if still I held them dear.
They would not find me changed from him they knew—
Only more sure of all I thought was true.

From "Into My Own"
By Robert Frost

Turn the page for a first look at
Kaira Rouda's new novel . . .

IN THE MIRROR

Available Soon!

None of us is guaranteed to wake up tomorrow.

When Jennifer Benson, a headstrong entrepreneur, is diagnosed with cancer she enters an experimental treatment facility to tackle her death sentence the same way she's tackled her life – head on. Unexpectedly, she finds herself confronting the truth about her past as she fights for her future . . .

I woke up with a start, a dream about a high school date still warm on the edges of my mind. The smell of wet fall leaves, the crisp air that makes it hard to take a deep breath, and Alex's arm around my shoulder. We were sitting on a blanket, in the shadows away from the heart of the bonfire. I knew he was going to ask me to Homecoming, but still, the anticipation made me jumpy, goofy even. He'd just leaned in for a kiss when, bam, the sound of a door banging open startled me out of sleep. Away from the most vivid, colorful dream I'd had in a year.

I squeezed my eyes shut tight, hoping I could drift back to sleep, back to Alex, back to the past.

The bright light from the hallway bounced across my face. "Sorry about the noise," Hadley mumbled. I kept my eyes closed, feigning sleep until I heard her leave. Even with my eyes squeezed shut, I could picture her pinched face, gray hair pulled tightly up into a bun, and large upper arms swinging below her crisp nurse's uniform. Now I was really awake. But smiling.

In my dream, I'd had long blonde hair hanging straight halfway down my back and my face was fuller as it had been in my senior year photos, with high cheekbones and crinkly blue eyes. I wore a nubby light blue wool sweater and my favorite jeans. In high school, I hadn't been carefree at all – I always was a worrier. But my dream self had been smiling all night.

As I rolled over to get out of bed, I caught a glimpse of myself in the mirror and cringed. The reflection in the mirror said it all. Everything had changed. I averted my eyes and noticed the calendar. It was Monday again. That meant everything in the real world and nothing at Shady Valley. We lived in the "pause" world, between "play" and "stop." Suspension was the toughest part for me. And loneliness. Sure, I had visitors, but it wasn't the same as being surrounded by people in motion. I'd been on fast-forward in the real world, juggling two kids and my business, struggling to stay connected to my husband, my friends. At Shady Valley, with beige-colored day after cottage-cheese-tasting day, my pace was, well —

I had to get moving.

I supposed my longing for activity was behind my rather childish wish to throw a party for myself. At least it gave me a mission of sorts. A delineation of time beyond what the latest in a long line of cancer treatments dictated. I embraced the deadline.

Tossing back the covers, I noticed the veins standing tall and blue and bubbly atop my pale, bony hands. I felt a swell of gratitude for these snake-like signs of life. The entry points for experimental treatments; without them, I'd be much more than paused by now. I pulled my favorite blue sweatshirt over my head, and pulled up my matching blue sweatpants. It wasn't the same as the outfit in my dream, but I was trying.

Moving at last, I brushed my teeth and headed next door to Ralph's. He was my best friend at Shady Valley - a special all-suite, last-ditch-effort experimental facility for the sick and dying—or at least he was until I began planning my party. I was on his last nerve with this, but he'd welcome the company, if not the topic. He was paused, too.

My thick cotton socks helped me shuffle across my fake wood floor, but it was slow going once I reached the grassy knoll — the leaf-green carpet that had overgrown the hallway. An institutional attempt at Eden, I supposed. On our good days, Ralph and I sometimes sneaked my son's plastic bowling set out there to partake in vicious matches. We were both highly competitive type A people in the "real" world and the suspended reality of hushed voices and tiptoeing relatives was unbearable at times.

"I've narrowed it down to three choices," I said, reaching Ralph's open door. "Please come celebrate my life on the eve of my death. RSVP immediately. I'm running out of time."

"Oh, honestly," Ralph said, his head rolled back with disgust onto the pillows propping him up.

"Too morbid? How about: Only two months left. Come see the incredible, shrinking woman. Learn diet secrets of the doomed," I said, smiling then, hoping he'd join in.

"Jennifer, give it a rest would you?" Ralph said.

"You don't have to be so testy. Do you want me to leave?" I asked, ready to retreat back to my room.

"No, come in. Let's just talk about something else, okay, beautiful?"

Ralph was lonely, too. Friends from his days as the city's most promising young investment banker had turned their backs - they didn't or couldn't make time for his death. His wife, Barbara, and their three teenage kids were the only regular visitors. Some days, I felt closer to Ralph than to my own family, who seemed increasingly more absorbed in their own lives despite weekly flowers from Daddy and dutiful visits from Henry, my husband of six years. So, there we were, two near-death invalids fighting for our lives and planning a party to celebrate that fact. It seemed perfectly reasonable, at least to me.

"Seriously, I need input on my party invitations. It's got to be right before I hand it over to Mother. I value your judgment, Ralph, is that too much to ask?"

"For God's sake, let me see them." Ralph said, as he snatched the paper out of my hand. After a moment, he handed it back to me. "The last one's the best. The others are too, well, self-pitying and stupid. Are you sure you can't just have a funeral like the rest of us?"